A DANGEROUS PURSUIT

Regency Spies & Secrets #1

Laura Beers

ARE YOU SIGNED UP FOR DRAGONBLADE'S BLOG?

You'll get the latest news and information on exclusive giveaways, exclusive excerpts, coming releases, sales, free books, cover reveals and more.

Check out our complete list of authors, too!

No spam, no junk. That's a promise!

Sign Up Here

www.dragonbladepublishing.com

———————— ～ ————————

Dearest Reader;

Thank you for your support of a small press. At Dragonblade Publishing, we strive to bring you the highest quality Historical Romance from the some of the best authors in the business. Without your support, there is no 'us', so we sincerely hope you adore these stories and find some new favorite authors along the way.

Happy Reading!

CEO, Dragonblade Publishing

CHAPTER ONE

England, 1814

MISS MADALENE DOWDING leaned lower in the saddle as she urged her horse forward, coaxing a little more speed out of the white gelding. She knew she was racing at a breakneck pace, but that did little to deter her. She did not fear falling off her horse. Frankly, she feared very little since her mother's death.

Her mother.

It had been six months since her mother had died, leaving her utterly devastated. The familiar feeling of grief washed over her, and she fought hard to push down the bitterness that threatened to rise up inside of her. Never had she felt so alone, despite constantly being surrounded by people. She struggled to find the contentment that she once knew, but it was proving to be a much more difficult task than she had ever imagined.

The sun sat high on the horizon, filling the valley with light. She inhaled the slight crispness of the air as she reined in her horse at the top of a hill. How she preferred living at her country home, far away from Town!

Her mother had always enjoyed the sights and sounds of London, and they would spend every Season there without fail. That was, until her mother got sick and the doctor suggested she remove herself to the country. For the next four months, Madalene had watched her mother wither away, and there had been nothing she could do to stop it.

A tear snuck out of her eye and slowly rolled down her cheek.

Why am I even thinking about this, she chided herself. Reaching up, she wiped the tear away with her riding glove. Her mother was gone. She had to accept that and move on. So why did the ache in her heart never cease to go away?

Madalene tightened the hold on the reins as her eyes scanned her land. At times, she could scarcely believe that she had become one of England's largest landowners upon her mother's death. It was a wonderful feeling to know that she could care for herself and for those she was responsible for.

Turning her horse back towards the manor, she kicked the gelding into a run and didn't stop until she reached the round gravel courtyard. She dismounted in a swift motion and extended her reins towards the lead groom.

"How was your ride?" the tall groom asked.

"It was wonderful, James."

James placed his hand on the gelding's neck and asked, "Will you be riding again this evening?"

"Most likely," she replied.

He tipped his head in acknowledgement. "Then I'd better go brush down your horse and give him something to eat."

"Thank you."

Madalene started walking towards the main door when it was opened by her short, black-haired butler. Graham had been with the family for as long as she could remember, and he had the most pleasant disposition about him.

"Good morning, Miss," Graham said, stepping to the side to grant her entry. "I take it by the smile on your face that your ride went well."

"It did," Madalene replied as she started to remove her gloves.

"Nothing pleases me more than riding in the morning hours."

Graham gave her a knowing smile. "I daresay that riding at any hour gives you great pleasure."

"That it does."

With a side glance at the drawing room, Graham grew serious and lowered his voice. "Mrs. Ridley and her son, Mr. Ridley, have requested to speak to you and are waiting for you in the drawing room."

Madalene stifled the groan that had formed on her lips. "Did they state why?"

Her butler gave her an apologetic look. "Mrs. Ridley did not, and I did not question her any further," he replied. "I did, however, inform her that you were on a ride, but that seemed to do little to deter her."

"That doesn't surprise me. Mrs. Ridley is much too determined for that," Madalene said as she extended her gloves towards Graham. "Will you inform Mrs. Foster that I require her presence in the drawing room?"

"Yes, Miss," Graham responded before he stepped back.

Madalene turned reluctantly towards the drawing room door. How she tired of these house calls. She had grown to dread them. Scheming mothers would parade their sons in front of her in hopes that she would fall for their flowery words. It grew rather tiresome.

She walked over to the door and peered in. Mr. Ridley was standing next to the window, looking out towards her well-maintained gardens, as his mother sat rigidly on the sofa. She had to admit that he wasn't entirely unfortunate to look upon with his sharp features and straight nose, but he had one flaw that she could not overlook. His mother. Mrs. Ridley was intolerable. She was a gossiping busybody and had deemed most people of the village beneath her.

Smoothing down her dark blue riding habit, Madalene stepped into the room and greeted her guests.

"Good morning, Mrs. Ridley." She tipped her head at the woman's son. "Mr. Ridley."

He turned from the window and faced her. His eyes perused the length of her, and she could see the approval in them. "You are looking especially lovely this morning, Miss Dowding."

"Thank you," Madalene replied graciously.

Mrs. Ridley spoke up from the sofa, her words sounding less than genuine. "I must agree with my son, Miss Dowding. You are looking quite beautiful this morning."

Madalene smiled politely at her. "My morning ride must have agreed with me, then."

"Oh, do you like to ride?" Mrs. Ridley asked innocently.

"I do."

"My son also loves to ride," Mrs. Ridley said, glancing over at him. "Don't you, Roger?"

"I do." Mr. Ridley cleared his throat. "Very much."

"Is that so?" Madalene asked, attempting to feign interest.

"It is," Mr. Ridley confirmed. "I also like dancing."

"Dancing is a most wonderful pastime." Madalene wasn't entirely pleased at the direction this conversation had taken.

Mr. Ridley took a step closer to her, and his face was now red with a thin line of perspiration on his upper lip. "I was hoping you would save me a dance at Mrs. Brooks' ball tomorrow evening."

Madalene clasped her hands in front of her, delaying her response. She didn't want to encourage the poor man, but she didn't want to be rude either. "I'm afraid I haven't decided if I will be in attendance yet," she admitted honestly.

Mrs. Ridley gasped. "But you must!"

Fortunately, before she could respond, her companion, Mrs. Foster, walked into the room. "I am sorry that I am late," she said with a smile on her lips.

Madalene stepped closer to her silver-haired companion. "Thank you for joining us, Mrs. Foster."

"It is my pleasure," Mrs. Foster replied before turning her attention towards Mrs. Ridley. "How are you doing this fine morning?"

"I am well," Mrs. Ridley replied with a forced smile.

"I am happy to hear that," Mrs. Foster said.

Mrs. Ridley turned her attention towards Madalene. "I believe my son is still waiting for your response."

Madalene attempted to keep her face expressionless as she replied, "I would be happy to save Mr. Ridley a dance, if I attend the ball."

Mrs. Ridley clapped her hands together. "You two will make such a dashing couple on the dance floor."

"Thank you, Miss Dowding," Mr. Ridley remarked as he wiped the sweat off his upper lip. "You have made me immensely happy."

A silence descended over the room, and Madalene watched as Mrs. Ridley gave her son a pointed look. Mr. Ridley reached into the pocket of his waistcoat and pulled out a small piece of paper. He unfolded it and studied it for a moment.

"Do you like to draw, Miss Dowding?" he finally asked.

Madalene glanced curiously at the piece of paper in his hand. "I do, very much."

"It would appear that we have something else in common, Miss Dowding," Mr. Ridley said as he slipped the paper back into his waistcoat pocket.

Mrs. Ridley smiled approvingly at her son. "Is there anything else you wanted to ask Miss Dowding?"

Mr. Ridley gave his mother a blank stare. "I don't believe so."

"Nothing at all?" Mrs. Ridley pressed.

With a frown on his brow, Mr. Ridley removed the piece of paper from his waistcoat pocket and reviewed it again. He looked up and asked in a hesitant voice, "Would you be interested in going on a carriage ride with me tomorrow?" It was evident by his expression that he was waiting for her to reject him.

Madalene felt compassion towards him, and she didn't have the heart to turn him down.

"A carriage ride sounds like a splendid idea," she responded.

Relief washed over Mr. Ridley's features. "I shall come by tomorrow afternoon to retrieve you."

Abruptly, Mrs. Ridley rose from her seat. "If you will excuse us, we will be on our way," she declared. "Thank you for agreeing to meet with us."

"Of course, it was my pleasure," Madalene replied.

After Mrs. Ridley and her son left the drawing room, Mrs. Foster shook her head. "That poor man was so nervous around you that he was reading notes from a piece of paper."

"You noticed that, as well?"

"I did," Mrs. Foster said. "I found it rather sweet."

Madalene walked over to the window and watched as Mrs. Ridley and Mr. Ridley stepped into their carriage. "Mr. Ridley is a nice enough man, but I have no interest in matrimony at this time."

Her companion came to stand next to her. "I'm relieved to hear that, because you are still much too young to marry."

"I daresay that is not true," Madalene replied. "I am twenty-one."

Mrs. Foster grinned. "That is quite young, my dear," she commented. "Marriage is a lifelong commitment, and the decision should not be taken lightly."

"What if I decide not to marry?"

With a half-shrug, Mrs. Foster remarked, "Then that is your decision. But I would hope that is not the case."

"Why do you say that?"

"Because falling in love is one of the greatest feelings in the world, and it will consume you, body and soul."

Madalene gave her companion an amused look. "I see that you have been reading *Pride and Prejudice* again."

"I have not," Mrs. Foster replied. "I just remember what it felt like the first time I saw my husband from across the room. Our eyes met, and I knew that my life had changed forever."

"Not everyone finds a love match."

Mrs. Foster bobbed her head. "That doesn't mean you should ever stop looking."

"I tire of men and their flowery words," Madalene stated. "I have yet to find a gentleman who will speak his mind freely around me."

"Give it time," Mrs. Foster encouraged.

Madalene smiled. "That could be a problem, because one of my greatest flaws is that I lack patience."

"That you do," Mrs. Foster agreed. "You have been that way since you were a little child."

"My mother constantly chided me for making rash decisions, but I couldn't seem to help myself."

Mrs. Foster offered her a sad smile, her voice full of compassion. "Your mother was a good woman."

"That she was," Madalene agreed. "Speaking of which, we need to travel to London to tour the orphanage. We haven't been back since it was first opened."

"That sounds like a wonderful idea, especially since I wouldn't mind doing a little shopping while we are in Town."

"I am not surprised in the least."

Mrs. Foster laughed. "You could always join me on my shopping trips."

"I would rather not."

"And why is that?"

"Because searching through fabrics does not interest me," Madalene replied honestly. "I would much rather be reading a book."

"You shouldn't say such things," Mrs. Foster remarked, lowering her voice. "You could be labeled as a bluestocking."

"So be it."

Mrs. Foster shook her head good-naturedly. "It is a good thing that you are beautiful and rich. You get to write your own rules."

"Isn't that grand?" Madalene asked as she started walking towards the door. "If you need me, I am going to change for breakfast."

"I find it odd that Mrs. Ridley called on you so early this morning."

Madalene stopped at the door. "I don't," she replied, glancing back at her companion. "I have come to always expect the unexpected from that woman."

"Do you wonder what else Mr. Ridley wrote on that piece of paper?" Mrs. Foster joked.

"I do not," Madalene replied.

As Madalene stepped out from the drawing room, she headed towards the grand staircase that dominated one side of the entry hall. Her thoughts kept returning to Mr. Ridley. She would need to be mindful not to encourage the man. The last thing on her mind was marriage.

MADALENE GLANCED OUT the window of the coach in the unfashionable part of Town and watched as the street vendors hawked their goods on the crowded pavement.

Mrs. Foster removed a fan from the reticule around her left wrist and started fanning her face. "Are we almost there?"

"We are."

"Thank heavens," Mrs. Foster said, lowering her fan to her lap. "After spending nearly all of yesterday traveling to Town, I'm afraid I am growing rather tired of seeing the interior of this coach."

Madalene gave her an understanding smile. "I do appreciate you coming with me."

Mrs. Foster returned her smile and replied, "That is what a dutiful companion does, especially when you desire to visit an unsavory part of Town."

"Well, I am grateful that you are my companion."

"As am I, my dear," Mrs. Foster said, her voice sounding sincere. "There is no place I would rather be."

Madalene smoothed down her simple cotton gown. "I am most relieved that my mother had the foresight to convince you to stay on as my companion before she died."

"Your mother was always looking out for you."

"That she was," Madalene agreed in a soft voice.

"I just hope that I have helped you as much as you have helped me," Mrs. Foster remarked.

"Oh, you most assuredly have," Madalene replied. "I don't know how I would have endured these past few months without you by my side."

Mrs. Foster smiled tenderly. "You are a strong child, much stronger than you give yourself credit for."

Madalene lowered her gaze to her lap and admitted, "I don't feel very strong."

"Why do you say that?"

"Because I miss my mother dreadfully." Madalene blinked back her tears, knowing it was not the time to display such emotions.

"There is no shame in that," Mrs. Foster reassured her. "It has only been six months since your mother passed away. You must give yourself time to properly grieve."

"Will the pain ever cease?" Madalene asked, bringing her gaze back up to meet her companion's.

A look of anguish came into Mrs. Foster's eyes. "The pain will never go away, but it will fade with time. At least, that is how it is for me with my dear George."

"I am sorry for bringing it up."

"Nonsense," Mrs. Foster said. "I enjoy speaking about George. In my opinion, it helps keep his memory alive."

Before Madalene could respond, the coach came to a jerky stop in front of a large two-level brick building. A sign hanging above the door read *Elizabeth Dowding School for Orphan Girls*.

The coach dipped to the side as the footman left his perch and came to put the step down. After it was extended, he opened the door and reached into the coach to assist them onto the pavement.

"Would you care for me to announce you, Miss Dowding?" the footman asked as he released her hand.

"That won't be necessary, but I thank you kindly."

The footman tipped his head before he took a step back.

Madalene stood in front of the building and admired it. The red bricks may have started to fade, but new windows had been installed, and the main door had received a fresh coat of paint.

Mrs. Foster came to stand next to her. "Your mother would be proud of you and your accomplishments," she said.

"Do you suppose so?" Madalene asked as she offered her companion a side glance.

"I do," Mrs. Foster replied. "What you have done here is no small feat."

"I just wanted to find a way to honor my mother's legacy."

"And I believe you have succeeded," Mrs. Foster responded, glancing over at her.

"I hope so."

The door to the orphanage opened and the plump housekeeper, Mrs. Kipper, appeared in the doorway. "Please come in," she encouraged, ushering them inside. "You don't need to stand on the pavement and risk getting pickpocketed." She glanced up and down the street with a disapproving look on her face. "There are street urchins all about who are always up to no good."

Madalene stepped into the building and stopped in the small, tastefully decorated entry hall.

"The headmistress has been expecting a visit from you," Mrs. Kipper said once she'd closed the door behind them. "If you would please follow me, I will show you to her study."

As they followed the housekeeper down a narrow hallway, Madalene could hear their booted steps echo off the tile floor. "Is it always this quiet in the orphanage?"

Mrs. Kipper laughed as she responded over her shoulder, "Heavens, no. It can get quite boisterous with twenty girls afoot. But the girls are currently receiving their lessons."

Mrs. Foster spoke up. "What lessons are they receiving?"

"We teach the girls skills they need to find employment after they leave the orphanage, such as needlework," Mrs. Kipper explained. "Furthermore, we educate them and train them in household business, thus enhancing their opportunities for obtaining a job."

"What a blessing that is for them," Mrs. Foster acknowledged.

"I agree," Mrs. Kipper said as she stopped at a closed door and knocked before she proceeded to open it.

Madalene stepped into the square-shaped room as the blonde haired, petite headmistress rose from her desk to greet them. She was wearing a pomona gown with a high neckline, and her hair was pulled back into a tight chignon at the base of her neck.

"Sorry to disturb you, Miss Hardy, but Miss Dowding and Mrs. Foster have come to visit," the housekeeper announced, clasping her hands together.

Miss Hardy smiled. "It is good to see you again, Madalene," she said in a warm and inviting tone. "How have you been?"

"I have been well, Edith," Madalene replied.

Edith pointed towards two upholstered chairs that faced the desk. "Would you care to have a seat?"

Madalene stepped around the chair and sat down. "How have you been faring?" she asked as she eyed the large stack of paper on the desk.

"I have been quite busy, if you must know," Edith shared, returning to her seat. "I never thought running an orphanage would require so much paperwork."

"Would you like me to hire someone to help you with that?" Madalene asked.

Edith waved her hand dismissively. "That won't be necessary. I find that I enjoy the mundane task, assuming the girls leave me alone long enough to accomplish it."

"Do you not have enough staff to properly tend to the girls?" Madalene questioned.

"Heavens, that's not what I meant," Edith declared. "We have more than enough, but I prefer to spend as much time with the girls as possible."

"I am sure they appreciate that," Mrs. Foster commented.

A twinkle came to Edith's eyes. "They are wonderful, and they just want to be loved, especially the little ones."

"What are their ages?" Mrs. Foster asked.

"The girls range from four to fourteen," Edith shared. "They are mostly bright and inquisitive children and have already endured so much at such a young age." She paused, growing solemn. "Some of these girls were found on the streets in the rookeries, and some came from other orphanages where they were not treated as kindly as they should have been. Many of them were half-starved and their hair was so tangled that it had to be cut prior to being cleaned."

Mrs. Foster gasped. "How terrible."

"Sadly, we have only seen the physical scars on the girls, but many hold emotional scars, as well," Edith continued. "I must admit that I was ill-prepared to be headmistress of this orphanage."

"I disagree," Madalene said. "I believe you are more than qualified."

"How so?" Edith challenged.

Madalene grinned. "You are by far the most clever woman that I know, and you have bested me at shuttlecock every time we have played."

Edith laughed, as Madalene hoped she would. "I am unsure how that makes me qualified to run an orphanage."

"I could have hired any number of women to run the orphanage, but I wanted someone that would love the girls," Madalene said. "That is what my mother would have wanted."

"Well, I would rather be a headmistress than work as a governess somewhere in the country," Edith remarked with a slight shudder.

"You would be a terrible governess," Madalene joked. "You have always preferred being in charge."

"That is true," Edith agreed. "Furthermore, with the generous salary that you have allotted me, I will be able to move my mother and sister out of their rented room at Floyd's Coffeehouse."

Madalene moved to sit on the edge of her chair. "If you would allow me to give you the funds, they could move out today and into somewhere respectable."

"My father was the one who got us into this mess," Edith said with a shake of her head. "I will be the one that will get us out of it."

"That isn't necessary—" Madalene started.

Edith spoke over her. "This is not your problem to solve, Madalene," she remarked firmly. "You have done more than enough for me and my family already."

Madalene pressed her lips together. "You are being quite stubborn."

"No more than you are," Edith contended, softening her words with a smug smile.

"Fine," Madalene said. "But if you change your mind, I am more than willing to help."

"I know, and that is why you are one of my dearest friends." Edith reached for a paper on the desk and set it in front of her. "You will be happy to know that we have recently acquired a French teacher for the girls."

"That is wonderful news," Madalene declared.

"I thought you might enjoy hearing that," Edith said. "Her name is Miss Rebecca Gaillard, and she came highly recommended from your solicitor, Mr. Walker."

Edith glanced over at the long clock in the corner. "Most of the younger girls are practicing their plain needlework at the moment," she remarked. "They are being instructed on how to make and mend their own linen. Would you care to observe?"

Madalene rose from her chair. "I would love to."

"Just as I suspected," Edith replied, rising. "The older girls are washing, ironing, and folding the linens. In the afternoon, all the girls will begin their academic lessons."

"What does that entail?" Madalene asked.

Edith came around her desk as she explained, "We want all the girls to be able to read the Bible, write in a legible hand, and understand the basic rules of arithmetic."

"That is no small feat for some of these girls," Mrs. Foster remarked.

Edith stopped at the open door and gestured that they should go first. "You would be correct, but I have great confidence in this group. By the time they are fifteen, they should be able to find employment as a servant in a grand estate or work in the front of a shop."

"Will we be able to help them secure employment?" Madalene asked, stepping into the hall.

"That is my hope," Edith replied as she turned to walk down the hall. "I want to ensure that each one of these girls is placed in a safe environment."

"You have accomplished a great deal," Madalene commented as she followed Edith, "especially considering the orphanage has only been open for four months."

Edith smiled over her shoulder. "It is amazing how much someone can accomplish when the funds are forthcoming. We also hope to raise funds for the orphanage by taking in all kinds of plain needlework."

"That isn't necessary," Madalene insisted.

"I know, but I think it would be beneficial if the girls helped support the orphanage with their work," Edith explained.

"That is a brilliant idea," Madalene proclaimed.

"You sound surprised," Edith joked as she stopped in front of a closed door. She knocked, and a muffled voice granted permission for her to enter.

Edith opened the door and stood to the side to allow Madalene and Mrs. Foster entry first. As Madalene stepped into the room, she saw a tall, thin woman with brown hair sitting at a desk in the corner of the room. She had a narrow face, deep-set eyes, a sharp nose, and thin lips.

The woman rose and looked at them expectantly.

Edith came to stand next to them as she provided introductions. "Miss Dowding and Mrs. Foster, please allow me the privilege of introducing you to our French teacher, Miss Gaillard."

Miss Gaillard dropped into a curtsy. "It is a pleasure to meet you, Mademoiselle Dowding," she said, "and thank you for this opportunity."

Madalene tipped her head. "I am pleased that you are with us, Miss Gaillard."

"Will you be observing my class today?" Miss Gaillard asked.

"With your permission, I believe I shall," Madalene replied.

Miss Gaillard nodded vehemently. "Of course. It would be my privilege."

"Her class doesn't start for another hour," Edith interjected. "We have plenty of time to continue our tour of the orphanage."

"How delightful," Madalene murmured.

CHAPTER TWO

BALDWIN RADCLIFF, THE Marquess of Hawthorne, walked down the foggy streets of a disreputable section of Town. The sun had set, and lamps had been lit on the street corners. He was well aware of the men that were lurking in the alleyways, waiting for the opportunity to rob him of his coins. But he had little to fear. He had two pistols on his person, one concealed behind his blue jacket, and the other in his right boot. A small knife was in his left boot, as well.

He wasn't one to go in search of a fight, but he had no qualms with finishing one. He almost welcomed the chance to engage in fisticuffs. It had been far too long since he had boxed with his younger brother.

A lanky man dressed in threadbare clothing stepped out from the shadows of the alley and pointed a pistol at him.

"Give me yer money," he demanded.

Baldwin stopped in front of him and shook his head in disapproval. "May I ask what you are attempting to do?"

The man stared back at him in disbelief. "I am trying to rob ye of yer coins."

"With that stance?" Baldwin asked, pointing at the man's feet. "If you aren't careful, you could easily be relieved of your pistol."

The thug huffed. "I think not."

In a swift motion, Baldwin grabbed the man's wrist, ensuring the pistol was pointing away from him, and wrenched it out of the thug's hand. Then, he pointed the pistol back at the man. The thug put his hands up, and Baldwin could see a trace of fear in the man's eyes.

"As I was saying," Baldwin continued, keeping the pistol aimed at the man, "you have to keep your feet balanced." He gave the man a knowing look. "Have you never robbed anyone before?"

The thug lowered his hands and sighed. "I'm sorry," he said. "This is the first time I have even tried."

"If that is the case, then why start now?"

The man shrugged his thin shoulders. "Ye appeared to be an easy target."

"Ah," Baldwin said, lowering the pistol. "I would suggest you give up your life of thievery before it even begins."

"I have tried, but I can't find a job, though. I've been looking since I came back from the war," the man explained. "My kids and wife haven't eaten in two days."

"What about you?"

The thug lowered his gaze. "It has been longer for me."

"That is most unfortunate," Baldwin said, extending the pistol back to the man. He reached into his waistcoat pocket and pulled out three gold coins. "Here is three pounds. It should be enough to feed your family for weeks."

"Thank ye, Mister," the man said as he clutched the money in his hands. "I don't know what to say."

"If you are looking for honest work, then go to the Marquess of Hawthorne's townhouse on Grosvenor Street." Baldwin paused. "Are you familiar with Hawthorne House?"

"I have only heard tales about its grandeur."

"Very good," Baldwin replied. "Go around to the servants' entrance and they will be expecting you."

"How can ye be so sure they will even agree to see me?" the thug asked. "It will cost me nearly two shillings to travel there."

"You do not need to concern yourself with that," Baldwin remarked in a firm tone. "When you arrive at Hawthorne House, your travel expense will be reimbursed, as well."

The man gave him a humbled look. "Thank ye," he said in a sincere tone. "I don't know what I did to deserve yer kindness, but I am grateful for it."

In a stern voice, Baldwin warned, "If I hear that you have resorted to thievery, you will be dismissed. Understood?"

Straightening to his full height, the man replied, "Yes, sir."

"Good, because I expect my employees to be trustworthy."

The man's eyes widened as his voice resonated with awe. "Ye are the Marquess of Hawthorne?"

"I am," he replied, seeing no reason to deny it.

"Do ye not know how dangerous Drake Street is at night?"

Baldwin smirked. "I am well aware, but I have business I must attend to."

"Would ye like me to escort ye out of here?" the man asked.

"That won't be necessary," Baldwin replied, "but I thank you for your offer. Besides, I intend to meet up with some of my associates soon."

The man bowed slightly. "Thank ye, milord. It will be a pleasure to work for ye."

Baldwin tipped his head as he resumed walking down the street. It wasn't long before he approached a dilapidated brick building and heard the sound of a bird call coming from further down the street. He stopped and repeated the sound.

A long moment later, a husky man with a pistol tucked into the waistband of his trousers stepped out from the shadows.

"Are you lost, Mister?" the man asked as he placed his hand on the butt of his pistol.

Baldwin shook his head. "I am not, but the king requested to see me."

"The king?" the man asked, his eyes narrowing. "What makes you think the king wants to see you?"

"Because I have something he needs to hear." Baldwin hoped that the code had not changed since he had been gone.

"What did you say your name was?" the man asked, removing his pistol from his trousers.

"I am known as Falcon."

"Falcon?" the man repeated, surprise in his voice.

"Yes."

"I heard you were dead."

Baldwin raised his hands wide. "As you can see, I am very much alive."

"Come with me," the man ordered, pointing the pistol at him. "I have someone who will be very interested in meeting you."

"Finally, we are getting somewhere," Baldwin remarked in an amused tone.

The man gestured with his pistol towards a plain brown door that was in desperate need of painting. "You go first."

Baldwin approached the door and opened it, revealing a dark, narrow passageway.

"Walk," the man commanded.

As Baldwin walked down the dark passageway, he saw a lone candle burning on a table. A stern-faced man was seated next to it, a pistol in his hand. "What do we have here?" he asked.

The man spoke up from behind him. "This man claims he is Falcon."

"I heard Falcon died."

"Me, too."

Baldwin began to open his mouth to respond but stopped when a door behind the man opened, the light illuminating the passageway.

A familiar voice came from within. "Falcon!" The dark-haired man stepped into the passageway, his eyes perusing the length of him. "It is about time you finally showed up. I expected you days ago."

"Hello, Corbyn," Baldwin greeted. "What happened to the other guards?"

Corbyn chuckled. "There have been a lot of changes since you have been gone." He ushered Baldwin into the room. "We have much to discuss, Falcon."

Baldwin noticed that the guards had lowered their weapons and were staring at him with a newfound respect in their eyes. A look that he had grown accustomed to over the years.

He brushed past them and headed into the office. His eyes scanned the sparsely decorated walls. "I see you haven't made any changes to your office since I left for France," he commented.

Corbyn huffed. "I'm afraid I haven't had the time."

"In three years?"

Corbyn appeared unconcerned. "It makes it much easier to move offices, if the need arises," he remarked.

"That is a good point."

Corbyn walked over to the drink cart in the corner. "Can I get you something to drink?"

"Yes."

Angling his body towards him, Corbyn picked up the decanter and removed the stopper. "Pardon me for saying so, but you look terrible," he said as he poured the drinks.

"That is understandable since I just stepped off the ship," Baldwin shared.

Corbyn picked up the two glasses and walked one over to him. "I expected you days ago."

"We ran into some unexpected trouble," Baldwin responded. "It isn't easy to cross the Channel undetected."

"You got caught."

"That we did."

"By us or the French?"

Baldwin took a sip of his drink. "The *HMS Victory*," he replied, "but Captain Hampton was being a real stickler, despite the war being over."

"Did you not have the proper documentation to cross?"

"We did, but we weren't able to produce it until after they shot a few cannons at us."

Corbyn walked over to his desk and sat down. "Were you using a French schooner to cross?"

"We were," he confirmed. "We paid a French merchant to take us."

Corbyn lifted his brow. "Willingly?"

Baldwin smirked. "He was compensated enough, and we left him and his crew alive at the dock."

"That was nice of you."

"Wasn't it?" Baldwin asked before taking the last sip of his drink. He walked over to the drink tray and set it down. "If the schooner leaves in the middle of the night, it should be able to cross back into French waters without an altercation."

"I was worried that you wouldn't receive my message," Corbyn said, placing his drink on the desk.

"What message?"

"The one that ordered you home."

Baldwin furrowed his brows. "I received no such message."

"Then why did you come back to England?" Corbyn asked.

Baldwin walked over to the chair in front of the desk and sat down. "The group of royalists that I had been working with discovered a credible threat against England," he revealed.

"Which is?"

"A French spy is traveling to England to meet with a group of radicals who are secretly plotting a rebellion."

Corbyn leaned forward in his seat. "What is this radical group called?"

"I am not entirely sure, but the informant managed to overhear that members of the group meet at Floyd's Coffeehouse on Baker Street."

"We have gone on much less," Corbyn said with a bob of his head. "I will assign this case to another agent at once."

"With all due respect, I am more than capable of completing this assignment."

"That you are, but it is time for you to retire."

Baldwin reared back slightly. "May I ask why?"

Corbyn gave him an understanding look. "We need you to take up your seat in the House of Lords and assume your place in Society."

"Why is that?"

"These are troubling times, and we need an advocate in the House of Lords."

"For anything in particular?"

Reaching for the newspaper on the corner of his desk, Corbyn held it up. "Lord Desmond has just introduced a bill to establish an agency within the Home Office that will be responsible for the overseeing of the workhouses."

"Did he state why?"

"The Home Office is responsible for safeguarding the rights and liberties of all the people, and he feels the parishes are not doing a good enough job with the overseeing of the poor," Corbyn explained. "He believes the Home Office has adequate funds to establish this new agency, and he is rallying the people in defense of the bill. If his bill succeeds, then we will lose some of our funding."

"Who does Lord Desmond think is keeping England safe from domestic and foreign threats?"

"That isn't his concern at the moment," Corbyn replied. "He wants to run for Prime Minister and use the workhouses as his platform."

"That is just asinine."

Corbyn took a sip of his drink. "People in the rookeries are dying at an alarming rate, and the reformers are tired of the Tories being in charge of Parliament. The people have been rioting for years."

"Regardless, the Alien Office wards off potential threats and keeps the people safe. We have agents all over the world protecting England's interests."

"As far as the Alien Office is concerned, we don't exist," Corbyn stated flatly. "Which is why we are not bound to the same rules as the other agencies in the Home Office."

"What does Addington say as the under-secretary of the Home Office?" Baldwin asked. "Surely he is fighting this bill?"

"He is," Corbyn confirmed, "as is the Home Secretary, but Lord Desmond is relentless, and he is getting the votes. That is why we need you in your seat at the House of Lords."

Baldwin rose from his chair and walked over to the window overlooking a small brick courtyard. He heaved a heavy sigh. "I can't just walk away from being an agent of the Crown," he insisted. "Frankly, I am too invested in this agency."

"You are a marquess, and you knew this day would eventually come."

"But I could be no less ready for it."

Corbyn's lips twitched. "You need not fret. We do have other competent agents, including Oliver."

"I have no doubt that my brother is more than competent, but I want this assignment," Baldwin retorted.

Corbyn grew silent for a long moment, studying him thoughtfully. Finally, he spoke. "All right, but you must also resume your seat in the House of Lords."

"Thank you, Corbyn."

"But after this assignment, you are finished working as an agent," Corbyn said, leveling his stern gaze at him. "Do we have a deal?"

"I suppose I have no other option."

Corbyn rose from behind his desk. "Go home, Falcon," he encouraged. "You have been gone for far too long."

Stepping away from the window, Baldwin admitted, "I suppose it is time."

"I can't help but notice that you seem reluctant."

Baldwin nodded. "I am. I'm not sure if I'm ready to go back."

Corbyn came around his desk and said, "Take all the time you need. I have to leave to interrogate a suspect."

"Do you require any assistance?" Baldwin asked hopefully.

"Thank you for the offer, but I can handle this suspect on my own," Corbyn replied as he walked over to the door. He placed his hand on the handle and stopped. "I believe it is time for you to face your past so you can embrace the future."

Baldwin lifted his brow. "Since when did you get so sentimental?"

"A lot has changed since you have been gone," Corbyn said. "I do find it odd that you can go undercover in France for three years, but you are too scared to return to your own townhouse. A rather remarkable townhouse, I might add."

"I have my reasons."

"And no doubt they are foolhardy," Corbyn quipped.

Baldwin winced. "You are right."

"Of course I am right," Corbyn said. "I wasn't offered this position because of my good looks."

With a shake of his head, Baldwin remarked, "You are entirely too full of yourself."

"With good reason, like the fact that I'm not afraid to go home," Corbyn joked.

"I will go, but only because I tire of this conversation," Baldwin said, closing the distance between them.

"That is a good enough reason for me."

———— ~ ————

BALDWIN SAT IN the filthy hackney as it made its way towards Hawthorne House. He was dreading going home. It wasn't long after his father had died that he had accepted the assignment to join a group of royalists in France. But a month-long mission turned into three years.

The hackney lurched to a stop in front of a high black iron gate. A guard approached the driver and asked, "What business do you have with us?"

The driver shouted down, "This fellow paid me to take him to Hawthorne House."

"It is too late for callers," the guard declared, taking a step back. "Be gone with you."

Baldwin put his hand through the open window and pushed down the handle. As he stepped onto the pavement, he said, "I would like admittance to my own home, if you don't mind."

The guard's eyes grew wide. "Lord Hawthorne," he responded, clearly stunned. "Yes, of course. Give me a moment."

The guard rushed to the gate, unlocked it and pushed it open. Baldwin reached into the pocket of his waistcoat and removed a few coins, then extended them towards the driver.

"Thank you, milord," the driver said with a tip of his hat.

After the driver deposited the coins into his pocket, he urged the hackney forward and disappeared down the darkened street.

Baldwin stepped into the cobblestone courtyard and took a moment to admire Hawthorne House. It was a rectangular building with two protruding wings. The doors and windows had gold embellishments around the frames, and a large portico hung over the door.

The guard spoke up from behind him. "I apologize for the misunderstanding, milord," he said in a hesitant voice. "I hadn't heard that you had returned home."

"No harm done," Baldwin replied.

He heard the gate being closed and locked behind him as he started across the cobblestone courtyard. Stopping in front of the double ebony doors, he sighed. This home offered so many memories of his father; memories that he longed to forget.

Baldwin placed his key in the lock and turned it, then pushed the door open. He paused on the threshold and took in the familiar scent. The entry hall was square in shape with marble-tiled floors and columns that preceded a dominating staircase that led up to the second level. The pleasant sound of the pianoforte could be heard drifting out from the drawing room.

The raised heel of his Hessian boots made clicking noises on the floor as he approached the drawing room. He came to a stop just outside it and peered in. He could see his sister, Jane, playing the pianoforte, her eyes closed as her hands drifted over the ivory keys with ease. Her brown hair was pulled into a high chignon and she was wearing a white gown with a blue sash around her waist. His mother listened to the music with her back to him, and he could see her once vibrant brown hair was now starting to fade.

Baldwin took a moment to gather the nerve to announce himself. He knew they would be angry for his departure, and subsequent abandonment, but he hoped they would forgive him in time.

He stepped into the room and cleared his throat. The music came to an abrupt halt, and he heard his mother gasp as she turned to face him.

His mother and sister both stared at him with wide, disbelieving eyes.

He felt the need to break the silence. "I hope I am not intruding," Baldwin attempted.

His mother rose from her seat. "You are finally home." Her voice was soft, almost reverent.

"I am."

She slowly approached him and hesitantly placed her hand on his right cheek, as if she were trying to convince herself that he was real. "I have prayed for your safe return for so long."

Unsure of what to say, Baldwin remained quiet. He saw his sister rise from her seat and walk closer to him.

"I thought you were dead," Jane accused in a critical tone.

Baldwin smiled, hoping to disarm his sister. "As you can see, I am very much alive."

His mother's eyes searched his face. "Where have you been?"

"I'm afraid I am unable to say," Baldwin replied.

Jane placed a hand on her hip and asked defiantly, "You have been gone for three years and you can't tell us where you have been?"

Baldwin turned his attention towards his sister. He had left when she was eighteen and preparing for her first Season. Now he barely recognized the young woman standing before him. Her pointed chin was jutted out and her eyes held an intensity, challenging him.

"Where Baldwin has been is not important, only that he has returned," his mother declared.

His brother's voice came from behind him. "Well said, Mother."

Baldwin turned towards the door and saw his younger brother, Oliver, standing in the doorway. He was dressed in a green jacket with a white waistcoat and dark trousers, a look that accentuated his dark hair.

"Welcome home, Brother," Oliver said.

"Thank you," Baldwin replied.

Oliver stepped further into the room. "It is about time that you returned," he stated, but there was no animosity in his voice.

"It is good to be home."

Oliver perused the length of him and commented, "You look awful."

Baldwin glanced down at his wrinkled clothes. "I could use a bath," he admitted, "and a fresh change of clothes."

His mother nodded. "That you could," she agreed. "You have a slight odor coming off your person."

"A slight odor," Jane huffed. "Baldwin smells like he rolled around in horse manure and deposited some in his pockets for later."

His mother frowned at Jane's comment. "It is rather a pungent smell, but nothing a long soak wouldn't cure." She walked over to the door and stopped. "Jane and I will see to the bath, won't we, dear?" she asked, giving Jane a pointed look.

Jane cast him an annoyed look before saying, "Yes, Mother."

Baldwin watched as Jane kept her head high and followed his mother out of the room. His gaze remained on the open door. "It would appear Jane is not pleased that I returned home," he observed.

"She will come around," Oliver insisted.

"I hope so."

"You must understand that it has been nearly three years since they have heard from you," Oliver said. "Most of the *ton* speculated that you were dead."

"Did you not receive my messages?"

Oliver nodded. "I received them, but they were quite vague."

"They had to be," he argued. "If they had gotten into the wrong hands, I would have been exposed."

"I am well aware of that fact." Oliver walked over to the door and closed it. "Did you already report to Corbyn?"

"I did," Baldwin confirmed. "I was pleased to see that the location of our headquarters remained unchanged."

"Was Corbyn pleased to see you?"

Baldwin walked over to a maroon velvet settee and sat down. "He appeared to be."

"Was your mission successful?"

"It was," Baldwin confirmed. "I did discover that a French spy intends to rendezvous with a group of radicals on English soil."

"For what purpose?"

"That is what I intend to find out," Baldwin stated.

Oliver came to sit across from him in an upholstered armchair. "You should take a break and let the other agents handle this case."

"Like you?"

Oliver shrugged. "If Corbyn deems me worthy of the assignment, but I am currently working on another case."

Baldwin leaned his head back and revealed, "Corbyn wants me to retire."

"Would that be the worst thing?"

"It would," Baldwin said. "The last thing I want to do is resume my place in Society."

"Is being a marquess really that troublesome?" Oliver joked.

Baldwin huffed. "I never wanted to be a marquess, at least not at the expense of Father."

"I am well aware of that, but it doesn't change the fact that Father died," Oliver reminded him.

"You don't need to remind me of that," Baldwin said in a sharper tone than he intended.

Oliver leaned forward in his seat. "Did Corbyn state why he wanted you to retire?"

"He did," Baldwin confirmed. "He wants me to resume my seat in the House of Lords and vote down Lord Desmond's bill."

Oliver let out a low whistle. "Lord Desmond is quite influential in the House of Lords. Did Corbyn mention that he intends to run for Prime Minister?"

"That he did."

"Just so you are aware, he is still just as despicable as he was when you last saw him," Oliver shared.

"That doesn't surprise me." Baldwin stared up at the white embellishment on the ceiling as the candles on the tables cast shadows around the outskirts of the room. "Being home feels so odd," he admitted.

"In what way?"

"For starters, I lived in single rooms above coaching inns for nearly three years," Baldwin shared. "I learned how to preserve candles for as long as possible."

"That must be a rather difficult thing for you to overcome," Oliver said with amusement in his tone. "A rich marquess who had to learn to be frugal."

Baldwin grew reflective. "Despite the hardships, I am not ready to give up being an agent of the Crown."

"What did Corbyn say to that?"

"He is going to let me work this last case," Baldwin shared, "but then I am to retire."

Oliver made a clucking noise with his tongue. "You were recruited right out of Oxford to be an agent."

"As were you."

"But, unlike you, I haven't been working as an agent for nearly ten years," Oliver pointed out. "You are thirty years old and have managed to survive being an Englishman living in France during a time of war."

"That is true."

"Furthermore, you are a marquess and require an heir," Oliver said. "How are you going to accomplish that feat if you are traipsing all over England and Europe?"

"It matters not, especially since you are my heir."

Oliver shook his head. "I don't want to be your heir. I have no intentions of ever marrying."

"Why is that?"

A haunted look came into Oliver's eyes. "A lot has changed since you left."

Before Baldwin could ask his brother what he meant by that, the door to the drawing room opened and his mother stepped into the room.

"The water for your bath is being prepared as we speak," his mother announced in a cheerful tone. "Would you care to retire to your bedchamber?"

Baldwin rose from the settee. "That sounds delightful."

"I also took it upon myself to inform Pratt that you were home, and he will notify the staff," his mother shared.

Baldwin came to a stop at the door and gestured his mother through first. As they stepped into the entry hall, Pratt approached them and bowed. "It is good to see you, milord."

Baldwin acknowledged the fastidious butler with a tip of his head. "Likewise, Pratt."

"I have sent Stevens up to act as your valet," Pratt said. "Do you require anything else?"

"Yes. A man will be coming by the servants' entrance in the coming days to inquire about work, and I want you to hire him."

"Does he have any qualifications?"

"He didn't say, and I didn't ask," Baldwin replied frankly. "Furthermore, I want you to reimburse him for his travel expenses."

Pratt lifted his brow, but wisely did not say anything on the matter. "Yes, milord. I will see to it."

"See that you do, and report back to me when the man has been situated."

His mother gave him a curious look and asked, "What is this man to you?"

"He attempted to rob me earlier."

"And you wish to employ him?" his mother questioned.

"I do," Baldwin replied. "He was just desperate to feed his family and couldn't see any other way."

"And how did you know that?"

"I could see it in his eyes," Baldwin admitted plainly.

His mother arched an eyebrow. "How is that possible?"

"Because eyes never lie, Mother," Baldwin said. "You must remember that."

"I will make note of it." His mother gestured towards the stairs. "Let's get you bathed and fed. I have requested Mrs. Hutchings to prepare supper for you."

"Thank you for seeing to that."

"It is my pleasure."

As Baldwin walked up the stairs, he knew that he should feel elated at being home, but uneasiness had settled about him instead.

CHAPTER THREE

"Do you mind if I go shopping today?" Mrs. Foster asked as she sat across the table in the dining room.

"Not at all," Madalene replied, reaching for her cup of chocolate.

"You could always come with me."

"I would rather not."

Mrs. Foster smiled kindly. "I have never met a woman who was so opposed to shopping as you."

"I only shop when the situation warrants it." Madalene returned her cup to the saucer and picked up a piece of toast from her plate. "You will miss my boxing lesson," she added.

"I find it rather odd that you enjoy such a barbaric sport."

"It keeps me nimble and healthy."

With a shake of her head, Mrs. Foster reached for her fork and said, "Be sure to have a footman near you during your lessons."

"I always do."

Mrs. Foster took a bite of her food and chewed thoughtfully. "Will you be calling on your friend from boarding school while we are here in Town?"

Madalene brushed the crumbs off her hands before saying, "I intend to. I will send a letter to Lady Jane today."

"I always think it is a treat to see a dear friend."

"I agree," Madalene said. "Jane and I were exceptionally close during our time at Miss Bell's."

Mrs. Foster glanced over at the footman standing near the door and lowered her voice. "Don't you find it rather peculiar that her brother, Lord Hawthorne, hasn't been seen in polite Society for three years?"

"I do not."

"Many speculate that he is dead."

Shrugging, Madalene said, "I care not what the gossipmongers say, and you shouldn't either."

"Perhaps he is an invalid and can't get out of bed?" Mrs. Foster mused.

"Or he is perfectly well and abhors Society."

Mrs. Foster shook her head. "That can't possibly be it. A marquess can't abhor Society."

"Whyever not?"

"It just simply isn't done."

Madalene laughed. "I daresay your argument is rather faulty," she teased.

"It is entirely too early in the morning to argue with you," Mrs. Foster said amusedly, placing her fork on her plate.

The butler stepped into the room. "Mr. Payne has arrived, Miss," he announced. "He is waiting for you on the lawn."

"Thank you, Graham," Madalene acknowledged as she pushed her chair back.

"Do be careful," Mrs. Foster remarked. "After your last boxing lesson, you had bruises on your arms that we had to conceal with powder."

"I will be mindful of that."

Madalene exited the room and stopped at a table in the entry hall to pick up her mufflers. The padded gloves helped her greatly during her boxing lessons. She headed towards the rear of the townhouse and a footman opened the door for her. He discreetly followed her outside and stood guard.

"Miss Dowding," Mr. Payne greeted in a pleasant tone as he put his own mufflers on.

Madalene stopped a short distance away and smiled. "Good morning, Mr. Payne." She took a moment to study her young, slender teacher. He was dressed in a brown jacket with a matching waistcoat and buff trousers. She always thought he looked deucedly uncomfortable as he sparred with her.

"Put your mufflers on, if you don't mind," Mr. Payne ordered.

Slipping her hands into the padded gloves, Madalene motioned to the footman, who quickly tied the strings to secure them onto her hands before returning to his post.

"Are you ready to start your boxing lesson?" Mr. Payne asked as he punched his two tan mufflers together.

"I am."

"Good," Mr. Payne said. "Adopt the proper posture, please."

Madalene set her body by placing her shoulders forward, slightly bending her knees and bringing her fists up.

Mr. Payne nodded approvingly. "That is good," he declared. "Now, I want you to hit me as hard as you can."

"I couldn't possibly," she attempted.

"Hit me," he ordered.

In a swift motion, Madalene brought her fist up and hit him squarely in the jaw, causing him to stagger back.

Mr. Payne looked at her in surprise. "That was an impressive blow," he said as he brought his muffler up to rub his reddened jaw. "You must be practicing at your country estate."

"I have been."

"Well, I won't be underestimating you again, that is for sure." Mr. Payne walked closer to her and stopped.

Madalene gave him an apologetic smile. "I'm sorry if I hurt you."

"This is boxing," Mr. Payne said. "You don't apologize for a well-timed blow." He brought his mufflers back up. "Are you ready for round two?"

"I am."

They continued to spar on the lawn until the sun was high in the sky. Madalene felt the sweat trickle down her back as she blocked his blows and returned a few of her own.

Mr. Payne put his gloves up and stepped back. "I believe our lesson is over," he announced, his breathing labored.

"Must it be?"

Chuckling, Mr. Payne said, "You have become an admirable opponent, Miss Dowding."

"That is kind of you to say." Madalene motioned again to the footman, who untied the strings of her mufflers, and she removed them from her hands.

"There is nothing kind about it," Mr. Payne pressed. "It is merely the truth."

Another footman approached them with a tray in his hands and extended it towards them. Madalene accepted a glass of water and took a long, lingering sip.

"How long do you anticipate being in Town?" Mr. Payne asked as he removed his mufflers.

"Only for a few more days."

"Would you care for another lesson before you depart?"

Madalene placed her empty glass back onto the tray. "I would, very much so," she replied eagerly.

"In two days' time, then?"

"That would be delightful."

With a slight bow, Mr. Payne said, "Good day, Miss Dowding."

She tipped her head in response. "Good day, Mr. Payne."

The words had barely left her mouth when the butler approached and announced, "Mr. Walker is here to see you, Miss."

"Will you show him into the drawing room?"

"As you wish," Graham replied before rushing off to do her bidding.

Pointing towards the townhouse, Madalene asked her boxing instructor, "Would you care to exit out the main door this time?"

Mr. Payne shook his head. "I shall depart through the back fence, assuming you don't mind."

"Not at all," she replied. "Whatever is most convenient for you."

With a parting smile, Mr. Payne turned and started walking towards the back fence. She couldn't help but smile when she heard him whistling a jaunty tune.

Madalene headed towards her townhouse and extended her mufflers to the waiting footman. She found herself curious as to why her solicitor had decided to call upon her. Did I forget about an appointment, she wondered.

Stopping at a large oval mirror in the entry hall, Madalene saw that her face was still flushed, and tendrils had escaped her tight chignon. She tucked the locks of brown hair behind her ears and smoothed down her pale blue cotton gown.

"Oh, dear," she muttered under her breath, "I'm afraid it won't get much better than this." She didn't dare take the time to go change; that would make Mr. Walker wait entirely too long.

Madalene stepped into the drawing room and saw her stout solicitor staring out the window, his hands behind his back. He was wearing a plain grey suit with matching trousers and his brown hair was combed neatly to the side.

"Good morning, Mr. Walker," she greeted politely.

Dropping his arms, Mr. Walker turned to face her with a frown on his face. "Good morning, Miss Dowding," he responded curtly.

"Whatever is wrong?"

His frown intensified. "There is no easy way to say this." He paused. "Miss Hardy is missing."

"Missing?" she gasped as her hand covered her mouth.

"I'm afraid so."

Madalene walked over to the settee and lowered herself down onto it. "When did this happen?"

Taking a step closer to her, Mr. Walker explained, "Miss Hardy was noticeably absent this morning, and Miss Gaillard took it upon herself to visit the headmistress' room. When she arrived, she discovered that the room was in disarray, and Miss Hardy was nowhere to be found."

"Was the constable notified?"

Mr. Walker nodded. "He was, and the constable suspects foul play. He believes the room was ransacked."

Pursing her lips together, Madalene murmured, "Poor Edith."

"After the constable left, I came here directly to tell you the horrific news," Mr. Walker said, his voice saddened. "I wanted you to be the first to know."

"I appreciate that."

"With your permission, I would like to hire a Bow Street Runner to run a parallel investigation into Miss Hardy's disappearance."

"Please do," Madalene remarked firmly. "What else can we do?"

Mr. Walker gave her a sad smile. "Frankly, I am not sure there is anything else we can do. The constable will do his due diligence and investigate this case, but his workload is great. Hence the need for a Bow Street Runner."

"How soon do you think it will take before the Bow Street Runner will take the case?"

"Hopefully, straight away, but there is a chance it might take a few days before they truly start investigating," Mr. Walker replied.

"That won't do," Madalene mused. "Has anyone spoken to her family yet?"

"I hadn't realized that Miss Hardy had any family," Mr. Walker said, giving her an odd look.

Madalene nodded. "She isn't entirely forthcoming about them."

"Do you know where they are residing?" Mr. Walker asked. "I would be happy to notify them myself."

"I do," Madalene replied, wincing. "But I daresay Miss Hardy would be furious if I revealed where they are living."

Mr. Walker lifted his brow in disbelief. "Miss Hardy is missing. Why would it matter if anyone discovered where her family is residing?"

"I can't explain the reasons without betraying her trust," Madalene explained.

Mr. Walker wiped his hand over his mouth, the disapproval evident on his features. "A woman's life is at risk, Miss Dowding. I am surprised that you would do something to hamper the investigation."

"Perhaps I could go speak to Mrs. Hardy and her daughter and ask them to seek out the constable directly," Madalene suggested.

Frowning, Mr. Walker said, "That seems like rather a foolhardy thing to do."

"I disagree," Madalene replied, coming to her decision. "I shall go speak to them immediately." She rose from the settee.

"With all due respect, Miss, I believe we should let the constable and Bow Street Runner handle this case," Mr. Walker stated.

"If nothing comes from seeking out Mrs. Hardy, then I will notify you at once of their location," she said, her voice firm.

"As you wish, Miss Dowding." He bowed. "I will be awaiting word from you."

"Thank you, Mr. Walker."

After her solicitor had departed from the room, she walked out into the entry hall and saw Graham standing next to the staircase.

"Has Mrs. Foster already left to do her shopping?" Madalene inquired.

"Yes, Miss," Graham confirmed.

Drat! It was evident that she was going to have to do this errand by herself.

"I have an errand to run," Madalene explained, "will you ensure the coach is brought around to the front?"

Graham bobbed his head. "As you wish."

Madalene glanced down at her gown. Fortunately, this gown was perfect for her errand. It would garner much less attention than her afternoon gowns. Now she just had to have her lady's maid fix her hair.

Her plan was simple. Go to Floyd's Coffeehouse and speak to Mrs. Hardy about her daughter's disappearance. With any luck, Edith would be with them and this whole mess would be sorted out.

THE SUN MAY have been high in the sky outside, but the inside of Floyd's Coffeehouse was dimly lit by sconces fastened to the wall. Baldwin sat with his back against the wall and watched as the patrons flocked in and out of the establishment. Some were dressed in raggedy coats and others in the finest clothing, but they were all seated at the same round tables. Despite this, he knew it wouldn't be long before he rooted out the radicals. That, he was sure of.

Coffeehouse conversation always seemed to conform to a specific manner. Politeness was essential to the conduct of debate and conversation, thus hoping to keep out the undesirables. If people did not conform to the unwritten rules, then they would be asked to leave, never to return again.

Most of the conversations centered around fashion and politics, and he had yet to hear anything that was suspect or traitorous.

An older woman with faded red hair sashayed up to him with an empty tray in her hands. "Can I get ye anything to eat, love?"

Baldwin smiled politely at the woman, never knowing when she might become useful to his investigation. "No, thank you. But could I get another cup of coffee?"

"This is yer third cup," the woman said, leaning closer to him. "Ye must really be enjoying our coffee."

"It is true," he said as he picked up his cup and extended it towards her.

"We also serve food, and it is nearly midday."

"Perhaps after my next cup I will order something to eat."

The woman glanced at the empty chairs next to him. "Are ye expecting someone?"

"I am not."

Glancing over at the next table when they burst into laughter, she asked, "Why not join their lively conversation, then?"

"I prefer to be alone." He reached into his pocket and removed a few coins. "Will you ensure that no one is seated next to me?" he asked as he extended her the coins.

The woman looked down at the coins and her eyes grew wide. "Yes, Mister."

"Thank you," he said. "What is your name?"

"Sarah," she replied as she deposited the coins into the pocket of her white apron.

Baldwin tipped his head in acknowledgement. "What a beautiful name."

A rosy blush came to her cheeks as she averted her gaze from his.

"If I was to join a conversation," he began, "which one do you suppose I should join?"

Sarah pressed her lips together before saying, "The table in the corner is discussing the skirmish over in America, the table next to it is discussing Prinny's excessive debts, and the one next to ye is discussing the merits of workhouses."

"I'm afraid those subjects are of little interest to me."

Leaning closer, Sarah lowered her voice and said, "At night, a group of men come in to discuss things that are much more serious in nature."

"Such as?"

"The state of the government and whatnot."

Baldwin put his hand up. "I am not interested in doing anything illegal."

Placing the tray onto the table, Sarah sat down next to him. "I never said they were doing anything illegal," she assured him. "But they do keep their voices hushed and stop speaking when I deliver their coffee to them."

"That is rather odd, is it not?"

She shrugged a half-shoulder. "It is not unusual here. The men don't want women to overhear their conversations."

"That is terrible."

"I am used to it," Sarah remarked.

"Are any of those men here now?" he asked hopefully.

Sarah's eyes scanned the room. "I don't see any of them now, but they usually come later and stay till closing."

An older man with white hair shouted across the room. "Sarah!" he exclaimed. "Get back to work!"

Sarah hastily rose from her seat and grabbed the tray. "I apologize for tarrying. I will go get yer coffee now."

"Please do not hurry on my account," Baldwin encouraged.

He watched as Sarah hurried across the room and stopped to speak to the older man before she disappeared through a back door.

Baldwin sat back in his chair. He had garnered the information he needed by speaking kindly to the waitress. Men often overlooked women, who noticed more than they ever let on. He had learned prostitutes were the greatest source of information, because men would often brag to them about their exploits. Sometimes it was too easy to discover what he needed to know, costing him only a few coins in the process.

Perhaps he would bring Oliver back with him later this evening in hopes of rooting out the radicals. After doing so, he would infiltrate them, and they would lead him to the French spy. If all went according to his plan, this mission would be wrapped up in less than a week.

The door to the coffeehouse opened, and a young woman with an elaborate chignon walked confidently into the hall. She was dressed in a pale blue gown, marking her as a woman of means. With an oval face, delicate features, and green eyes that appeared defiant and intense, she was a vision of perfection.

The room went silent as all eyes turned to look at her expectantly, many of them lewdly perusing her body.

To his astonishment, the young woman appeared to grow more determined by the attention she was garnering. "I would like to speak to the man in charge," she said firmly.

A man at a table next to him shouted, "Come here, pretty little thing. I will be whatever you want me to be!"

She jutted out her chin. "I do not appreciate your insinuation," she remarked in a haughty tone.

The man laughed at her indignation.

Sarah walked out of the back room and saw the young woman standing in front of the door. "Settle down!" she exclaimed to the group. "Ye have all seen a lady before."

"Not as pretty as her!" another man yelled.

Shaking her head, Sarah approached the young woman and started conversing with her. It was a long moment before she bobbed her head.

Sarah started weaving between the tables and the young woman followed. They both disappeared up a set of stairs in the back of the room.

Curious as to what this young woman wanted, Baldwin rose from his chair and headed up the stairs. He had just stepped into the hall when he heard someone knocking on a door around the corner, followed by Sarah saying, "Mrs. Hardy. It is me, Sarah."

Baldwin flattened himself against the wall and crept closer to the edge of the hall. He could hear the door creak open and an unfamiliar voice asked in a slightly muffled voice, "Is everything all right?"

"Your daughter is missing from the orphanage," another voice said. He assumed this was the young woman from downstairs. "I was hoping she was with you."

"No, she is not. I rarely see Edith since she moved into the orphanage," the woman said.

"Do you know where she could be?" the young woman asked.

Silence.

"Do not fret," the young woman attempted, but he could hear the strain in her voice. "The constable and a Bow Street Runner will be on the case, and they will find her shortly."

"What will we do about money until then?" the woman asked.

Baldwin peered around the corner and saw the young woman reach into her reticule. She pulled something out and extended it towards the woman.

"This should help until Edith returns home."

"Thank you," the woman said in a grateful tone. "You have no idea how much this means to me and my daughter."

"You are more than welcome."

The woman stepped into the hall and lowered her voice. At that moment, loud, boisterous laughter came from downstairs, blocking out the conversation between the women.

Baldwin watched as the woman disappeared back into her room and closed the door. He realized he had better leave or he would be discovered.

He hurried down the stairs and returned to his chair. As he reached for his now cool cup of coffee, he saw Sarah and the young woman descending the narrow stairs.

Three men rose from a table in the corner and went to approach the young woman as she stepped off the stairs.

"What's your hurry?" he heard one of the men ask as they blocked her path to the door. "Come join us for a cup of coffee."

"No, thank you," was the young woman's reply.

"What is your name?"

The young woman stiffened. "That is none of your concern."

"Leave her be," Sarah ordered firmly.

The men dismissed Sarah's comment and continued to pester the young woman with unwelcome questions.

Baldwin rose from his chair, knowing it was his duty as a gentleman to help a woman in need. He walked over to the group of men, shoved past them and reached for the young woman's arm. "Allow me to escort you to your coach," he said.

One of the men blocked his path. "Maybe this woman doesn't want to go with you."

Baldwin met the man's gaze, his eyes narrowing dangerously. "It is time for this lady to leave, and I intend to ensure she is met with no harm." His words brooked no argument.

The man's eyes flickered with fear as he moved to the side. "That is good of you, Mister."

Baldwin addressed the young woman when he asked, "Is your coach outside?"

"It is," she replied.

He acknowledged her words with a nod as he started leading her towards the door. As they stepped outside, he saw a black coach waiting on the street. A footman jumped off his perch when he saw the young woman and went to put the step down.

Baldwin dropped his hand from her arm as they came to a stop in front of the coach. "Get in the coach and never come back," he barked.

The young woman's lips twitched downward, but her words were cordial, reiterating to him that she was a genteel woman. "I would like to thank you for escorting me—"

Baldwin cut her off. "Save your words."

"I beg your pardon?"

He took a step closer to her, and the young woman looked up at him in surprise. "Women are not allowed in coffeehouses," he stated. "Reputations have been ruined for less."

"I am aware of that, but I needed to speak to someone renting a room upstairs. I assure you that the matter was of the utmost importance."

"Why didn't you send a footman in to do your bidding?"

Uncertainty flickered in her eyes. "I wanted to be discreet."

"Discreet?" he questioned. "The very presence of a woman in a coffeehouse caused a stir amongst the patrons."

"I had not realized my presence would cause such a disturbance."

"Then you are a fool."

The young woman's lips parted in disbelief, making it evident that she was not used to being treated in such a fashion. "That is rather ungentlemanly of you to say."

Baldwin let out a dry chuckle. "I never claimed to be a gentleman."

"Your actions prove otherwise," the young woman challenged.

Realizing that they were drawing the attention of the people on the street, he held out his hand and said, "Allow me to assist you into your coach before anyone recognizes you."

The young woman reluctantly placed her hand in his and stepped into the coach. Once she was situated, she slipped her hand out of his.

"Thank you—" Her words were barely out of her mouth as he closed the door of the coach.

Baldwin watched as the coach drove away from the coffeehouse, finding himself immensely relieved that he would never have to see that infuriating young woman again.

CHAPTER FOUR

THE MORNING SUN streamed through the window as Baldwin sat in his chair and perused the ledgers on his desk. His brother had done a fine job of ensuring all their investments had grown over the years. When Baldwin left for his mission, Oliver had balked at the responsibility that had been handed him, but Baldwin had faith that he would rise to the challenge. And he had been correct.

Oliver had increased their holdings by buying up the parcels of land surrounding their country estate in Sussex.

"Well done, Brother," Baldwin muttered to himself as he closed one of the ledgers and reached for another. Perhaps he should leave his brother in charge more often.

As if on cue, Oliver walked into the study with his cravat untied, the top buttons of his waistcoat undone, and his hair tousled about.

"What has you up so early?" his brother asked with a yawn.

"I wanted to get a start on reviewing the ledgers," Baldwin lied. He didn't want to tell his brother that he hardly slept anymore. He couldn't. Images would come to his mind, images that he wanted to forget.

Oliver sat down in the chair in front of the desk, his eyes red. "May I ask why?"

"I thought I should become reacquainted with the finances. Although, I must admit that you've done an admirable job with them."

With a smirk, Oliver admitted, "It wasn't me."

"No?" Baldwin asked. "Then who was it? Our man of business, Mr. Owen, or one of our solicitors?"

"It was Jane."

Baldwin lifted his brow. "Jane?" he asked. "She did all of this?"

Oliver nodded. "Our sister is quite clever when it comes to managing the properties and balancing the ledgers."

"You don't say," Baldwin replied, wiping a hand over his mouth. "I had no idea."

"I hadn't, either, but she saw me struggling with the ledgers one night and offered to take a look," Oliver shared. "After that, she just sort of took over and started working with our man of business."

"And Mr. Owen worked with her willingly?"

"Once he saw Jane's vision, and how much money was to be made by her, he came around."

"For which I am immensely grateful." Baldwin paused, perusing his brother's haggard appearance. "I must say that you look awful."

Frowning, Oliver said, "That was not a very nice thing to say to your favorite brother."

"I am only speaking the truth," Baldwin replied. "Were you out all night?"

"I was. I went to the gambling halls."

"Is that where you went after dinner?"

Oliver nodded. "I spend nearly every night out. Sometimes I am at the gambling halls, and other times I am at social gatherings, balls or soirées."

"Since when did you start enjoying social events?"

Crossing his arms over his wide chest, his brother said, "I don't, but Corbyn tasked me with identifying any radical thinkers amongst the *ton*."

"Ah, I understand now."

"At first, I enjoyed the gambling halls," Oliver admitted. "I even made a small fortune at the tables, but now I find them rather irksome."

"You should ask for a new assignment."

Oliver shook his head. "I am in a perfect position to spy. Furthermore, the scheming mothers generally avoid me for their matchmaking because of my despicable reputation." He lifted his brow. "But I daresay that you won't be so lucky."

"I intend to avoid the marital noose."

Oliver chuckled. "It wouldn't be so terrible for you to marry, assuming you find someone you can tolerate."

"That is the problem," Baldwin replied. "I don't tolerate very many people."

"No, you don't," Oliver joked. "I see that you haven't changed."

Baldwin winced at his brother's remark, knowing that wasn't true. He had changed drastically over these past few years, and not for the better.

"What is it?" Oliver asked.

"Nothing," Baldwin said.

"It clearly is something," Oliver pressed, eyeing him with concern.

Baldwin sighed deeply. "I have seen some terrible things, Brother," he admitted. "Things that I cannot unsee."

"We have that in common, you and I," Oliver replied with a look of compassion.

"The royalist group I worked with was merciless," Baldwin confessed. "They wanted to get their message across at any cost, and they didn't care who got hurt in the process, including children."

"That is awful."

Baldwin grew silent as he turned his gaze towards the window. "I am not the same man I was before I left for France," he admitted.

"In what way?"

"I'm angry," Baldwin shared, bringing his gaze back to meet his brother's. "I'm angry that there are people out there intending to harm innocent people to advance their own selfish agendas."

Oliver uncrossed his arms. "That is why we do what we do," he said. "We go after the radicals and rein them in."

"But who reins us in?"

Oliver gave him a questioning look. "Why would you need to be reined in?"

Baldwin ran his hand through his brown hair, finding the familiar rage brewing inside of him. He couldn't seem to explain his emotions clearly, nor could he understand them himself. All he knew was that every day was a struggle to go on. His haunted past was colliding with the present, making his life unbearable.

"Forget I said anything," Baldwin remarked dismissively.

"Baldwin—"

But Baldwin spoke over his brother. "I mean it." His voice was firm.

Oliver frowned, but he wisely changed subjects. "How did your time at Floyd's Coffeehouse go?"

"It went well," he admitted. "I discovered that a group of men meet late at night, near closing, and they tend to keep to themselves."

"Do you suppose they are the radicals that you are looking for?"

Baldwin shrugged. "I'm not sure, but it's a start."

"That it is," Oliver agreed.

"I should note that an odd thing did transpire yesterday."

Oliver sat straighter in his seat. "Which was?"

"A lady came to the coffeehouse and went upstairs to visit a female tenant," he explained. "They exchanged a few words and then she departed by way of coach." He intentionally left out a few parts of the story that were not important.

"That is peculiar," Oliver commented. "Why would this lady risk her reputation to visit a coffeehouse?"

"That is what I have been pondering myself, but I am at a loss," Baldwin answered.

"Women are rather unusual creatures," his brother mused.

"That they are," Baldwin agreed. "Perhaps you would care to join me this evening at the coffeehouse?"

Oliver nodded. "I believe a coffeehouse is a splendid way to spend one's evening."

"That it is."

"Besides, it is either the coffeehouse or attending a ball with Mother and Jane." Oliver shuddered.

Baldwin laughed. "I won't tell Mother you said that."

"What won't you tell me, dear?" his mother inquired as she glided into the room.

With a smile on his face, Baldwin asked, "Would it be all right if Oliver joined me at the coffeehouse tonight instead of escorting you and Jane to the ball?"

A look of displeasure crossed his mother's expression as she turned her attention towards Oliver. "But what will we say to Lady Haskins when she asks about you?"

"You could always tell her that I am at a coffeehouse," Oliver attempted. "I doubt that she would take offense."

His mother pouted. "You promised to escort Jane and me, and I have been looking forward to it all week."

Oliver huffed. "Fine," he said. "I will escort you to the ball, and I will accompany Baldwin to the coffeehouse another time."

His mother's pout turned into a victorious smile rather quickly. "See there," she remarked, "I knew you would come to the correct decision on your own."

Baldwin couldn't help but be impressed by his mother's theatrics. The agency could use someone like her.

His mother now focused her attention on Baldwin with a twinkle in her eye. "I think we should have a ball in your honor," she announced.

"Pardon?" He had not been expecting that.

"A ball," she repeated, "to celebrate your return to Society."

Baldwin shook his head. "I do not want a ball."

"But you must!"

"And why is that?"

His mother looked at him like he was a simpleton. "You have been gone for the past three years, and many members of the *ton* believe you to be dead."

"Good," Baldwin said. "I can't stand most of those busybodies anyway."

His mother placed a hand on her hip. "Most of those busybodies are my dear friends, and I will not have you make disparaging comments about them."

Baldwin leaned forward in his chair and rested his arms on his desk. "Regardless, I do not want a ball."

"I'm afraid it is too late."

"Meaning?"

His mother looked at him innocently. "I was so sure that you would want a ball that I already sent out the invitations."

"How is that possible?" Baldwin asked in disbelief. "I just returned home."

"I thought it would be best if we planned it straight away."

"We?"

His mother blinked. "Don't you want to be involved in the details?"

"No, I don't," Baldwin declared bluntly.

"That is a shame," his mother said as she walked towards the door. "But, fortunately, Jane and I will be happy to plan the whole thing since we know how busy you are."

"Mother…" he growled.

She stopped in the doorway. "You won't have to worry about a thing, my dear. Just leave all the details to us."

"I would prefer it if you called it off."

His mother gasped. "But the invitations have already gone out. What would people think of us?" she asked, bringing her hand to her chest.

"Frankly, I don't care."

"But I do," his mother stated. "Besides, Jane isn't married yet, and we have her reputation to think of."

Baldwin frowned, knowing he was fighting a losing battle. He didn't have the heart to disappoint his mother in this, not after everything he had put her through these past few years.

"I understand, Mother."

She smiled broadly. "You are a good son," she said before departing from the room.

Oliver eyed the empty doorway. "Why is it that I feel we just got duped?"

"Because we did, Brother," Baldwin said. "We did."

"SO THIS MAN just escorted you to your coach, without so much as a by-your-leave?" her lady's maid asked in disbelief as she brushed Madalene's long brown tresses.

Madalene nodded. "The man grabbed my arm, led me outside, and then proceeded to insult me."

Teresa shook her head. "That was poorly done by him, but he did save you from an unsavory situation."

"I should think not," Madalene replied. "I had the situation in hand."

"You did?"

Madalene reached for a bottle of lotion on the dressing table. "Those three men in the coffeehouse were nothing I couldn't handle."

"And why do you say that?"

"Because they were just trying to impress me," Madalene said. "I don't believe they intended to do me harm."

"I think you are too trusting, Miss."

Madalene started rubbing the lotion on her arms. "Either way, that man at the coffeehouse was just awful, and I hope never to see him again."

"I should say so," Teresa responded as she began to pull Madalene's hair into a coiffure. "Although, I must wonder if he was handsome."

"Why should that matter?"

Teresa shrugged. "I'm just trying to understand the entire situation."

Madalene pressed her lips together before admitting, "If you must know, he wasn't terrible to look at."

"Meaning?"

"Some might even consider him handsome with his chiseled jaw, sharp features, and broad shoulders."

"But you don't?"

Madalene gave her lady's maid an exasperated look. "I'm afraid I don't find men who insult me to be overly attractive."

"Fair enough," Teresa replied. "Will Mrs. Foster be accompanying you to visit Lady Jane this afternoon?"

"No, Mrs. Foster will be visiting with some of her own friends."

"Do you think that is wise?"

Madalene lifted her brow. "Lady Jane lives two blocks over," she explained. "I have no doubt that I can arrive at Hawthorne House unscathed."

"If you say so," Teresa said with a smile. "I can't help but think that trouble often has a way of finding you."

"I can assure you that it is through no fault of my own."

"Of course not, Miss." Teresa took a step back. "Are you pleased with your hair?"

Madalene turned to admire her hair in the mirror. It was piled high on top of her head and small ringlets framed her face. "It is lovely," she acknowledged. "You truly outdid yourself."

"Thank you," Teresa responded. "Would you care to dress now?"

"I would." Her lady's maid walked over to the bed and picked up a white gown with a lovely pink sash. "I thought you might like to wear this gown to visit Lady Jane."

"What a fine choice," Madalene agreed as she walked closer to the bed.

A short time later, she exited her bedchamber and headed towards the entry hall. She had just stepped down onto the last step when Mrs. Foster swiftly crossed the tile.

"I just wanted to confirm that you don't need me to accompany you to visit Lady Jane," Mrs. Foster said, her breathing labored from her quick pace.

"That won't be necessary," Madalene assured her as she walked over to a table and picked up her white gloves. "Go enjoy some tea with your friends."

Mrs. Foster smiled, but it didn't quite reach her eyes. "I do worry about you."

"There is no reason to worry about me. The coach will drop me off in front of Hawthorne House and will wait to deliver me back home."

"Don't forget to keep your distance from Lord Oliver," Mrs. Foster warned. "You wouldn't want to become associated with that man. He has the most horrid reputation as a gambler and rakehell."

"Which I believe is grossly exaggerated amongst the *ton*."

"Why is that, my dear?"

"Because the few times I have associated with Lord Oliver, he was extremely polite and courteous to me."

Mrs. Foster huffed. "Do not be fooled by the affectations of men."

"What a terrible thing to say."

"It is the truth, and as your companion, it is my duty to keep you protected from those types of men."

Madalene offered her a reassuring smile. "I will be fine," she said. "No harm will come to me at Hawthorne House, I am sure of it."

Graham stepped into the entry hall. "Your coach is waiting out front, Miss," he announced, opening the door.

Madalene turned to Mrs. Foster. "Please do not fret about me."

"Just promise me that you won't go to any more coffeehouses."

"I can promise that."

Mrs. Foster grinned. "Off with you, then."

Madalene exited her townhouse and stepped into the waiting coach. It wasn't long before they arrived at the gate in front of Hawthorne House. After her driver spoke to a guard, they were admitted entrance into the courtyard.

As Madalene exited the coach, she took a moment to admire the enormous townhouse before approaching the main door, which was promptly opened.

The butler greeted her with a kind smile. "Good morning, Miss Dowding," he said, stepping aside to allow her entry. "It is good to see you again."

"Likewise, Pratt."

Pratt closed the door. "Lady Jane has been expecting you," he revealed. "I shall inform her that you have arrived."

"Wonderful," Madalene replied. "I shall wait for her here."

Pratt tipped his head in acknowledgement before heading towards the stairs. Madalene turned and started admiring the paintings and tapestries that hung on the wall. She had always been fascinated with all the works of art that Hawthorne had amassed.

She was so enamored with the paintings that she failed to hear someone approach. In the next moment, she felt someone grab her arm and could feel the warmth of his breath on her ear as he asked,

"What do you think you are doing here?"

Madalene turned her head and her heart dropped. It was that horrid man from the coffeehouse. Realizing that she needed to take control of the situation, she yanked back her arm and turned around to face him.

"I have every right to be here."

His eyes narrowed. "Did you follow me here?"

"Why would I do that?" she asked in an exasperated voice.

"Coming here was a huge mistake for you."

"And why is that?"

The man placed his hand on the wall behind her and leaned in, his words low. "How did you find me?"

"Trust me, I wasn't looking for you," she replied, attempting to appear unaffected by his nearness. There was a gleam in his eyes that she knew she should find terrifying, but instead she found herself intrigued.

"Who sent you?" he demanded.

She cocked her head. "Why would anyone send me to find you?"

"You may play coy—"

Speaking over him, she said, "I am not playing coy with you. Frankly, I want this conversation to be over with."

"Not until you answer my questions."

"Are you always this insufferable?"

A smirk came to his lips, but it held no humor. "You have no idea who you are dealing with."

"That may be true, but I still find you to be irksome," she said.

Slowly, methodically, his intense eyes roamed over her face. "Why are you here?" he asked. "Do you have a message for me?"

"I am not here for you nor would I ever have a message for you."

A huff passed his lips. "I grow tired of this game."

"I assure you that there is no game, and I grow tired of *your* insinuations," Madalene challenged.

"Clearly, you are more clever than I have given you credit for."

Madalene arched an eyebrow. "Was that supposed to be a compliment?"

The man opened his mouth to respond when Madalene heard Lady Jane exclaim, "Baldwin! What do you think you are doing?"

Baldwin dropped his hand and stepped back. "This does not concern you, Jane."

"It most certainly does," Jane insisted, coming to stand next to her. "Madalene is my dear friend, and I will not have you treat her in such a horrendous fashion."

"You befriended my sister?" Baldwin asked, his voice skeptical.

"Madalene and I went to boarding school together," Jane explained. "I know I have spoken about her."

"I don't recall you ever mentioning a Madalene before," Baldwin said, stepping back to create more distance between them.

Jane frowned at her brother. "I daresay that I must question if you ever listened to any of my stories."

"I assure you that I listened."

With a look that implied she didn't believe him, Jane remarked, "I hadn't realized that you two knew each other."

"We don't, at least not officially," Madalene replied.

"Oh, then allow me to rectify that situation," Jane stated, glancing between them. "Miss Dowding, allow me to introduce you to my brother, the Marquess of Hawthorne."

Madalene dropped into a curtsy, knowing what was expected of her. "My lord," she murmured respectfully.

Lord Hawthorne's face was expressionless, but his eyes still held animosity towards her. "It is a pleasure to meet you." His words sounded forced.

Jane placed a hand on her shoulder and asked, "As pleasant as this is, would you care to adjourn to the drawing room for some refreshment?"

Dropping Lord Hawthorne's gaze, Madalene replied in a relieved tone, "I would love to."

As she turned to follow Jane towards the drawing room, she couldn't help but notice that Lord Hawthorne remained rooted in his spot, and she could feel his eyes boring into her back.

They stepped into the drawing room and Jane spun around to face her. "I am sorry about my brother," she said quickly. "It would appear that he has forgotten how to have a polite conversation."

"Your brother seems rather…" Madalene's voice trailed off as she attempted to think of the right words.

"High-handed, pompous, a jackanapes…" Jane rattled off.

Madalene giggled and brought her hand up to cover her mouth. "Yes, all of those things."

Jane sighed as she dropped down onto a settee. "My brother is not the same man that he was when he left three years ago."

"Why do you say that?"

"Do you recall how I used to share stories about my brothers when we were younger?" Jane asked.

"I do," Madalene replied. "I was always so envious about how close you were with your brothers."

"Well, it has all changed now."

"In what way?"

Jane gave her a sad smile. "Oliver is a rakehell now, and my other friends have distanced themselves from me in fear of associating with him."

"How awful."

"And Baldwin has been cantankerous since he arrived home a few days ago."

Madalene came to sit down next to her friend. "Where was Lord Hawthorne before?"

Jane tossed her hands up in the air. "I have no idea!" she exclaimed. "He left right after our father died, with no word, and then he just showed back up with no explanation."

"He won't tell you where he has been?"

Jane shook her head. "But I have a few theories."

"You do?"

A playful smile came to Jane's lips as she glanced over at the door. "I think my brother was a pirate," she whispered.

Madalene laughed. "A pirate?"

"It makes perfect sense," Jane stated. "After all, his skin has darkened, and he barks orders like he has been bossing around a crew all day."

"Your logic sounds flawless," Madalene joked.

Jane's smile grew. "How I have missed this."

"As have I."

"We haven't seen each other since your mother died," Jane said.

"But we have written each other."

"That is true," Jane replied. "Will you be staying for the rest of the Season?"

Madalene shook her head. "I intend to return home to my country estate in a few days, but first I must take care of something important."

"Oh?" Jane asked. "You have piqued my interest now."

A young blonde maid entered the room with a tray in her hands and placed it in front of them on a table.

"Would you care for me to pour, milady?" she asked Jane.

"No, thank you," Jane replied. "I shall see to it."

The maid dropped a curtsy and departed from the room.

As Jane poured the tea, Madalene walked over to the door and closed it. "I don't want any prying ears to overhear our conversation."

"You mean Baldwin?" Jane asked in an amused tone.

Madalene smiled. "Perhaps, but what I am about to reveal must be kept in the strictest confidence."

"You have my word."

Returning to her seat, Madalene shared, "Do you remember Edith

Hardy from boarding school?"

Jane picked up a cup of tea and extended it towards her. "Of course, I remember Edith. You hired her as the headmistress of your mother's orphanage."

Madalene took a sip of her tea. "Edith has gone missing," she revealed.

"Missing?"

"My solicitor informed me that Edith didn't show up for work, and her room appeared to be ransacked."

Jane gasped. "How awful!"

"The constable came to investigate, but I received word that he has no leads," Madalene continued. "But he does believe that she has been abducted."

"What terrible news," Jane murmured.

Madalene lowered her cup and saucer to her lap. "I went to a coffeehouse where Edith's mother and sister rent a room upstairs."

"That was rather a foolhardy thing to do," Jane said, giving her a pointed look.

"I had to," Madalene defended. "Edith didn't want anyone to know that her mother and sister reside at a coffeehouse."

"Why didn't they come live at the orphanage with her?"

"I offered to let them come work, but Edith is stubborn."

Jane smiled. "No more than the rest of us."

"Good point," Madalene remarked. "Anyway, that is where I met your brother."

"My brother was at a coffeehouse?"

"He was, and he escorted me to my coach."

Jane eyed her curiously. "That doesn't sound like my brother."

"After he escorted me to my coach, he soundly insulted me and told me never to return to the coffeehouse."

"Now, that, sounds exactly like my brother," Jane said, laughing.

Madalene grew serious before admitting, "The last thing Mrs.

Hardy told me was that Edith could have been abducted by the same men that her late husband owed money to."

"Oh, no!" Jane exclaimed.

"I informed Mrs. Hardy that I would have no issue with paying a ransom, assuming there is one," Madalene revealed. "Furthermore, Mrs. Hardy said she would seek out the constable to speak to him."

"That is a good start, then."

Madalene bit her lip. "Edith confided in me that she has been making payments to the Queen's Gambling Hall on Bond Street."

"For what purpose?"

"To settle her father's debts," Madalene explained. "Once he died, the debt was transferred to his wife, and they have been harassing her."

"But if Edith was making payments to the gambling hall, why would they then have her abducted?"

"Perhaps she wasn't paying them back fast enough?" Madalene mused. "Regardless, I am going to the Queen's Gambling Hall to ask them."

Jane's eyes grew wide. "You can't be in earnest."

"I am."

"That is entirely too dangerous," Jane protested. "They could decide to abduct you, as well."

Madalene placed her cup on the tray. "I have to do something, Jane," she asserted. "The constable informed me that his workload was full and that he didn't have time to complete a thorough investigation."

"He said that?"

Madalene nodded. "My solicitor intends to hire a Bow Street Runner, but that could take days."

"Do you truly intend to march into a gambling hall and ask the nearest person about Edith?" Jane questioned.

"I haven't worked out all the kinks to my plan."

"Do you even have a plan?"

Rising, Madalene walked over to the window and stared out into the courtyard. "Lots of women go to gambling halls," she contended.

"Not the reputable ones."

"That is not entirely true," Madalene said, turning back to face her friend. "The Duchess of Winchester is a frequent visitor of the Queen's Gambling Hall."

"Yes, but she is also notoriously in debt," Jane pointed out, "and a duchess."

"But isn't it worth the risk if it means that I could save Edith?"

"I worry that there are too many variables at play."

"You are right, of course," Madalene said with a sigh.

Jane gave her a knowing look. "But that isn't going to stop you, is it?"

Madalene's lips twitched. "Not really."

"Just be careful," Jane urged.

"Aren't I always?"

Jane let out a light, airy laugh. "Hardly," she proclaimed. "You were always the first person to get into mischief at school."

"That may be true," Madalene replied as she returned to her seat near her friend, "but you were always right behind me."

Reaching for the teapot, Jane poured herself another cup of tea. "That is why we will always be the best of friends."

"Agreed."

CHAPTER FIVE

B ALDWIN STARED OUT the window, the drink in his hand long forgotten. He wasn't able to quite decipher the irritating Miss Dowding. She appeared to be an innocent in so many ways, but he couldn't seem to shake the feeling that she was more than she appeared.

And how did she have the uncanny ability to unnerve him?

"Devil take it," he muttered to himself.

A familiar voice came from the doorway. "Is this not a good time?"

Baldwin turned and saw Corbyn watching him with an amused look on his face. "Come in," he encouraged, waving him in.

"I couldn't help but notice that you were distracted," Corbyn remarked as he walked further in the room.

Baldwin frowned. "I don't like to be scrutinized."

"I wasn't scrutinizing you," Corbyn contended. "It was merely an observation."

Leaning back, Baldwin sat on the windowsill. "I was just thinking about this woman—"

"Enough said," Corbyn interrupted. "Women have the ability to drive men to distraction."

"It's not like that. This particular woman is infuriating—"

"Aren't all women?" Corbyn joked.

Baldwin shot his friend an annoyed look. "Will you stop interrupting me?" he asked. "I find it rather annoying."

"Go ahead, then."

"This woman, a Miss Dowding, showed up at Floyd's Coffeehouse and went upstairs to speak to one of the tenants," Baldwin shared.

"What did they speak about?"

Baldwin crossed his arms over his wide chest. "The gist of it was that the tenant's daughter had gone missing and Miss Dowding had come to inquire about her whereabouts."

"Was she successful?"

"No, but Miss Dowding did mention a constable and a Bow Street Runner were on the case."

"Bah," Corbyn huffed. "Both of them are useless. You might as well have a half-witted child look for the girl then."

"Not all Runners are terrible."

"Yes, they are," Corbyn protested. "There is a reason we don't consult with them when we work on our cases domestically."

Baldwin shook his head. "Regardless, Miss Dowding was foolish enough to come unaccompanied to the coffeehouse to inform the mother."

"I would agree with you there." Corbyn hesitated for a moment before asking, "When did this girl go missing?"

"I don't rightly know, but I would assume it was rather recent."

Corbyn had a thoughtful expression on his face. "I can't help but wonder if this girl has been abducted along with the rest of the missing girls."

Baldwin uncrossed his arms and asked, "What missing girls?"

"About a week ago, a slew of girls went missing from the disreputable part of Town," Corbyn explained. "It made the news because one of the girls was the sister of the man who wrote the article in the morning newspaper."

"It wouldn't be the first time that women were snatched in those parts of Town."

"Sadly, it would not be," Corbyn agreed. "Women go missing from the rookeries all the time. It is a very unsavory thing to think about."

"Who is on the case?"

Corbyn gave him a pointed look. "Who do you think?" he asked, before answering his own question. "It is those worthless Runners."

"Why do you distrust the Bow Street Runners so much?"

"I have my reasons."

Straightening from the windowsill, Baldwin walked over to the drink cart. "Which are?"

Corbyn stiffened. "They are mine, and mine alone."

"Secrets, I see."

"We both have them."

Baldwin placed his glass down onto the cart before he picked up the decanter. Then, he topped off his drink and poured another. "No truer words have ever been said." He picked the glasses up and walked one over to Corbyn. "May we get back to Miss Dowding now?"

Corbyn accepted the glass and took a sip. "Go on," he encouraged.

"Earlier this morning, Miss Dowding showed up here unexpectedly and began to snoop through my townhouse."

"She did?"

Baldwin nodded. "At least, that's what I thought she was doing."

"What did you do?"

After taking a sip, Baldwin placed the glass on the desk. "I confronted her and demanded to know why she was in my townhouse."

"What did she say?" Corbyn asked.

"She didn't say, but rather, insulted me."

Corbyn lifted his brow. "She insulted you?" he repeated back slowly.

"Yes, repeatedly."

"I like this girl," Corbyn said with a smile.

"You wouldn't if you met her," Baldwin declared. "She is argumentative and refuses to answer even the most basic questions. It is maddening."

Corbyn studied him, then asked, "Is she beautiful?"

"She is," he admitted, seeing no reason to deny it, "but that is beside the point."

"Then what is the point?"

Baldwin glanced over at the open door and lowered his voice. "Miss Dowding is a friend of Jane's from boarding school, but I can't help but wonder if she has been sent here to spy on me."

Corbyn was silent for a long moment, his brow furrowing into a frown. "Are you in earnest?"

"I am."

"I think you are just overthinking this." Corbyn rose and put his glass on the desk. "After all, what reason would this young woman have to spy on you?"

"Perhaps she learned that I was a spy—"

Corbyn interrupted again. "How?" he asked, his voice matching Baldwin's in volume. "If that did happen, then we would have an even bigger problem. We would have a mole in the Alien Office."

Baldwin ran a hand through his hair. "I just can't seem to get a read on this young woman."

"If Miss Dowding shows up again, then I think you might be able to make a case against her," Corbyn remarked. "Until then, and I hate to say this, I believe it was just a coincidence."

"I don't believe in coincidences," Baldwin said gruffly.

"Usually, I don't, either. But in this case, I do."

Walking around his desk, Baldwin sat down in his chair. "You are probably right," he agreed.

"You will find that I am generally right," Corbyn stated, puffing out his chest. "It makes being in charge easier."

"I see humility is not a requirement to lead."

Corbyn smirked. "Not in the least," he replied. "Now, back to the original reason I came to visit you at your modest townhouse."

"Which is?"

The smile faded from Corbyn's face. "A tip came in," he said.

"Is it credible?"

"I vetted it myself," Corbyn shared. "It would appear that the Queen's Gambling Hall has been frequented by some radicals lately."

"How would you know this?"

"Apparently, some of them had become quite inebriated and were kicked out," Corbyn shared, "but not before they loudly shared their views with the other patrons."

Leaning forward in his chair, Baldwin asked, "Do you think this is the group we are looking for?"

"Could be."

Baldwin glanced towards the window and saw that the sun was starting to set. "I will depart immediately."

"And forgo dinner?" Corbyn tsked.

"I can eat at the gambling hall."

Corbyn placed his hand on the back of the chair. "That is a shame, especially since I have heard you employ a French cook."

"We do," Baldwin confirmed, rising. "My mother saw to that."

"I would imagine gambling hall fare would pale in comparison to the dinner your French cook will serve."

Baldwin adjusted his white cravat as he replied, "I would agree."

Corbyn opened his mouth to respond but closed it when Jane walked into the room. Her expression was hard, but it softened when her eyes landed on Corbyn.

"Lord Evan," Jane greeted politely. "I hadn't realized you were here."

Corbyn bowed. "Lady Jane. You are looking as lovely as ever."

A barely discernable blush came to Jane's cheeks as she smiled at Corbyn. Then it disappeared, and her face grew expressionless. It had happened so quickly Baldwin feared he had imagined it.

Jane clasped her hands in front of her as she turned her attention back to Baldwin. "Mother mentioned that you would like to speak to me." Her words were devoid of emotion.

"I would," Baldwin confirmed.

Corbyn tipped his head and said, "If you will excuse me, I have a meeting that I must attend to on the other side of town."

Jane watched Corbyn leave the room before she turned and gave Baldwin an irritated look.

"I would like to compliment you on the job that you did overlooking our investments while I was gone," Baldwin said, picking up one of the ledgers on the desk. "You did an impressive job."

"Thank you," she replied. "If that will be all..." Her voice trailed off.

Baldwin stared at her for a moment. "Are you angry with me?"

Jane blinked. "Why would I be angry with you, Brother?" she asked dryly. "Could it be that I have spent the past three years wondering if you were dead or alive?"

"I know that must have been hard—"

Her mouth dropped. "Hard?" she repeated, cutting him off. "No, what was hard was hearing Mother crying down the hall because she missed her son, or watching her stare out the window, wondering if he would ever return."

Baldwin let out a deep sigh. This is not how he intended this conversation to go. "I would like to apologize—"

Jane put her hand up, stilling his words. "Don't you dare apologize," she stated. "Father died, and instead of staying with your family, who needed you during our time of grief, you abandoned us." Her voice hitched. "You willingly left us."

"I did."

Jane pursed her lips before asking, "Where did you go?"

"I'm afraid I can't say," Baldwin answered regretfully.

Taking a step closer to him, Jane met his gaze unflinchingly. "You show up after three years, with no explanation of where you have been, and you expect me to just accept your apology and move on?"

"I understand that it may take time, but I am hoping we can return to the way we used to be," Baldwin remarked as he placed his hand gently on her shoulder.

"I used to adore you," she said, shaking his hand off. "I would follow you around and bask in any attention you gave me. Now I can't even stand to be around you."

Baldwin let his hand drop, unsure of what to say. He hadn't anticipated Jane would hold such animosity towards him.

Jane took another step closer towards him. "You will not disappoint Mother again," she asserted. "You will go to the ball in your honor and you will pretend to enjoy yourself."

Putting his hand up in front of him, Baldwin replied, "I will do so, assuming you do not invite Miss Dowding to the ball."

"But I have already sent her invitation."

"Rescind it, then," Baldwin said firmly.

Jane tilted her head as her words came out slowly, deliberately. "We both know that you have no real power here. If you fail to attend the ball, then you would intentionally embarrass Mother in front of her friends and Society." She lifted her brow. "And you wouldn't be as cold and unfeeling as that, now would you?"

Baldwin frowned, knowing that she had called his bluff. "No, I would not."

"I am glad to hear that. Madalene will come to your ball, whether you like it or not," Jane announced as she turned to leave.

Staring at her retreating figure in disbelief, Baldwin couldn't help but admire the woman his sister had become. Unfortunately, she hated him quite profusely, and he wasn't sure how he could fix that.

———————⁓———————

DRESSED IN A pale green muslin gown with a square neckline, Madalene descended the stairs of her townhouse with light steps, being mindful to avoid anyone's notice, especially Mrs. Foster's.

Her butler met her at the base of the stairs with a frown on his face. "I don't like this, Miss."

"Please do not fret over my decision," she said.

"How can I not?" Graham asked. "Are you sure I cannot accompany you?"

Madalene shook her head. "There is no need. Besides, I believe I already explained my reasons for visiting the Queen's Gambling Hall."

"You did," Graham replied, "but why not just send a footman to do your bidding?"

"Because I want this matter resolved as quickly as possible," Madalene replied. "I will speak to the men in charge and petition for Edith's release."

Her butler sighed. "Is there anything that I can say to change your mind?"

She gave him a reassuring smile. "I'm afraid not."

"Then I shall be waiting up for your return," Graham said. "If you aren't home by midnight, I will send for the constable."

"Thank you."

As Graham went to open the door, he remarked, "Mrs. Foster will be furious when she discovers you went out this evening."

"Most likely," Madalene agreed, "but I choose not to dwell on that."

Graham held open the door. "I took the liberty of speaking to the driver and footmen. I informed them of the clandestine nature of this errand and ordered them to remain vigilant."

"I don't know what I would do without you, Graham," Madalene said, hoping her voice conveyed her sincerity.

The lines around his eyes crinkled. "Let's hope we never find out, shall we?"

With a parting glance, Madalene exited the townhouse and headed for the waiting coach. She stepped inside and smoothed out her gown. The coach jerked forward, and she took a deep breath to soothe her growing nerves.

She didn't know why she was particularly nervous. She would go into the gambling hall, speak to the man in charge, and pay Edith's debt. Then Edith would be released, and everything would be as it should. So why did it feel too easy?

Glancing out the window, Madalene watched as they started driving through the unfashionable part of Town. The buildings darkened, men in tattered clothing were loitering on the pavement, and the pungent smell of excrement grew increasingly stronger.

Reaching into her reticule, Madalene removed a handkerchief that had been doused with rosewater. She brought it up to her nose and took in the scent. Problem solved, she thought. Now, on to the next problem.

The coach came to a stop in front of a nondescript brick building. There was no sign hanging above the door identifying the establishment, and the front windows were dark, making it appear as if the building were empty.

The footman put the step down and opened the door. "We have arrived," he informed her as he assisted her out of the coach.

"This is the Queen's Gambling Hall?" she questioned.

"It is," he confirmed. "You go through the main door and you will come to another set of doors that lead to the gambling hall."

"I understand."

"Would you like for me to go with you?"

Madalene met his gaze. "Are women generally escorted by men in the gambling hall?"

"No, Miss," the footman acknowledged. "But they are usually here for a very different reason."

Squaring her shoulders, Madalene said, "I will do this on my own."

"We will remain here until you return," the footman informed her.

Madalene acknowledged his remark with a tip of her head before she approached the main door. She reached down and turned the handle. The door opened, and she stepped into a dark entry hall. The sound of men's voices could be heard drifting down the hall.

She followed the noise until it grew increasingly louder. Stopping outside of a set of double doors, she placed her hand on the handle and turned it.

As Madalene stepped inside, she was astonished to see that the hall was filled to capacity. Round tables were set up strategically through-out the room with solemn-looking gentlemen surrounding them. The acidic smell of cigar smoke dominated the space as women, wearing gowns with scandalously low necklines, walked around the room delivering drinks.

No one gave her any heed as she stayed by the door. Her eyes scanned the room as she looked for someone who appeared to be in charge.

The door opened, bumping her further into the room.

"My apologies," the man muttered as he entered, not bothering to spare her a glance.

Madalene knew she couldn't stay by the door for the entire even-ing, so she started walking between the tables. The men glanced up at her, eyeing her with approval, but their focus returned back to the cards in their hands.

A serving woman approached her with an empty tray in her hand and asked, "Are you lost, dear?"

"Why do you say that?"

The woman gave her an amused look. "You aren't the type of woman we usually cater to."

"Oh," Madalene replied. "I was hoping to speak to the man in charge."

"May I ask why?"

Madalene took a step closer to the woman so as to be heard over the boisterous noise in the hall. "I have some business I need to discuss with him," she asserted.

The woman considered her for a moment before saying, "Follow me." Then, she spun on her heel and started circumventing the tables.

Following close behind, Madalene gripped the strings to her reticule tighter. She hoped that the man in charge would be somewhat pleasant.

At the end of the hall, there was a closed door that the woman approached and banged on. It opened and a rough-looking man stared back at her.

"This woman would like to speak to Eddy," the woman announced, gesturing back at her.

The man turned his beady eyes towards her, and Madalene resisted the urge to shrink back. "Come on in," he said, opening the door wide.

The woman turned back to face her and mouthed, "Good luck."

Madalene walked hesitantly into the small room and was startled when the door slammed behind her.

Another man sat at a large, imposing desk placed next to a window. He had a big head, a crooked nose, and thinning black hair combed over to the side. He smiled at her, but it appeared forced.

"I'm Eddy," he said. "You wished to see me."

Madalene nodded. "I did," she replied, hoping her voice sounded more confident than she felt. "I would like to conduct some business with you."

"Interesting. And what kind of business would you like to do with me?"

Taking a step closer to the desk, Madalene shared, "My friend, Edith Hardy, has gone missing, and I understand that her father owed you some money."

"I am sad to hear about Miss Hardy going missing, but you are correct that Mr. Hardy did owe me some money," Eddy revealed. "Quite a lot, actually."

"If I pay the money back, would you let Miss Hardy go free?"

Eddy leaned back in his seat, eyeing her curiously. "What makes you think I had something to do with Miss Hardy's disappearance?"

"Mrs. Hardy mentioned the possibility."

With a loud laugh, Eddy said, "You must not believe everything you hear, darling."

Madalene tensed at his condescending tone, but it was not the time to back down. "Do we have a deal or not?" she boldly asked.

The humor was stripped from Eddy's face. "We do not, because I had nothing to do with Miss Hardy's disappearance. After all, why would I hurt the lady who has been gracious enough to pay me back these past few months?"

When she didn't say anything, Eddy continued. "But I do intend to make Mrs. Hardy pay for making such slanderous accusations against me, especially since she isn't in a position to pay me back for her worthless husband's debts."

"Please don't do that," Madalene pleaded. "Allow me to pay off her debts."

Eddy made a clucking noise with his tongue. "It is rather a large sum," he stated. "Thirty pounds, to be precise."

"I can pay it." Madalene held up her reticule. "I have the amount right here."

Eddy blinked. "You are carrying thirty pounds around in your reticule?"

"Miss Hardy had previously informed me of the amount she owed for her father's debts, and I wanted to resolve this matter quickly," Madalene explained.

Stepping up to the desk, Madalene reached her hand into the reticule and started pulling out handfuls of money, placing them in front of Eddy.

Once she had removed the last pound, Madalene stepped back. "Mrs. Hardy's debt has been paid, and you will leave her alone," she demanded.

Eddy's eyes never left the money as he replied, "Yes, of course. I am relieved that I don't have to see that insipid widow ever again."

"By chance, do you have any idea who might have abducted Miss Hardy?" Madalene asked hopefully.

Meeting her gaze, Eddy said, "Women go missing around here all the time. I would just be grateful that it wasn't you who was abducted."

"But Miss Hardy is my friend."

Eddy gave her a look that could be construed as compassion. "My advice is to get a new friend," he stated. "Wherever Miss Hardy is, she is long gone."

"I refuse to give up looking for her."

Eddy shook his head. "It has been my experience that people don't like when other people start asking too many questions," he advised. "You don't want to anger the wrong people."

Before she could reply, Eddy snapped his fingers and the other man jumped up from his chair. He grabbed her arm, opened the door, and shoved her out of the room, slamming the door behind her.

Madalene turned back and stared at the door in astonishment. Never before had she been treated in such a horrendous fashion. But what did I expect, she thought. She wasn't exactly dealing with gentlemen here.

She had failed to find Edith, but at least she had paid off her father's gambling debts. Now Mrs. Hardy wouldn't live in such fear of her creditors.

Turning around, Madalene started walking between the tables as she headed back towards the main door. She had just passed a crowded table when a man's hand reached out and grabbed her arm.

"Let me go," Madalene cried out as she yanked back.

The man didn't relinquish his hold as he turned in his seat to face her. To her surprise, she was staring into the eyes of Lord Hawthorne. And by the furious glint in his eyes, he didn't look pleased to see her either.

He rose abruptly from his chair and led her towards the corner of the room. Once they arrived, he remained close and asked, "What are you doing here?"

"I could ask you the same thing."

"It is perfectly acceptable for a gentleman to be at a gambling hall," he responded curtly. "Whereas, being seen at one could ruin a young lady's reputation."

"I am aware of that fact."

Lord Hawthorne's eyes wandered over her face. "So, I must beg the question, what are you truly doing here?"

"Gambling," she lied.

"Yet I didn't see you place any bets."

Arching an eyebrow, she asked, "You were watching me?"

"I was," he replied, unabashed, "and I can't seem to figure out the game that you are playing."

"As I have told you before, I am playing no game."

"Then why are you here, Miss Dowding?" he asked again. "And I want the truth this time."

Madalene jerked her arm back, successful in freeing it this time. "If you must know, my friend was abducted, and I was trying to buy her release."

Lord Hawthorne's eyes narrowed slightly, as if he were attempting to gauge her sincerity. "Why don't you start from the beginning?"

"My friend went missing a few days ago, and her mother thought Eddy might have something to do with it since they owed him money."

With a baffled look on his face, he asked, "Who is Eddy?"

Madalene tried to distance herself from Lord Hawthorne by taking a step back, but she was stopped by the wall behind her. "He is the man in charge of the gambling hall."

"I see, and you just waltzed right into his office to accuse him of abducting your friend."

Madalene winced slightly at the harshness of his words. "I did, but I ended up paying off her debts instead."

"Why did your friend owe Eddy money?"

Clasping her hands in front of her, Madalene explained, "Edith's father gambled all their money away and then died in debtor's prison. Eddy refused to let the debt die and insisted that Edith's mother pay back the money."

"Was she able to?"

"Heavens, no," Madalene replied with a shake of her head, "but Edith is working as the headmistress at my orphanage and has been paying Eddy back a bit at a time."

"Pray tell, then what purpose would he have to abduct her?"

Madalene shrugged. "Mrs. Hardy thought it was a possibility, and I thought I should at least attempt to find Edith."

"You are either incredibly brave or stupid, Miss Dowding," Lord Hawthorne remarked. "And, frankly, I haven't decided which one you are yet."

"Do you intend to keep insulting me, or am I free to go?" Madalene asked dryly.

"You can't keep going on the way you have been. You must think of your reputation."

Madalene held his gaze in silent challenge for a long moment before saying, "I would rather risk my reputation than lose my friend entirely."

Lord Hawthorne muttered something incoherent under his breath as he slowly shook his head. "I might regret saying this, but I am going to help you."

"In what way?"

"I have a certain set of skills that will enable me to find your friend much more efficiently than you," Lord Hawthorne answered.

"What kind of skills?"

"I am not at liberty to say."

"And if I refuse your help?"

A cocky grin came to Lord Hawthorne's lips. "That would be a rather foolish thing to do."

Madalene considered the infuriating lord for a moment. She wanted to refuse his help, and wipe that smug smile off his face, but she was out of options. After all, she was no closer to finding Edith than she had been before. She needed help, but why did it have to come from him?

Forcing a smile to her lips, Madalene said, "I will accept your help."

"Good."

"But I have a condition."

His grin dimmed. "Which is?"

She jutted out her chin. "I want to be involved in the investigation."

"No."

"Whyever not?"

Lord Hawthorne leaned closer, and she could feel the heat of his breath mingling with hers. "I work alone," he stated firmly with a hint of coldness she'd not heard before.

"Will you at least keep me abreast of the investigation?"

"I would be willing to do that, assuming you do not become a nuisance."

"Thank you." Madalene worked hard to pretend that his nearness wasn't affecting her. She had never been this close to a man before, and she found it rather unnerving.

To her great relief, Lord Hawthorne stepped back and offered his arm to her. "Allow me to escort you to your coach," he said. "I assume it is out front."

"It is," she replied as she placed her hand on his sleeve.

As Lord Hawthorne led her towards the doors, he remarked, "I should note that the longer your friend is missing, the less likely it is that we will be able to find her."

"I assumed as much."

"And there is a good chance that she is already dead."

Madalene gasped. "You don't truly believe that, do you?"

Keeping his gaze straight ahead, he replied, "I do."

"I truly hope that isn't the case."

Lord Hawthorne opened the door and stepped to the side to allow her to go first. "I will come by tomorrow to discuss the particulars."

"I shall be looking forward to it."

They exited the main door, and Lord Hawthorne walked her to the coach. He opened the door and put his hand out for her.

Madalene accepted his assistance and stepped inside. "Thank you," she murmured.

Lord Hawthorne didn't close the door right away. Instead, he said, "I don't want you to get your hopes up. No good will come from that."

"I understand, but I still have hope that Edith will be returned unharmed."

"Do you not understand what I am saying to you?"

Madalene smiled ruefully. "I do, but I choose to ignore half of what you say."

Lord Hawthorne didn't smile as she had intended, but rather his eyes sparked with annoyance. "Go home, Miss Dowding," he ordered before closing the coach door.

She found herself watching Lord Hawthorne re-enter the building as the coach pulled away from the pavement. What a perplexing man, she thought. She wasn't entirely sure why she'd accepted his help, but there was something about him that made her feel safe. And it was that something that compelled her to trust him.

CHAPTER SIX

BALDWIN RUBBED HIS tired eyes as he rode in his coach to the House of Lords. He had spent nearly the entire night before at the Queen's Gambling Hall, and he was exhausted. He had identified a few schoolboys that were quite vocal about their radical beliefs, but they were just deep into their cups. He doubted any of them had any real conviction.

Bringing him back to no leads. Sadly, he was no closer to identifying the radical group than he had been when he first started looking.

He intended to go back to Floyd's Coffeehouse tonight and watch for the group of men the serving woman had informed him about. Perhaps that would yield a clue.

Baldwin clenched his fists as his thoughts turned to Miss Dowding. Why had he agreed to help her find her friend? Don't I already have enough to worry about at the moment, he thought. But when she had revealed her plight, he found his heart softening towards her, which was so unlike him. Emotions were burdens that needed to be suppressed at all costs. They could get a man killed.

The coach came to a stop in front of Westminster. He exited the coach and entered the building by way of two large wooden doors. As he stepped into the White Hall, he could feel everyone's eyes on him, but he didn't let it affect him.

Baldwin walked over to where the Tories were gathered and sat down in the back row.

His friend, Lord Brinton, approached him with an obnoxious smile on his face. "As I live and breathe, is that Lord Hawthorne, gracing us with his presence from on high?" he greeted.

"What is it that you want?"

Lord Brinton sat down on the seat next to him. "I am relieved that I finally have a friend in Parliament," he said.

Baldwin gave him a skeptical look. "You didn't have one before?"

"No," Lord Brinton replied. "For some reason, people find me too charming."

With a shake of his head, Baldwin remarked in an amused tone, "I see that you have not changed, Percy."

Percy turned in his seat to face him, lowering his voice. "May I ask where you have been these past three years?"

"Here and there," Baldwin replied. "But mostly I spent my time at our Scottish estate."

"I see," Percy said. "The last time I saw you was at your father's funeral."

"I believe it was."

Shifting in his seat, Percy faced the center of the room. "You are in luck, because Lord Desmond will have the floor today and will be arguing for his new bill."

"How is it being received?"

"Very well," Percy replied, "at least by the Whigs."

"Not the Tories?"

Percy shrugged. "He has some votes amongst us, but not many."

"Do you think it will pass?"

"Who can say?" Percy replied. "But there is always a chance."

"Why do you say that?"

"Because Lord Desmond is rallying the people behind it," Percy explained.

"Are you for the bill?"

Percy shook his head. "Heavens, no," he said. "I believe we are in need of more workhouses, but I don't believe the Home Office should oversee them. It is the parishes' job to administer to the needs of the poor."

Baldwin frowned as he saw the thickset Lord Desmond walk into the room with a satchel over his right shoulder and take a seat in the front row on the opposite side of the room. His long, bushy sideburns drew attention to the sagging skin under his neck.

"I hate Whigs," Baldwin muttered.

"What do you hate about them in particular?" Percy asked. "Could it be that they believe the power belongs to the voice of the people or that they want to reform the monarchy?"

"Precisely, they are a bunch of radical fools," Baldwin responded.

"I would agree with you. England could not survive without a monarchy."

"I should say not," Baldwin agreed. "If I wanted to live in anarchy, then I would move to the American colonies."

Percy chuckled. "That is terrible of you to say."

"America isn't satisfied with what it has, hence the reason we are currently engaged in a skirmish with them."

"That is because they foolishly thought we would let them invade Canada without a fight."

The room grew quiet as the Lord Chancellor said a few words of introduction. Then, he turned the floor over to Lord Desmond.

Lord Desmond rose from his seat and walked over to a table positioned in the center of the room. The silence was deafening as he picked up a stack of papers and shuffled them. He placed them back down and turned to address the side of the room where the Tories were sitting.

"As we sit in our grand townhouses, men, women, and children are dying on the streets," Lord Desmond stated, his voice echoing off the dome-shaped roof. "Honest, hardworking men can't find work, or they are turned away because of a war injury. These men want to feed their families, to make an honest wage, but they can't. No one will let them."

Lord Desmond started pacing the center of the room. "You may have heard, but there is a food shortage, as well. The war with France has taken a toll on Society, but who is going to speak for the poor, the needy, the half-starved?"

"Hear, hear," a man shouted.

Turning towards the Whigs, Lord Desmond continued. "We cannot stand by and let our own people perish in the streets. We must help them!" He placed his hands on the lapels of his blue jacket. "Our job is to speak for the people."

"Oh, botheration," Percy muttered under his breath.

"We need more workhouses in the rookeries," Lord Desmond declared. "We need to make them accessible to the poor. The parishes cannot handle the influx of the poor and the needy. It is time for us to make a stand and help them."

Lord Frampton jumped up from his seat near Baldwin and declared, "No one is disputing that we need more workhouses, but we take issue with how you intend to pay for it."

"I am glad you brought that up." Lord Desmond walked over to the table and grabbed the stack of papers. "The Home Office has one of the largest budgets of any of the government departments. One of its purposes is to safeguard the rights and liberties of individuals. I believe that the poor fall under this category. With nearly nineteen hundred workhouses in England alone, how are we ensuring the poor are being treated with civility?

"We aren't!" Lord Desmond declared, responding to his own question. "Some workhouses are clean and comfortable havens to the poor, but others are dark and foreboding places. Many people are contracting terrible diseases and are being buried in unmarked mass pauper graves." He shook his head. "When a parish does open in the rookeries, it is met with serious rioting because it has been discovered that the death rate for workhouse children under the age of five is over ninety percent. Ninety percent!"

Lord Desmond frowned. "Some people are so reluctant to enter a workhouse or plead for relief that they resort to begging or prostitution. I am sure that everyone in this room has witnessed these terrible and sinful practices as you walk around the streets of London."

Turning towards the front of the room, Lord Desmond said, "In 1722, legislation passed that entitled parishes to provide poor relief and specifically referenced the building of workhouses. But I say that we need to update our laws and protect our people, especially the ones who can't stand up for themselves."

Baldwin watched as some of the Tories nodded their heads in agreement, and he knew that Lord Desmond was starting to sway some of them.

Rising, Baldwin asked in a loud voice, "How do you intend for the Home Office to fund this new agency to oversee the workhouses?"

Lord Desmond looked at him in disbelief. "Lord Hawthorne," he said. "I hadn't realized you had returned from your travels."

"Yes, I arrived a few days ago."

With a polite smile, Lord Desmond greeted, "Welcome home."

"Thank you, but you still haven't answered my question."

The smile dropped from Lord Desmond's face as he asked, "Have you had a chance to read the bill?"

"I have not had the privilege yet."

"Well, I can assure you that the Home Office wouldn't have an issue budget-wise with the creation of a new agency within their department," Lord Desmond said as he moved to address another question.

Baldwin wasn't satisfied with that answer. "They would have to reallocate funds from other functioning agencies to pay for this new agency," he pressed.

"Yes, they would."

"And you believe these other agencies deserve to have their funding cut?"

Lord Desmond put his hands out wide. "In case you haven't heard, England is not at war with France anymore. We won!"

"I am well aware of that, but that doesn't mean we don't have any more enemies just waiting to pounce."

"And who would that be?" Lord Desmond scoffed. "I hope you don't intend to say those pesky Americans." He chuckled.

"We have other threats."

Lord Desmond lifted his brow. "And you would know that how, Lord Hawthorne?"

"One can hardly read the morning newspaper and not get the sense that England is not as beloved by other nations as we want to believe," Baldwin stated. "We can't leave England unprotected from domestic or foreign threats."

"I am not proposing cutting our military funding," Lord Desmond argued. "Although, I do believe there is some waste in there, as well."

"I am not surprised you would think that," Baldwin huffed.

Lord Desmond eyed him critically. "You seem remarkably informed about the state of world affairs for a man who has isolated himself for the past three years."

Ignoring his snide remark, Baldwin said, "That doesn't mean I haven't stayed abreast on the issues."

"Then you would know that the war greatly affected our economy, our food supply, and created an unprecedented level of unemployment."

"I do."

"What do you propose that we do, Lord Hawthorne?" Lord Desmond asked scornfully. "After all, I would imagine that you don't have any problem acquiring food for yourself and your family."

Baldwin smirked. "It would appear from the looks of you that you don't have that problem either, Lord Desmond."

Lord Desmond slammed the papers back down onto the table. "If you read the bill, you will see the advantages of having the Home Office oversee the poor. It would free up the parishes to deal with other matters within their borders."

"How exactly did you determine that?"

In a dismissive tone, Lord Desmond replied, "It is much too complicated for you to understand."

"Allow me to be the judge of that," Baldwin responded.

"The Poor Laws are outdated, and the parishes cannot create workhouses fast enough to help with the growing number of the poor. The government needs to provide these workhouses and contract out the management of them."

"Aren't some workhouses already contracted out in that manner?"

"They are," Lord Desmond confirmed, "but most parish workhouses appoint a person or group of people within the parish to manage it, called the overseers of the poor."

"And it is your opinion that contracting out the work to someone is much more efficient than using the overseers of the poor."

Lord Desmond nodded. "It is, especially since some overseers are far more effective than others."

"Then why don't you draft a bill that changes how the workhouses are managed rather than burden us with a bill that creates a new agency within the Home Office to oversee the poor?"

"Because we need more workhouses in the rookeries, and we need them now," Lord Desmond declared. "The Home Office has resources that would allow us to build these workhouses without delay."

The Lord Chancellor rose from his chair and announced, "I'm afraid it is time we move on to other pressing matters." He shifted his gaze to Lord Westinghouse. "You now have the floor."

As Baldwin returned to his seat, Percy leaned closer and whispered, "I wouldn't look now, but Lord Desmond is staring daggers at you."

"I am not the least bit surprised."

Percy studied him curiously. "I hadn't realized that you were so opposed to Lord Desmond's bill."

"I find anything that will weaken our national security to be an issue for me."

"Well said."

Turning his attention towards Lord Desmond, Baldwin saw the lord was, in fact, glaring at him. He met his gaze and tipped his head.

Lord Desmond scoffed and turned his attention to Lord Westing-house, who was currently speaking about the Corn Laws.

Baldwin sat back and listened as the other lords debated about the price of grain and the effects it had on the economy. This was to be his life now, he realized. He stifled a groan at that terrible thought.

"I SHALL TIE you to a tree," Mrs. Foster declared as she pulled her needle through the fabric. "That way you won't be able to sneak out again."

Madalene pushed her own needle and thread through the white handkerchief she was working on. "That sounds deucedly uncomfort-able," she said.

"As well it should be."

"Why not just lock me in my bedchamber?" Madalene asked, amused.

Mrs. Foster huffed indignantly. "You would just leave by way of the window."

"True," Madalene replied. "The stones on the townhouse would make excellent footholds. I haven't tried, but I am sure I could climb down."

"Do be serious, Madalene," Mrs. Foster contended.

Madalene lowered the handkerchief to her lap. "I am sorry that I snuck out last night, but I had no choice."

Mrs. Foster frowned. "One always has a choice," she contended, "and you chose very poorly. You must safeguard your reputation at all costs."

"You are right, of course."

"It is not a matter of simply being right."

Placing the fabric onto the settee next to her, Madalene reached for her cup of tea on the table. "I was hoping to buy Edith's freedom."

"Your intentions were noble, but you failed in that regard."

"That may be true, but now Mrs. Hardy is out of debt to that horrid man."

Mrs. Foster's face softened. "You have a good heart, much like your mother, but you need to think things through a little more carefully."

"Patience has never been one of my virtues."

"I know, child," Mrs. Foster replied, "but I don't know what I would have done if you had been abducted last night."

"I can take care of myself."

"You are naïve in the ways of the world," Mrs. Foster said with a sigh. "You could never fight off a man who is intent on doing you harm."

"You underestimate me."

"Perhaps, but it is my job to keep you safe."

Madalene took a sip of her tea before saying, "And you are doing a splendid job."

"Am I?" Mrs. Foster questioned. "In the past few days, you have snuck out twice, to go to a coffeehouse and a gambling hall."

"All with good reason."

Mrs. Foster shook her head. "I don't know what I am going to do with you. I daresay that I would have a more productive conversation with a cat."

Madalene placed her cup on the table. "I know that I am making light of this conversation," she replied, "but I assure you that no harm was done from me visiting the coffeehouse or gambling hall."

"Except that Lord Hawthorne saw you," Mrs. Foster said, giving her a knowing look. "Both times."

"That may be true, but he has agreed to help me find Edith."

"I don't want you to get your hopes up," Mrs. Foster remarked. "What would a marquess know about finding a missing person?"

"It is different with Lord Hawthorne."

"In what way?"

Madalene pressed her lips together as she considered her response. It was evident that Lord Hawthorne held secrets. She could see it in his eyes, but they were safely guarded. Furthermore, he did claim to have a certain set of skills that could help her find Edith.

"There is more to Lord Hawthorne than meets the eye," Madalene said.

"What are you referring to?"

"I can't explain it," Madalene admitted, "but I feel as if I can trust the man."

Mrs. Foster didn't appear pleased by her admission, apparent by the frown that appeared on her lips. "You shouldn't give your trust to a man with whom you are hardly acquainted."

"I know it sounds foolish—"

Speaking over her, Mrs. Foster said, "It does, and, frankly, I am back to wanting to tie you to a tree."

Madalene laughed at her companion's unexpected remark. "I will be mindful to be cautious around Lord Hawthorne."

"It pleases me immensely to hear that."

"Why do you say that?"

Mrs. Foster pointed at the window that faced the street. "I just saw

Lord Hawthorne ride up on his horse."

Before she could respond, Graham appeared in the doorway and met her gaze. "Lord Hawthorne is here, Miss. Are you available for callers?"

"I am," Madalene answered, smoothing her primrose muslin gown.

"Very good," Graham replied before exiting.

In the next moment, Lord Hawthorne stepped into the room. He was dressed in a blue jacket, a matching waistcoat, and buff trousers. His brown hair was brushed forward and he had a wry smile on his lips. She wondered what it would take to truly see him smile, one that exuded happiness.

Lord Hawthorne bowed stiffly. "Good afternoon, Miss Dowding," he greeted. "Thank you for agreeing to speak with me."

Madalene tipped her head respectfully. "Of course, my lord," she responded before gesturing towards Mrs. Foster. "Allow me to introduce you to my companion, Mrs. Foster."

Lord Hawthorne turned his gaze towards her companion. "It is a pleasure to make your acquaintance."

"Likewise, Lord Hawthorne," Mrs. Foster acknowledged.

Silence descended over the room, and before it threatened to become awkward, Madalene asked, "Would you care for some tea?"

"No, thank you," Lord Hawthorne replied. "It is such a pleasant day that I was hoping to take a turn with you in the garden."

"What a splendid idea," Madalene responded, rising from her seat on the settee. "Would you care to join us, Mrs. Foster?"

Mrs. Foster shook her head. "I thank you for the kind offer, but I'm afraid I have letters I need to write," she said. "I do hope you enjoy yourself."

As Madalene approached Lord Hawthorne, he offered his arm and she accepted it. She led them towards the rear of the townhouse, and a footman opened the door for them, then discreetly followed them outside and stood guard at the door.

Once they were walking on the gravel footpath, Madalene dropped her arm from his. "Thank you for coming today."

"I told you that I would."

"You did, but I imagine that you are a very busy man."

Lord Hawthorne nodded, keeping his gaze straight ahead. "I just spent the morning at the House of Lords, and we adjourned for a few hours."

"Was anything interesting discussed?"

"Nothing that would interest you," he remarked dismissively.

Stopping, Madalene turned to face him. "Why would you say that, my lord?"

"We discussed politics and whatnot."

"And women can't be interested in politics?"

Lord Hawthorne's expression was unreadable as he stopped and turned to her. "A respectable lady wouldn't be interested in discussing politics with a man," he replied.

"I see," she muttered. "Am I to assume that you don't find me respectable?"

"I never said that," he answered, shaking his head.

"But you implied it."

"I'm afraid you misconstrued my words, Miss Dowding." Lord Hawthorne turned and resumed walking down the footpath.

Madalene shook her own head before she went to catch up with him.

With a side glance at her, Lord Hawthorne said, "You mentioned that Miss Hardy worked at your orphanage."

"That's right," Madalene replied. "It is known as the Elizabeth Dowding School for Orphan Girls. I named it after my mother, in honor of her legacy."

"That is most charitable of you."

Glancing over at him, Madalene said, "My mother doted on me

something fierce, but I knew she was saddened that she wasn't able to have any more children."

"That is most unfortunate."

"My mother spent most of her time acting as a patron for various organizations that focused on nurturing children," Madalene shared.

"Your mother sounds like an impressive woman."

A sad smile came to her face. "She was," Madalene replied. "She was the best of women, and I was fortunate enough to be able to call her Mother."

"How long ago did she pass away?"

"Six months ago."

"And when did you open the orphanage?"

"Four months ago."

"That is quite the undertaking," Lord Hawthorne said.

Madalene nodded. "It was, but I started working on opening the orphanage before my mother passed away," she shared. "She even helped with some of the planning."

"I see."

"My mother had a weak heart, and I watched her wither away for months before she died," Madalene admitted.

"That must have been hard to see."

"It was, but I was grateful for that time with her."

A pained looked came to Lord Hawthorne's expression. "My father died unexpectedly three years ago. I didn't even have the chance to say goodbye."

"I am sorry for your loss."

He stiffened at her words.

"What is it?" she prodded.

Barely sparing her a glance, he replied, "Those words seem empty to me. They are what people say when they don't know what else to say."

"I agree with you there."

"You do?"

Madalene smiled at the astonishment in his voice. "Try not to sound so surprised," she joked.

"My apologies, but we do not usually see eye to eye on things."

"That may be true, but at least we are conversing without arguing."

Lord Hawthorne's lips twitched, but still he did not smile. "That is a start, then."

"Yes, it is," Madalene replied.

They came to a stop at the back fence and Lord Hawthorne gestured towards an iron bench situated under some trees.

"Would you care to sit?" he asked.

Madalene sat down, but Lord Hawthorne remained standing. He met her gaze. "How did you meet Miss Hardy?" he asked.

"We met at boarding school."

"Is my sister acquainted with her?"

"She is," Madalene confirmed, "but Edith was a year older than us."

Clasping his hands behind his back, Lord Hawthorne asked, "Did you see to the hiring of Miss Hardy yourself?"

"I did."

"And you trust her to be a good, hardworking young woman?"

Madalene bobbed her head. "Very much so."

"You mentioned that Miss Hardy's father owed money to Eddy, but did he owe money to anyone else?"

"Not that I am aware of."

Lord Hawthorne was silent for a long moment. "It is common for people to hide their true natures from the people around them," he said. "How well do you *think* you know Miss Hardy?"

"Edith wasn't like that. She was quick to laugh and spoke freely."

He huffed. "Then you are easily deceived."

"Perhaps, but I know my friend. She wasn't involved in any disreputable business," Madalene pressed. "She was working hard to pay off her father's debts so her mother and sister could build a new life."

"How admirable," Lord Hawthorne muttered.

Madalene cast him a frustrated look. "Are you always this cynical?"

Lord Hawthorne didn't hesitate in the least as he replied, "Yes."

"I pity you, then."

His brow rose. "You pity me?" he repeated slowly.

"I do," she said. "Not everyone has a devious nature."

"It has been my experience that they do."

"Regardless, Edith was abducted, and we must try to help her."

Lord Hawthorne unclasped his hands and said, "I will do my best to find her, but London is a very big town."

"I could always—"

"No! You will do nothing," he barked.

Madalene's shoulders slumped slightly. "I am just deeply worried about my friend."

"You should be."

"Where will you start looking for her?"

"I have contacts all over London who should be able to assist me in finding Miss Hardy," he revealed.

Finding herself curious as to what kind of contacts a marquess would have, she asked, "May I ask who your contacts are?"

"You may not," he said firmly, "but I can assure you that they can be trusted."

"I just think…"

He spoke over her. "That is wholly unnecessary."

She lifted her brow in amusement. "You don't wish for me to think, my lord?"

The irritation was evident on Lord Hawthorne's expression as he replied, "You are a very vexing young woman."

Madalene decided to take the opportunity to ask another question that had been on her mind. "You previously mentioned that you had a certain set of skills that could help me find Miss Hardy," she said. "I am curious to what those are."

"You do not need to concern yourself with that," he remarked dismissively.

"Whyever not?"

Lord Hawthorne clenched his jaw. "I am not willing to divulge that information and you must take me at my word if you want my assistance."

Madalene knew that she had pushed him too far and she didn't dare risk losing his help in finding Miss Hardy. Frankly, she had no other options but to trust Lord Hawthorne.

"I will take you at your word, for now," she said, "but I do hope one day you will trust me enough to confide in me."

Lord Hawthorne extended his hand to assist her in rising. "Trust is to be earned, Miss Dowding."

Madalene accepted his hand and rose. "Regardless, I am thankful that you are assisting me in finding Miss Hardy."

"Let's not get ahead of ourselves," Lord Hawthorne remarked as she removed her hand from his. "I did warn you not to get your hopes up, especially since there is a good chance we may never find Miss Hardy."

"You did mention that, but I am choosing to focus on the positive."

Lord Hawthorne shook his head. "Your eternal optimism is quite irritating."

"Thank you."

"That wasn't intended as a compliment."

Madalene smiled up at him. "I know, but I decided to take it as one."

"On my word, it is extremely frustrating to get through a conversation with you," Lord Hawthorne declared. "I am not entirely sure why I ever agreed to help you in the first place."

She had been wondering the same thing. "Why did you offer to help me?" she asked.

Lord Hawthorne didn't speak for a long moment. Finally, he said, "I suppose I felt some compassion towards your plight, and I know my sister would be saddened if anything ever happened to you."

"Well, I thank you for your assistance."

"Don't thank me yet." Lord Hawthorne put his arm out towards her. "Allow me to escort you back inside. I need to return to the House of Lords shortly."

CHAPTER SEVEN

B ALDWIN HAD JUST situated himself in his darkened coach when the door was flung open and Corbyn stepped inside.

"You are helping the chit now?" Corbyn asked as he sat down across from Baldwin, his voice dripping with disapproval.

"I see that you got my letter," Baldwin replied as the coach jerked forward.

"I did, and I have some questions."

"I'm not surprised."

Corbyn untied his white cravat and tossed it to the side. "If I understand your letter correctly, you want me to use the agency's resources to find this woman, this Edith Hardy."

"Yes."

Frowning, Corbyn asked, "For what purpose?"

"You said yourself that Miss Hardy could be one of the women that were reported missing in the newspaper."

"She might likely be, but the Bow Street Runners were assigned the case," Corbyn said. "No one asked for our assistance."

"That hasn't stopped us before."

Corbyn shook his head. "I know Runners are incompetent at best, but that doesn't mean we interfere every time they botch an investigation."

"All I am asking is that we send out a few inquiries to the other agents around Town and see if they have seen anything that would warrant some concern."

Leaning forward, Corbyn removed his grey jacket and promptly turned it inside out, making it brown in color. "I have agents residing in the rookeries," he shared, setting the jacket next to him. "Everything they see is suspicious. Crimes are rampant there, and some Runners won't even go into certain parts of Town."

"Someone must have seen these girls being abducted," Baldwin pressed.

"Most likely, but we have more pressing matters at hand," Corbyn argued. "You are supposed to be trying to find a French spy and stopping a radical group."

"I can do both."

"Can you?"

Baldwin reared back. "What are you implying?" he asked.

"You seem awfully preoccupied with this Miss Dowding."

"That is not true."

Corbyn gave him a knowing look. "Miss Dowding keeps showing up where you are, and she has a sad, distressing story to get you to do her bidding."

"What are you inferring?"

"Maybe you were right," Corbyn said with a slight shrug. "Perhaps Miss Dowding is more than what she is letting on."

"I do not believe that to be the case," Baldwin replied. "Her eyes do not speak of a devious nature."

"Just promise me that you will be cautious."

"Aren't I always?"

Chuckling, Corbyn replied, "I believe we both know that to be untrue. Sometimes I wonder if you have a death wish."

As Corbyn started unbuttoning his ivory waistcoat, Baldwin asked, "What are you doing?"

Corbyn's hands stilled. "I am changing."

"I can see that, but why?"

"I have an appointment in the rookeries," Corbyn explained.

"Pray tell, why didn't you change before you got into my coach?"

Corbyn removed his waistcoat and placed it on the bench. "I'm afraid I didn't have the time, and I needed to speak to you." He shrugged on his jacket and shared, "I had my valet design my jackets to be worn on either side."

"That is rather ingenious."

"I thought so, as well," Corbyn remarked as he reached up and tousled his brown hair.

Baldwin found himself curious and asked, "Who are you meeting?"

A smile came to Corbyn's lips. "I do not reveal my informants."

"But why you?" Baldwin asked. "Why not assign an agent to meet with this informant?"

"I enjoy getting out into the field every so often, and this is *my* informant." Corbyn had been folding his waistcoat into a small square and now stuffed it into one of his pockets.

Baldwin glanced out the window as the wheel of the coach hit a rut in the cobblestone street. "Isn't that taking an unnecessary risk?"

"Not for me."

Bringing his gaze back to meet Corbyn's, Baldwin said, "I want your help with finding the missing girls." Corbyn opened his mouth, no doubt to object, so Baldwin hurried on. "You owe me one."

Corbyn gave him a skeptical look. "You are truly calling in your favor for Miss Dowding's sake?"

"I am."

"Fine," Corbyn responded with a deep sigh. "I will send out some inquiries amongst the agents, but I can't promise anything."

"Thank you."

Corbyn hit the top of the roof with his fist and the coach began to slow down. "This is where I get out," he stated as he reached for the handle. "I will expect to see you in my office tomorrow morning. I want to be briefed on the progress of your assignment."

Baldwin winced. "It hasn't progressed as quickly as I would have liked."

The coach came to a halt, and Corbyn opened the door. "You have all night to find something," he noted in a stern voice. "Don't let me down."

After Corbyn closed the door, Baldwin watched as he disappeared down a darkened alleyway. He thought briefly about following his friend, but he decided that would be a foolhardy thing to do. Corbyn was almost as good a spy as he was... almost. Although, it came as no big surprise when he learned that Corbyn had been promoted to the head of the agency at the Alien Office. He was exactly the type of leader the agents needed to rally around.

It wasn't long before the coach stopped in front of Floyd's Coffeehouse. He exited the coach and entered the building in a few strides. His eyes scanned the room as he looked for Sarah. When he didn't see her, he took a seat at a table in the corner.

A thin, blonde woman approached him with empty cups in her hands. "What can I get you, Mister?"

"Just some coffee."

"If you want something to eat, I can recommend the mutton stew," she suggested.

Reaching into his pocket, Baldwin pulled out a coin and slid it across the table. "Just coffee for me."

The woman reached for the coin and said, "I will be back shortly."

Baldwin placed his arms onto the table and leaned forward as he tried to listen to the conversations going on around him. Nothing he heard was cause for any great alarm, just the usual conversations that he would expect to find in a coffeehouse.

The serving woman walked up to the table and placed a cup of steaming coffee in front of him. "Here you go."

"Thank you," he said, placing his hands around the warm cup.

She looked curiously at him. "You must be the bloke that Sarah told me about."

"She talked about me?"

Glancing over her shoulder, the woman lowered her voice. "She said you were asking a bunch of questions the last time you were here."

"I am just trying to find some like-minded individuals, such as myself."

She seemed unconvinced, but she bobbed her head. "Let me know if you need my help."

Baldwin watched as the woman walked towards a group of three young men who were hurling their words about. As she reached for their empty cups, one of the men eyed her backside lewdly.

The woman didn't seem to pay it any heed and quickly moved on to another table.

He watched as one of the men pulled out a bottle from his jacket pocket and poured the contents into his cup. Then, he passed the bottle to another person at his table.

Baldwin shook his head at the young men. It was only a matter of time until they were kicked out of the coffeehouse for their rowdy behavior, since alcohol was generally banned from reputable establishments.

Reaching for his cup, Baldwin was about to take a sip when he heard one of the young men say, "I wonder if the boss would want her."

Another young man with a large forehead swiped at his arm. "I doubt it. She is old," he said, slurring his words.

"How old do you suppose she is?"

"I don't know, but she is at least thirty."

The young man whistled. "She doesn't look too bad for her age."

Baldwin followed their gaze and realized they were making the disparaging comments about the woman who had served him.

The young men returned their attention to one another, keeping themselves hunched over their drinks. They weren't dressed in the finest apparel, but they were dressed in the latest fashion. Their boots had scuff marks on them, implying they did not care for them as they should. Which also meant that they did not employ a valet, or at the very most, a terrible one.

Finding himself curious by the conversation he had overheard, he rose from his seat and approached the table where the young men were situated. He sat down on an empty chair and placed his cup on the table.

All the young men's eyes were on him. "That seat is taken, mate," one of them said.

"That is a shame, because I was hoping to buy you all a cup of coffee," Baldwin responded.

They exchanged glances before a dark-haired young man smiled broadly. "Well, you should have led with that, Mister."

Baldwin chuckled. "Next time I will." He caught the eye of the serving woman and motioned her over. "Can I get a round of coffee for my new friends?"

The woman nodded her head. "As you wish."

He turned his attention back towards the men. "She is quite beautiful," he commented.

"That's what I said earlier," the dark-haired man remarked, his eyes red-lined.

The man with the large forehead spoke up. "You just want to bed her."

"That is true."

The last young man had curly brown hair that hung low over his forehead. "What is your name?" he asked.

"Baldwin," he replied simply.

The young man tipped his head. "I'm Edgar."

"Just call me Sam," the dark-haired one said.

Baldwin turned his gaze towards the last man, who had the large forehead. "And you are?"

"My name is Paul."

"It is nice to meet you," Baldwin said. "I just got released from the Royal Navy a few weeks back, and I moved to Town to find some work."

They all scoffed before Edgar declared, "You moved to the wrong place."

"Why do you say that?" Baldwin asked innocently.

"There ain't enough work to go around here," Sam declared, leaning back in his chair. "People are trying to make ends meet by stealing and swindling people."

"Is that how you three are making money?" Baldwin inquired.

They grew silent. "We got ourselves nice jobs," Paul finally admitted.

"Which are?"

"Can't say," Paul replied, "but the pay is real good."

Baldwin bobbed his head. "I can respect that," he said.

The serving woman walked up with a tray and placed a new cup of coffee in front of each of them. "Will there be anything else?"

"No, thank you," Baldwin said as he handed her a coin, then reached for his cup.

Sam watched him curiously. "You mentioned you were in the Royal Navy."

"I was," Baldwin huffed, "but that hasn't helped me find any work. I have been scrambling about trying to find a purpose in my life."

Edgar pulled out the bottle from his pocket. "Want to add a little brandy to your coffee?"

Baldwin smiled as he put his hand out to accept it. "How did you smuggle that in?" he asked, pouring a small amount into his coffee.

"The owner of the establishment don't care as long as we keep on paying," Sam said loudly as he reached for the bottle.

Paul put his finger up to his lips. "Why are you talking so loud?"

"I'm not," Sam argued.

Baldwin kept his face expressionless, but it was evident that these men were heavily inebriated, which was a good thing for him. People's defenses were generally down when they'd had too much to drink.

Leaning forward, Baldwin said, "You all appear to be exceptionally clever men."

Edgar bobbed his head in agreement. "We are."

"I thought so," Baldwin replied, glancing over his shoulder. "I am looking for a group of free thinkers."

"That is what we are," Sam declared, straightening in his chair.

Baldwin clenched his fist and pounded it onto the table, causing the young men to jump in their seats. "That is good, because I want to join the fight against tyranny. I want to fight for the people's rights."

Edgar lifted his brow. "You look like you would be good at fighting," he said.

"I fought in the Royal Navy for ten years, and I have nothing to show for it," Baldwin stated. "It is time to do something for myself."

Sam watched him as he gently bobbed his head. "We can help you with that, but it might be dangerous."

"I don't mind living dangerously," Baldwin said. "I lived that way every day I was in the Royal Navy, never knowing if the next battle was to be my last."

Paul leaned forward and lowered his voice. "We have a meeting tomorrow night at the Blue Boar on Whitechapel Street at ten. You should join us."

"The Blue Boar?" Baldwin repeated.

"We meet in the back room," Paul shared, bringing his finger up to his lips, "but you mustn't tell anyone."

Baldwin nodded. "I understand."

"That is good," Sam said in a low voice, "because Morton will kill you if you talk."

"Then I don't want to make this Morton fellow mad," Baldwin replied with a smile, hoping to lighten the mood of the group.

Sam let out a bark of laughter before saying, "No, you most assuredly don't."

Baldwin reached for his cup and slowly took a sip. He was grateful that he finally had a lead on a radical group. It may not be the one that he was seeking, but it was a good start.

———

MADALENE LET OUT a sigh as she reviewed the orphanage's ledgers at Edith's desk. She had always been good with numbers, but this was proving to be an impossible feat.

Mrs. Foster spoke up from an upholstered chair near the fireplace, where she was engaged in needlework. "Whatever is wrong?"

"Once Edith returns home, I am going to hire a bookkeeper to manage her ledgers."

"Why do you say that, dear?"

Madalene gestured towards the ledgers. "I don't know how she has time to balance these books and still be headmistress."

"She seems to do so splendidly."

"That she does," Madalene agreed, leaning back in her chair. "What am I going to do if Lord Hawthorne doesn't find Edith?"

"You mustn't think that way," Mrs. Foster chastised.

"I know, but it has been days and there has been no word from Edith's captors."

Mrs. Foster lowered the needlework to her lap. "It isn't like you to give up hope so easily," she replied.

"True, but I find Lord Hawthorne's words keep echoing in my

mind," Madalene said. "He is quite the naysayer."

"Maybe the constable has a lead on the case?"

"Perhaps," Madalene replied, unconvinced.

"Or Lord Hawthorne could have uncovered something useful?"

Madalene gave a slight shrug of her shoulders. "I suppose that could be the case," she replied. "Although, I hope my trust in him isn't misguided."

"He is only a marquess." Mrs. Foster pressed her lips together. "But I have already expressed my opinion on the matter."

"That you have."

The door to the office opened, and Mrs. Kipper stepped into the room. She met Madalene's gaze and announced, "Lady Hawthorne and her daughter, Lady Jane, have come to call."

Madalene rose from her chair. "Will you show them in?"

"Yes, Miss," Mrs. Kipper replied before departing from the room.

A few moments later, Jane glided into the room with a bright smile on her face. "What a charming orphanage."

Madalene walked around the desk to greet her friend. "How would you know exactly?" she joked. "You have only seen the entry foyer and Edith's study."

"I just know that I am going to love everything about this orphanage," Jane said matter-of-factly.

Lady Hawthorne walked into the room and came to a stop next to her daughter. "When you told us of your vision, I never imagined you would have brought it into fruition so quickly."

"I promised my mother that I would open the orphanage as quickly as possible," Madalene revealed.

With a tender smile, Lady Hawthorne said, "And you have succeeded in that regard, my dear. Your mother would be so incredibly proud of you."

Touched by her words, Madalene gave her a grateful smile. "Thank you for that, Lady Hawthorne."

Lady Hawthorne arched an eyebrow. "Since when have you started using my title?"

"My apologies, Harriet," Madalene replied.

"That is much better," Harriet said before she turned her attention towards Mrs. Foster. "How have you been faring, Leah?"

Mrs. Foster rose from her chair and placed her needlework on a side table. "Frankly, I am getting older, and I don't like it. Not one bit."

Harriet laughed. "I must agree with you there," she replied. "I find that growing old does not agree with me, either."

Jane spoke up. "Are you able to take us on a tour of your orphanage?"

"I am," Madalene confirmed. "The girls are in their lessons right now, so it is a perfect time to observe them."

Clasping her hands together, Jane said, "I do so love that you are educating these young minds. How very progressive of you."

"Our goal is for the girls to find respectable employment upon leaving the orphanage."

"That is most impressive," Harriet remarked.

Madalene walked over to the open door. "We hope, in due time, that the orphanage will earn a name for itself," she said.

"I have no doubt," Jane stated. "After all, you are in charge of it."

"That is kind of you to say," Madalene said as she led them through a narrow hall, "but the truth of the matter is that we are still new."

"How do you intend to place the girls in households with no recommendations?" Harriet asked.

Madalene glanced over her shoulder as she replied, "We are hoping to add more patrons to the committee for that reason."

Harriet nodded approvingly. "I would be happy to be a patron."

"That pleases me immensely to hear, but you haven't even seen the entire orphanage yet," Madalene said, stopping at the base of the stairs.

"I have no doubt that everything is up to the task," Harriet remarked. "Frankly, you could have shown me a dilapidated building and I would have still offered to be a patron."

"You are too kind," Madalene acknowledged.

Harriet smiled. "I want this orphanage to succeed because it is important to you. I will help you in any way you see fit."

"A recommendation from Lady Hawthorne would go a long way in helping to secure employment for these girls," Madalene revealed.

"Then consider it done," Harriet said. "Besides, we are constantly in need of new servants at Hawthorne House. I will speak to our housekeeper about that."

Jane glanced up the stairs. "Is it always this quiet in an orphanage?" she asked.

"Not at all," Madalene replied quickly, "but the girls are tucked away in their lessons." She smiled. "You should have heard the commotion when it was raining outside, and the girls were forced to play inside."

"I can only imagine," Jane said, "especially since we had a few bouts of unruly behavior ourselves at school."

"That we did," Madalene agreed with a chuckle as she started up the stairs.

Once they reached the top of the stairs, Madalene led them towards a closed door. "Miss Gaillard is our new French teacher," she revealed, "and she has quite a way with the girls."

Madalene opened the door and stepped into the room. The girls were sitting on chairs in a circle and Miss Gaillard was speaking French to them.

Miss Gaillard stopped speaking and met her gaze. "Good morning, Mademoiselle Dowding," she greeted in her usual thick French accent.

"Good morning, Miss Gaillard," Madalene replied. "I apologize for the intrusion, but we were hoping to observe your lesson."

Miss Gaillard nodded her understanding. "We are learning how to say our colors in French." She glanced down at the girls. "Would anyone like to demonstrate what they have learned for Mademoiselle Dowding?"

A lanky girl raised her hand. "I would, Mademoiselle Gaillard," she replied energetically as she kicked her feet under her chair.

Miss Gaillard gave her a look of approval. "Begin when you are ready, Tabitha."

Jumping up to her feet, the girl recited, *"Rouge, orange, jaune, bleu, violet, brun, noir, blanc."*

"Well done, Tabitha," Madalene praised.

The girl smiled proudly as she rocked on her heels. "Mademoiselle Gaillard says that I am a natural at speaking French."

"Does she now?" Madalene asked, smiling at the girl's exuberance.

Miss Gaillard interjected, "It is true. Like Tabitha, all my students are excelling at a very rapid pace."

"That is wonderful to hear," Madalene praised.

"Earlier, I was telling the children about my childhood home in France," Miss Gaillard shared, "and about all the brightly colored flowers that grew in fields that surrounded us, including the poppy flower."

Jane stepped further into the room. "I am not familiar with the poppy flower."

"It is a vibrant red flower that brings much joy to the people who look upon it," Miss Gaillard said with a wistful tone in her voice. "I miss gazing at them from my room."

"How long have you been in England?" Lady Hawthorne asked.

Miss Gaillard gave her a sad smile. "Since before the war," she replied. "My parents thought I would be safer at my cousin's home in Stratford."

"And your parents?" Lady Hawthorne inquired. "Have they been affected by the war?"

"I'm afraid I haven't heard from them in over a year," Miss Gaillard admitted, her voice hitching.

Compassion was in Lady Hawthorne's voice as she expressed, "I am sorry to hear that."

Tears came into Miss Gaillard's eyes, but she blinked them back.

"It is I that should apologize," she said. "I'm afraid I am letting my emotions get the best of me."

"You have no reason to apologize," Madalene asserted. "I can't imagine how hard it is, not hearing from your parents in all this time."

"Thank you," Miss Gaillard responded. "But I can't dwell on the negative, no? After all, there is no good that would come from that."

"Well said," Lady Hawthorne praised.

Tabitha raised her hand.

Miss Gaillard directed her attention towards the girl. "Yes, Tabitha?" she asked.

"Shouldn't this conversation be in French?" Tabitha asked innocently.

Smiling, Miss Gaillard explained, "I have a rule that only French will be spoken once you pass through that door, and I'm afraid the girls have taken it to heart."

"*Magnifique*," Madalene said. "*Au revoir.*"

After they filed out of the room, Madalene closed the door behind them. "I must admit that I have been rather impressed with Miss Gaillard."

"I can see why," Jane said. "She seems very bright."

Miss Foster spoke up as they walked down the hall. "Madalene has ensured that only the most delightful women instruct the girls."

"That may be true, but I can't take the credit for Miss Gaillard," Madalene shared. "My solicitor was the one who recommended her for the position."

Madalene came to a stop in front of another closed door. "Now for our next lesson," she said. "Miss Hanson teaches every kind of needlework. She used to work as a dressmaker before she was hired on here."

"She sounds quite proficient with a needle," Lady Hawthorne mused.

"I believe you will be rather impressed by her as well," Madalene remarked as she placed her hand on the round door handle.

CHAPTER EIGHT

D RESSED IN A threadbare grey jacket, Baldwin walked down the narrow and muddy street with his usual confident stride, despite feeling nearly every cobblestone beneath him. The boots he had selected to wear for the evening had thin soles and small holes along the top. His ill-fitting trousers were held up by twine, and his waistcoat was a faded black with tattered edges.

Leaving no room for chance, Baldwin had spent his day preparing for the meeting with the radical group. He was aware that he might be searched so he had left his overcoat pistols at home but retained a muff pistol in his right boot.

Baldwin stopped outside of the dirty building, ignoring the filthy odors in the air. He could hear riotous noise coming through the open windows. No sign hung above the door to identify it as the Blue Boar, but he knew he was at the right place. He opened the door and stepped inside of the hall. Lighted sconces hung on the wall and candles sat on the mantel above the fireplace.

Long tables ran the length of the hall and serving wenches hurried around to bring tankards to the patrons. He walked further into the room and caught the eye of a tall woman wearing a gown that had a scandalously low neckline.

She wiped her hands on her gown. "Welcome, stranger," she greeted. "Can I get ye something to drink?"

"I am looking for the back room."

The woman bobbed her head knowingly. "'Tis straight back," she said, gesturing towards the back wall with a closed door.

"Thank you..."

Baldwin had barely uttered the words when the woman turned away from him. He walked the short distance towards the back room and reached for the handle. He turned it, but it was locked. Balling his hand into a fist, he pounded on the door.

It opened slightly, and a man stuck his head out. "What is it that ye want exactly?"

"I'm here for the meeting."

"Go away," he ordered gruffly, pulling his head in and closing the door.

Baldwin waited for a moment before he pounded on the door again. This time, the door opened a little wider.

"I said 'go away'," the man repeated, brandishing a pistol in his hand.

"I spoke to Sam, Edgar, and Paul last night at Floyd's Coffeehouse and they invited me to the meeting," Baldwin explained.

"Oh, ye did, did ye?" the man asked in disbelief. "And I'm the king's brother."

A man's deep voice spoke up from behind the guard. "Let him enter."

The guard opened the door wide and put his hand out. "After ye, sir," he mocked as he bowed.

Stepping inside of the small, rectangular room, Baldwin saw two crowded tables and men standing along the wall. They all stopped talking and watched him enter the room, their eyes full of distrust.

A brawny man with long dark hair tied at his neck approached him. His eyes were cold and restless. "What business do you have with us?" he asked.

"I heard that you are free thinkers."

"We might be," the man replied, "but we don't know who you are."

Baldwin offered him a smile, hoping to disarm him. "My name is Baldwin Sparrow, and I want to join the fight against tyranny."

"How do we know you are who you claim?"

His smile faltered. "Meaning?"

The man took a step closer to him. "How do we know you are not a Runner after blood money for turning us in?"

"I can assure you that I am no Runner," Baldwin replied. "I have a rather unfavorable view of them myself."

A man in the back of the room shouted, "Search him!"

The brawny man nodded in agreement, his eyes not leaving Baldwin's. "A Runner would be carrying weapons on his person," he said. "You don't by chance have any on you?"

"I do not," Baldwin said, holding the sides of his grey jacket open. "I don't even have the funds to purchase one."

The man stepped closer. "Where do you live, Baldwin?" he asked.

"Two blocks over on Draper Street."

The man scrunched his nose. "You certainly smell like you live on Draper Street." His eyes dropped to his boots. "Are you down on your luck?"

"No more than I suppose the rest of you are," Baldwin replied.

"I want to search your place," the man said unexpectedly. "That will tell me all I need to know about you."

Baldwin furrowed his brow. "You want me to show you now?"

The man eyed him critically. "Unless you don't truly have a place on Draper Street, and are trying to deceive us."

"Not at all," Baldwin replied. "I have nothing to hide."

"Good." The man turned towards the group and gestured to a broad-shouldered man with a thin mustache. "Tom will come with us."

Tom rose from his chair and approached them. "I would be happy to."

"Follow me, then," Baldwin said, spinning on his heel.

Without saying a word, they exited the pub and walked down the street. Baldwin turned the corner and pointed towards a blackened building that was starting to fall in on itself. "That is where I live."

"We shall see," the man muttered, unconvinced.

Baldwin approached the main door and opened it, causing it to fall off its hinges. He rested it against the wall and headed up two flights of stairs, being careful to avoid the broken steps. He stopped at a door and reached for the handle.

"Isn't it locked?" Tom asked.

Baldwin chuckled. "The lock hasn't worked in ages." He opened the door to the cramped square room and stepped inside. The smell of tainted air immediately assaulted his lungs.

Two straw mattresses were pushed up against the wall and his brother, Oliver, was sitting on top of one. He was wearing dark trousers that were too short on his long legs and a dirtied blue shirt, the top hanging open.

"What are you doing home?" Oliver asked, moving so his back was leaning against the wall. "You weren't supposed to be home for hours."

Baldwin gestured towards the two men. "They wanted to see where I live," he remarked nonchalantly.

Oliver put his hands up. "Well, here it is. It ain't much, but it's ours."

The man stepped forward into the room and asked, "And who are you?"

"I'm Baldwin's cousin," Oliver replied as a black rat scurried across the room, stopping briefly at the dirty bowls sitting on the floor. "Who are you?"

The man's eyes followed the rat as it disappeared into a hole in the wall. "My name is Morton," he said.

"Well, Morton," Oliver drawled. "I wasn't expecting Baldwin home so soon, and I have a lady coming over. Do you mind?"

Morton turned back towards Baldwin. "I'm sorry I misjudged you, but one can never be too careful."

"I understand," Baldwin replied. "I would be the same way."

A redheaded woman stuck her head into the doorway. "This was not our arrangement," she declared after glancing around the room, and moved to turn away.

Oliver leapt up from the straw mattress. "Hey, lovely lady, come back here," he encouraged, closing the distance between them. "They were just leaving." He glared pointedly at the men.

The woman pouted as she glanced between them. "Good, because I need to get home shortly."

Smiling flirtatiously, Oliver said, "And you shall. After we have had some fun of our own." He turned to Baldwin. "You and your friends need to leave—*now!*"

Morton placed his hand on Baldwin's shoulder. "I think we can head back to the meeting now."

Baldwin nodded. "I would like that."

As they exited the room, Baldwin tipped his head at his brother before closing the door. They exited the building and headed towards the Blue Boar.

Morton glanced over at him. "Again, I would like to apologize," he said. "Having a meeting with any radical views is a good way to get oneself locked up. And Runners are merciless."

"I am well aware of that," Baldwin replied. "That is how I ended up in the Royal Navy."

"You are a criminal?"

"Aye," Baldwin confirmed. "I was robbing a shop to get my girl some pretty ribbon and a Runner came across me. The judge gave me a choice; prison or join the navy."

"Do you regret your choice?"

"Nearly every day," Baldwin asserted. "I was fighting for a monarchy that I don't believe in, and we were flogged for any infraction. When I was assigned to a ship that was bound for the Americas, I walked off and didn't look back."

"You deserted?" Morton asked.

Baldwin nodded. "I did, but I served my time. The Royal Navy refused to release me, citing stupid reasons. They just needed more men to fight in their blasted wars."

"Aren't you afraid you will get a court martial for desertion?" Tom asked as he walked next to Baldwin.

"Every day on that ship, I walked around like I was already dead," Baldwin revealed. "I won't go back. They will have to drag my bloody corpse back to the ship."

Morton gave him an approving look. "We have something in common, you and I."

"We do?"

"I'm willing to do whatever it takes to advance our cause," Morton shared, "including dying for it."

"I've come to accept that dying is easy, but living takes hard work," Baldwin said.

"Well said, Baldwin," Morton stated as they entered the Blue Boar. He walked to the back door and pounded on it.

The door was opened, and Morton brushed past the man guarding it. "I have seen the rubbish pile where Baldwin lives," he announced, stopping in the front of the room. "I have no problem with this man attending our meetings."

Baldwin stepped towards the wall and leaned his shoulder against it.

Morton straightened his shoulders. "The monarchy has abandoned us, gentlemen," he proclaimed. "We are in desperate straits due to high taxes, the obscene price of food, and unprecedented levels of unemployment due to wartime trade restrictions. Some of our own neighbors have no choice between joining the army or starving, leaving their loved ones behind to fend for themselves. And what happens if we dare speak up about the injustice?" He paused before answering, "We will be arrested and labeled as rebels."

Pacing the small room, Morton continued. "The people are rioting, and it scares our mad King George. He knows that the fate of the French monarchy could be his own. Perhaps we should put his head on a stake, too!"

"Hear, hear!" the men in the room yelled.

Morton put his hand up to quiet the men down. "I have just spoken treason for even uttering those words, but the king must know that we have rights! While the Prince Regent is acquiring more debt to fund his lavish lifestyle, the people are starving." He pointed towards a man who was sitting at one of the tables. "When was the last time you ate?"

The man smirked. "Tonight."

The room erupted in laughter, and Morton's face held an amused grin. "You are one of the lucky ones, my good man," he said, then grew solemn. "But men, women, and children are starving right here in Town. I have seen their disheveled, sunken faces as they beg on the streets. The hope in their eyes has vanished. It has been taken away by a merciless king who only cares for himself!"

A man spoke up from the back of the room. "What can we do about it?"

Morton turned his attention towards him. "We can fight!" he exclaimed. "France did it! As did the Americans!" He held his clenched fist up in the air. "What is stopping us from doing it?"

The men in the room cheered as Morton bobbed his head. When the room died down, Morton walked over to a box in the front of the room. "We need funds to start a revolution," he said, holding it up. "Give what you can but keep enough so you can eat. A starved man is not a useful rebel."

Morton placed the box on a table and stepped back. "If anyone is looking for work, then I might be able to help you. But it is not without risks, mind you."

The back door opened and two serving wenches walked in with trays filled with tankards. "Drink and remember, men," Morton said as he stepped away from the front of the room.

Baldwin went to intercept Morton. "I am interested in a job," he said.

Morton bobbed his head in approval. "Follow me," he instructed as he left the back room. He sat at an empty table in the main hall.

Baldwin sat down across from him and gave him an expectant look.

Morton leaned closer. "I have found a lucrative business," he said in a hushed voice, "but it is not for the faint of heart."

"You don't want me to kill anyone, do you?" Baldwin asked, keeping his face expressionless.

"No. Nothing like that," Morton chuckled, "but it might make you squeamish."

"You have seen the place where I live," Baldwin joked. "Nothing makes me squeamish anymore."

"That is what I wanted to hear," Morton said, glancing around him. "I found a merchant who will take some merchandise off our hands and sell it in India."

Baldwin nodded his understanding. "What do you want me to steal?"

Morton paused. "Women."

Baldwin lifted his brows. "Women?"

"We are careful who we abduct, so as not to attract too much attention," Morton explained. "We pluck them off the streets, and no one is the wiser."

"What happens to these women?"

Morton shrugged. "Who cares?" he asked. "But we make a hefty profit."

"What's my cut?"

A self-satisfied smile came to Morton's face. "I pay five pounds a girl."

"Five pounds?" he repeated back in astonishment. "Just to abduct some girl and deliver her to you?"

Morton leaned back in his seat and declared, "It is the easiest money that you will ever make."

"How much do you make off each girl?" Baldwin asked.

"Ten pounds, but my cut goes to help the revolution," Morton shared.

Baldwin wiped his hand over his chin. "What girl do you want me to abduct?"

"You choose," Morton remarked.

"How long do I have to get her?"

Glancing over his shoulder, Morton said, "The merchant will be arriving by the end of the week. We are keeping the abducted girls in a pub near the docks known as the Flailing Duck."

"I can find a girl before then."

"Excellent," Morton said as he waved a serving wench over. "Shall we drink on it?"

"YOU WANT TO do *what?!*" Corbyn shouted.

Unperturbed by his friend's outburst, Baldwin slowly repeated his request, "I want to abduct a girl and deliver her to the Flailing Duck."

Corbyn shifted his disbelieving gaze towards Oliver. "Your brother is mad," he declared.

Oliver wore an amused look on his face. "I won't disagree with you there."

"Hear me out first before casting judgment," Baldwin insisted.

"Proceed, then," Corbyn said as he sat back in his chair. "I find that I need a good laugh anyway."

"I will abduct a girl and deliver her to the pub," Baldwin explained. "Then, we tip off the Runners about the location of the missing girls and they will raid the pub. The girls will be saved, and I won't risk my cover being blown."

Corbyn shook his head. "How have you stayed alive for all these years?" he muttered under his breath.

"The plan will work," Baldwin insisted.

"No, it won't," Corbyn said. "I can't even begin listing how many ways your plan could go horribly, terribly wrong."

"Not if you and Oliver are in on it," Baldwin revealed.

Oliver shifted in his seat towards him. "What would you have me do?"

"You two cannot possibly be in earnest?" Corbyn asked. "I am all for taking risks, but not at the expense of an innocent woman."

"That is why we will find a woman who will go along with the plan willingly," Baldwin said.

Corbyn huffed. "And what woman would be stupid enough to let herself be abducted intentionally, putting herself in harm's way?"

Baldwin shifted in his chair. "I was thinking Miss Dowding would."

A heavy silence fell over the room as Corbyn and Oliver stared at him with wide eyes. Finally, Oliver spoke. "I doubt that Miss Dowding is up to the task."

"I believe you may be underestimating her," Baldwin said.

"And you may be giving her too much credit," Corbyn contended. "Furthermore, Miss Dowding is a genteel woman. If word got out that she was abducted, it could ruin her reputation."

"No one will find out," Baldwin asserted.

"How exactly can you be sure of that?" Oliver questioned.

"We will pay off the Runners for their silence," Baldwin explained. "They can announce in the papers that they found the women, but they will leave off their names."

Corbyn rose from his chair and walked over to the drink cart. "Your plan is foolhardy and far from flawless."

"Perhaps, but don't all plans come with some risk?" Baldwin asked.

Corbyn picked up the decanter. "Assuming Miss Dowding goes along with this plan, what would you have Oliver and me do?" he asked.

"Oliver would follow us as we head to the pub, and you would already be positioned inside the main hall," Baldwin explained. "After I deliver Miss Dowding, you both will stay to ensure she is safe."

"But I doubt that we will have eyes on her," Oliver pointed out.

"True, but you can ensure that they won't move her anywhere else until the Runners arrive," Baldwin said. "Oliver will keep an eye on the pub from the outside."

Corbyn took a long sip of his drink before asking, "What is the point of this plan?"

"The radical group are using these abducted girls to help finance their revolution," Baldwin shared. "They are selling them off to a merchant who sends them off to India."

"That is disconcerting, but we can't save every woman who shares a similar fate," Corbyn said. "That isn't what we do."

Baldwin frowned at his friend's callous remark. "Regardless, I need to earn Morton's trust, because I fear that this group of rebels is more than they appear to be."

"Do you believe they are the group that we have been searching for?" Corbyn inquired.

"I am not entirely sure, but I believe they have the capacity to be dangerous," Baldwin shared. "Before they even allowed me to stay for the meeting, they asked to visit where I lived."

"You took them to Hawthorne House?" Corbyn asked with a lifted brow.

Baldwin smirked. "No, I took them to my rented room on Draper Street."

"When did you acquire this investment?" Corbyn joked as he placed his empty glass back on the cart.

"I paid a hefty sum to a man to rent his room for a few weeks," Baldwin explained. "Oliver helped me with the subterfuge."

Corbyn picked back up the decanter and poured two glasses of brandy. "In what way?"

"Oliver was there when we arrived, and he even hired a woman to make an appearance."

Nodding, Oliver said, "It is true. I have worked with this actress before, so I knew she wouldn't let me down." He chuckled. "Although, the rat running around the room made a nice touch, as well."

"That it did," Baldwin agreed.

Corbyn walked over the two glasses and extended one towards each one of them. "I reviewed the extensive log with all the persons of interests in London, and Morton is not on the list."

"He isn't?"

"No, but I went ahead and added him," Corbyn said. "Can you tell me anything else about Morton?"

"I can tell by his manner of speech that he is clearly educated," Baldwin replied. "His clothing was in the latest fashion, and his Hessian boots were well tended to."

"That is a start," Corbyn remarked as he went around his desk and sat down. "I will instruct our agents to keep their eyes and ears open for this Morton fellow."

Baldwin took a sip of his drink, then lowered the glass. "Are you in?" he asked.

Corbyn sighed heavily. "I don't have a choice, do I?"

"You always have a choice," Baldwin said, "but I would prefer to work with you."

A smirk came to Corbyn's lips. "Like when we stormed the beach to stop the smugglers in Wembury and left with matching scars on our arms from a cutlass?"

"That was a fun assignment," Baldwin stated.

"Fun?" Corbyn repeated. "We barely left with our lives."

Baldwin smiled. "That is why it was so enjoyable."

"If I recall correctly, that was the first time you turned down a promotion," Corbyn said, eyeing him closely.

"I didn't want to be cooped up in an office somewhere," Baldwin responded. "I wanted to remain in the field."

Corbyn leaned forward in his chair and placed his arms on his desk. "This could have been your office, and you could have been the one reporting to the Superintendent of the Alien Office."

"But I wouldn't have been happy with this job," Baldwin remarked. "Besides, it suits you most admirably."

"I suppose you wouldn't have been interested in the pay either," Corbyn said knowingly.

"I don't work as an agent for the pay."

Oliver spoke up. "It is getting late," he pointed out. "We should be heading back to Draper Street."

Corbyn lifted his brow. "You intend to reside there?"

"For the time being," Baldwin replied, rising. "At least until we are satisfied that we aren't being watched."

Corbyn perused the length of him. "You look terrible."

"Frankly, I don't smell that good either," Baldwin admitted, "but I had to convince Morton that we lived in the rookeries."

Oliver rose and placed his empty glass on the desk. "I can handle the smell, but the fleas are horrendous."

"That they are," Baldwin agreed. "And the straw poking out of the mattress can be quite irksome."

"It is more comfortable to sleep on the floor, in my opinion," Oliver remarked.

Corbyn met his gaze, his expression stern. "When you are recruiting Miss Dowding for this assignment, be sure to inform her of all the inherent dangers that are associated with this abduction. I don't want her to be unprepared and turn into a simpering miss on us."

"I will," Baldwin replied. "I intend to teach her some basics on how to defend herself, as well."

"I wish you luck, and I want to be kept informed," Corbyn said. "If this assignment fails, it is on you, Falcon."

Baldwin tipped his head in acknowledgement as he and Oliver started towards the door. They walked in silence until they left the building.

"I sure hope you know what you are doing," Oliver muttered.

"It will work out."

"How can you be so sure?"

Baldwin glanced over at his brother. "We don't have much of an option in the matter. I need to establish a level of trust with Morton."

"But to choose Miss Dowding…" Oliver's voice trailed off. "That is a bold choice, Brother, even for you."

"I will ensure that Miss Dowding is ready for the assignment."

Oliver lifted his brow. "Why do you have so much confidence in her?"

"She is stronger than most people give her credit for," Baldwin replied, hoping his words were true. "Furthermore, she is desperate to find her friend, which is why I believe she will go along with this plan."

"What if this friend isn't with these abducted girls?"

Baldwin shrugged. "Then I made a valiant effort to find Miss Hardy, and I failed."

"And you would be all right with that?"

"I would, especially since I can't keep chasing after Miss Hardy," Baldwin replied.

Oliver skirted around a rotting animal carcass in the street as he remarked, "Jane will be furious if something happens to Miss Dowding."

"I am well aware of that fact."

"She might very well never forgive you."

Baldwin winced, knowing his brother's words were spoken in truth. "Then nothing can happen to Miss Dowding."

"Jane already holds a lot of resentment towards you for leaving," Oliver shared.

"I am well aware of that," Baldwin said. "She spoke some harsh words to me a few days ago."

Oliver gave him a side glance. "What are you going to do about it?"

"What can I do?" Baldwin asked honestly. "Jane made it perfectly clear that she hates me."

"Jane is hurting."

Baldwin huffed. "Aren't we all?"

"Yes, but you were the one who left," Oliver pointed out.

"I had my reasons."

"I miss Father, too," Oliver remarked, a note of sadness in his voice.

Baldwin stiffened as he stopped on the street and turned to face his brother. "Of course you do," he said. "Father was proud of you."

"He was proud of you, as well," Oliver argued.

"No," he replied. "I did nothing to earn Father's praise."

Oliver's brow knitted. "Aren't you being rather hard on yourself?"

"Father wanted me to help him manage our investments and properties, but I was too busy being an agent," Baldwin said, keeping his voice low. "I failed him."

"You did no such thing," Oliver asserted.

Baldwin shook his head. "It doesn't matter now," he declared. "Father is gone, and I will never be able to live up to the man that he was."

"You are making a blasted good effort, if you ask me," Oliver said, his voice filled with compassion.

"No, Jane was right," Baldwin asserted dejectedly. "I abandoned the family when you needed me the most."

"You were hurting," Oliver observed. "You still are."

"Forget I said anything," Baldwin huffed as he resumed walking.

"It's not too late to make amends," Oliver responded, matching his stride.

Baldwin pursed his lips together as they continued to walk down the street. His brother couldn't understand the overwhelming anguish that he struggled with on a daily basis. At times, it threatened to consume him, taking away every last ounce of happiness that he possessed. Which wasn't much.

Oliver's voice broke through his musings. "What I wouldn't give for a hackney right now," he joked.

Baldwin chuckled, grateful for the change in topics. "I agree. It is a shame that hackneys don't operate this deep in the rookeries."

"Fortunately, we are only a few blocks away," Oliver commented as his alert eyes glanced at the men loitering in front of the buildings. "Let's hope we get into a fight on our way there."

"You're looking for a fight?"

Oliver smirked. "No, but I wouldn't mind if one found us."

CHAPTER NINE

T HE WARMTH OF the afternoon sun streamed through the open windows as Madalene took a sip of tea.

"Please say that you will come," Jane said over the rim of her teacup.

Madalene frowned, lowering the cup in her hand. "I daresay that your brother won't want me at his ball."

"It doesn't matter what he wants," Jane countered. "I want you there."

Lady Hawthorne spoke up from next to her daughter. "Jane is correct. Besides, *we* both want you there."

"I suppose I could attend, assuming I haven't left for the countryside yet."

Reaching forward, Jane placed her empty teacup on the tray. "You must delay your trip."

"I already have for the sake of finding Edith," Madalene replied.

"Has the constable found any leads on where Edith could be?" Harriet asked.

Madalene shook her head. "I'm afraid not."

"You must be patient," Harriet encouraged. "After all, these investigations can take time."

"Time that Edith doesn't have," Madalene asserted, placing her cup and saucer onto the tray. "I just don't believe the constable is doing all he can on this case."

"Has the Bow Street Runner made any progress?" Jane asked.

"I'm not sure," Madalene replied. "My solicitor hasn't responded to my letter."

Jane gave her a knowing look. "You might be working yourself into a frenzy for no reason," she said. "The Bow Street Runner may have already found Edith, and she will be able to attend the ball in Baldwin's honor."

"I don't believe that to be the case," Madalene responded. "I'm sure I would have heard if that were true."

"It would be nice to have two friends at the ball," Jane commented. "I tire of pretending that I enjoy going to these social events."

"Attending these social events is expected of you," Harriet said, exasperated. "You are the daughter of a marquess."

"I know," Jane responded, "and I am expected to smile and pretend to enjoy all the busybodies that flutter around the room, openly judging one another."

"Not everyone is a busybody," Harriet pointed out.

"You are right," Jane said, her lips twitching. "How could I forget the gossipmongers?"

Madalene hid her growing smile behind her fingers. They both shared a mutual dislike for social events, but Jane wasn't in a position where she could refuse invites. However, that didn't stop her from complaining about it incessantly.

"If you don't stop, perhaps I will just arrange a marriage for you and be done with it," Harriet declared, but there was no real threat behind her words.

"Will you arrange a marriage with a pirate for me?" Jane asked, perking up.

"Why a pirate?" Harriet asked.

"Then I could travel around the world and learn to use a cutlass," Jane declared.

"Dear child," Harriet sighed, "whatever am I going to do with you?"

Jane laughed. "We shall grow old together, and I will read you books by the fireplace."

"What of grandchildren?"

"That is what Baldwin and Oliver are for," Jane replied quickly. "They need heirs, not me."

Harriet shifted her gaze. "What do you think about that, Madalene?"

Lowering her hand, Madalene replied, "I believe I shall join you by the fireplace and delight in Jane's storytelling."

"You both are terrible," Harriet remarked, softening her words with a smile. "One day, you will both be married and have lots of children running around your estates."

"I hope our estates are neighboring," Jane mused. "Wouldn't that be wonderful?"

Before Madalene could respond, Graham stepped into the room and announced, "Lord Hawthorne would like a moment of your time, Miss."

Jane eyed her curiously. "Why is my brother calling upon you?"

"Perhaps he has an update on Edith," Madalene replied.

"Why would that be the case?"

Madalene glanced over at the door before saying, "He offered to look into her disappearance."

"But my brother is a marquess," Jane said. "What could he possibly do to help Edith?"

"I'm not entirely sure, but it seemed like a good idea at the time to accept his help." Madalene turned her attention back towards Graham. "Will you send Lord Hawthorne in, please?"

"As you wish," Graham replied as he departed from the room to do her bidding.

A moment later, Lord Hawthorne stepped into the room wearing a dark green jacket, an ivory waistcoat, and buff trousers. His eyes widened with surprise when he saw his mother and sister in the room.

"Mother," he acknowledged. "Jane."

Jane frowned. "May I ask why you are calling on my friend?" she asked. "You don't intend to yell at her again, do you?"

"That is not my intention," Lord Hawthorne replied.

"Then what is?" Jane pressed.

Lord Hawthorne ignored the question, instead turning his attention to Madalene. "May I have a moment of your time, Miss Dowding?" he asked. "I have something private I would like to discuss with you."

Rising, Harriet announced cheerfully, "I believe this would be a good time for us to depart. Don't you agree, Jane?"

"I suppose it is," Jane replied reluctantly as she rose.

Harriet stepped over to Lord Hawthorne and kissed his cheek. "Will we see you for dinner tonight?"

"You will not," Lord Hawthorne said. "I regret to inform you that Oliver and I have business that we need to attend to."

"That is most unfortunate," Harriet remarked as she attempted to hide her disappointment, "but we understand."

"I don't," Jane muttered.

Lord Hawthorne glanced over at his sister and asked, "Would you care to go riding before breakfast tomorrow?"

"I'm afraid I am busy, but I thank you for the kind offer," Jane remarked dryly.

Despite Lord Hawthorne's face remaining expressionless, Madalene detected pain in his eyes at his sister's rejection.

"Come along, Mother," Jane said before she hurried out of the room.

Harriet watched Jane's retreating figure before she gave her son an apologetic smile. "We will see you soon, won't we?"

"You will," Lord Hawthorne assured her.

With a parting glance at Madalene, Harriet stepped out of the drawing room.

Madalene rose from the settee. "What did you wish to discuss with me?" she asked, finding herself increasingly curious.

In a few strides, Lord Hawthorne closed the distance between them and said in a low voice, "I need a favor."

"From me?"

He nodded, his eyes intently watching her.

"What would you ask of me?" she inquired, clasping her hands in front of her.

"I need to abduct you," he remarked simply.

"I beg your pardon?" Madalene went to take a step back, to create more distance between them, but the settee behind her prevented her retreat.

Lord Hawthorne appeared displeased by her reaction. "Perhaps I should start from the beginning," he suggested.

"I think that would be best."

"I have a credible lead on some missing girls, and there is a chance that Edith could be among them."

"That is wonderful news!" she gushed.

He nodded slowly. "It is, but we are unable to retrieve the girls right away."

Madalene tilted her head. "And why is that?"

"I'm not at liberty to say, but it is of utmost importance." His words may have been curt, but she could tell that he was in earnest.

"I believe you," she found herself admitting.

Lord Hawthorne stared at her with uncertainty in his eyes. "You believe me?" he asked. "Just like that?"

"I do."

"You don't require an additional explanation?"

Madalene shook her head. "Not unless you intend to divulge more."

"I do not."

"Then it would appear that my curiosity must be satisfied."

Wiping a hand over his chin, Lord Hawthorne looked puzzled. "It would appear that I have underestimated you yet again."

Madalene lifted her brow. "Now, will you kindly explain why you need to abduct me?"

"I would take you to a pub near the docks where the other missing girls are being held," Lord Hawthorne shared. "You will be in no immediate danger. I will have two people ensuring that you remain safe."

"Who are these people?"

"One is my brother, Oliver, and the other is none of your concern. With any luck, you won't even see him."

"I see."

"After you are with the missing girls, the Bow Street Runners will raid the pub and set you free."

"Will it truly be that simple?"

He winced. "There are some risks associated with this plan."

"Such as?"

"The Bow Street Runners might not come immediately, and you may be required to protect yourself," he said.

"And how exactly would I do that?"

Lord Hawthorne reached into his boot and pulled out a small pistol. "Are you familiar with how to use a muff pistol?"

"I am not."

"That is disconcerting," he replied, frowning. "It is not uncommon for a lady to carry one in her reticule."

Glancing down at the pistol, Madalene remarked, "I have never been in a position that required the use of one."

"I shall bring my spare with me tomorrow and give it to you," Lord Hawthorne said, returning the muff pistol to his boot.

"I am not opposed to that."

"Good," he replied. "Do you carry a knife on your person?"

"I do not."

With disapproval on his features, he asked, "Do you not have the slightest regard for your personal safety?"

"I can box," Madalene announced proudly.

Lord Hawthorne didn't appear impressed by her admission. "I doubt that very much."

"It's true," she asserted.

His next words seemed to catch her off guard. "Punch me, then."

Her lips parted in surprise at his odd request. "I couldn't possibly punch you, my lord."

Leaning closer to her, he said, "I give you leave to punch me."

"But what if I hurt you?"

Lord Hawthorne chuckled. "You couldn't possibly hurt me," he remarked smugly.

Tired of his pompous attitude, Madalene reared her fist back and punched him in the face. She felt gratified when she saw him stumbling backwards.

His right hand went to cover his nose and she saw blood on his fingers. "Oh, my lord!" she exclaimed. "I am so incredibly sorry."

Rushing over to the table, Madalene picked up the handkerchief she had been working on and brought it back to Lord Hawthorne.

"Allow me to retrieve some ice for your nose," she said.

Rising to his full height, Lord Hawthorne asserted, "That won't be necessary."

"But you are bleeding, my lord."

Dabbing his nose with the handkerchief, he remarked, "No harm done. It was just some blood."

"Again, I am terribly sorry—" she began.

Lord Hawthorne raised his hand, stilling her words. "I am impressed, Miss Dowding. You have quite a punch."

"I assure you that I have never drawn blood before."

"How often do you box?"

"I practice nearly every morning," she admitted.

He bobbed his head in approval as he lowered the handkerchief in his hand. "I am glad to hear that. No one would expect someone of your stature to hit so proficiently."

"I will take that as a compliment."

"I assure you that it was meant as one," Lord Hawthorne said.

Madalene glanced down at the bloody handkerchief. "Would you care for a clean handkerchief?" she asked.

Lord Hawthorne followed her gaze. "It would appear that I ruined this one."

"No need to concern yourself with that," she assured him. "I have many, many more."

He smiled, but it was quickly replaced by a grimace. "I'm afraid my nose is not ready for me to smile," he admitted.

"Did I break it?" she asked hesitantly.

Lord Hawthorne brought his hand up to touch his nose. "It doesn't appear so. But even if you did, it wouldn't be the first time I have broken my nose."

Unsure of what to say, she started, "I am truly sorry, and—"

"It was not your fault," he interrupted. "I was the one who told you to punch me."

"That may be true, but I shouldn't have hit you as hard as I did."

His lips quirked slightly upward in a hint of a smile. "I have a feeling you have been wanting to hit me for quite some time."

"No, of course not," she rushed to say.

Leaning closer, his eyes held an amused glimmer. "Liar."

A giggle escaped her lips, and she brought her hand up to cover her mouth. "Well, perhaps."

"I assumed as much," Lord Hawthorne remarked, taking a step back. "If you are not opposed, I shall call on you tomorrow to continue our discussion."

"I look forward to it."

Lord Hawthorne tipped his head. "Good day, Miss Dowding."

"Good day, Lord Hawthorne," she replied, dropping into a slight curtsy.

He opened his mouth as if he intended to say something, but then he closed it. Finally, he spoke. "Until tomorrow, then."

Madalene watched as Lord Hawthorne departed from the room, and she couldn't help but wonder what he had intended to say.

～

BALDWIN LAY ON the filthy straw mattress as he stared up at the dry rot on the ceiling. It was only a matter of time before the ceiling collapsed, he realized. He truly hoped he wouldn't still be around when that happened.

Most of the other side of the building had collapsed in on itself, but people were still residing in the rooms, at least the habitable ones. What horrible conditions these people had to live with every day just to survive. He could hear the wail of a little child further down the hall, and he couldn't help but wonder if it had enough to eat for the day.

Perhaps more workhouses would be a good thing, he thought to himself. It would give these people a chance to do more than just make it to another day. But the funding had to come from somewhere else besides the Home Office.

His swollen nose started throbbing and he brought his hand up to gently touch it. A small smile came to his lips at Miss Dowding's reaction after she hit him. He could hear the slight panic in her voice, as if he would be upset with her. But he wasn't. In fact, he was impressed by her strength. Every time he thought he had her figured out, she surprised him.

For some inexplicable reason, she believed in him. She took him at his word and didn't press him for more. What an interesting woman Miss Dowding was turning out to be. Perhaps when this was all over, he would take her on a carriage ride through Hyde Park.

A knock came at the door, breaking him out of his reverie.

"Enter," he ordered as he sat up on the straw mattress.

The door creaked opened, and Morton stepped into the room. "Evening, Baldwin."

Rising, Baldwin returned his greeting. "Evening."

"I have come to speak to you privately," Morton said. "Do you have a moment?"

Baldwin huffed. "Time is the one thing I have plenty of."

Morton closed the door and turned back around to face him. "Where is your cousin?" he asked with a side glance at the empty straw mattress.

"Chasing after women."

"Ah," Morton said, eyeing him closely. "Did you get into a fight?"

"Nothing that I couldn't handle."

Appearing amused, Morton remarked, "I just wanted to say that your story resonated with me, and I can't help but think you and my father were similar."

"How so?"

"My father was a criminal, but he was hanged for his crimes." Morton walked over to the broken window, which was stuffed with rags and paper to keep out the elements.

"What crime did he commit?"

"Murder," Morton replied. "He killed my mother."

Baldwin gave him a baffled look. "I am not sure how we are similar."

Morton chuckled. "My father was a man of principles. When he found out his wife was fornicating with his friend, he killed her for it."

"You think I am a man of principles?" Baldwin asked.

"I do," Morton replied. "You made the choice to stop fighting for the king and start fighting for yourself."

"That is true."

"You risk death if you are caught, but you still deserted."

"'Life, liberty and the pursuit of happiness' is what the Americans have, and I want that," Baldwin said, leaning his shoulder against the wall.

"Everyone deserves that," Morton responded.

"That they do."

"Have you thought of traveling to the Americas?"

Baldwin bobbed his head. "Yes, but I need funds to buy a ticket, and I'll only go after the skirmish is over between England and America."

Morton met his gaze. "What if I could come up with the funds for you to start a new life in America. Would you be interested?"

Baldwin straightened from the wall. "I would be very interested, but are we talking about abducting more girls?"

"No, abducting the girls is just a quick way to produce some money," Morton explained. "I am talking about much more than that."

"I assume this is illegal."

Morton smirked. "It only is if you get caught."

"I don't know," Baldwin said as he rubbed the back of his neck with his hand. "I may live in a rubbish pile, but at least it isn't jail. I can come and go as I please."

"Can you?" Morton asked. "After all, it will only take someone recognizing you once and you're dragged back to the ship and hung for desertion."

"I choose not to dwell on that."

Morton took a step closer to him. "I'm giving you the opportunity to make history."

"How could I make history?" Baldwin made sure his expression showed doubt with a good dose of hope mixed in. He wanted Morton to believe he was cautious but willing to be a part of the movement.

"We are recruiting a team to do a special assignment," Morton said. "The pay is good, and the plan is infallible."

Baldwin's face grew slack. "No plan is infallible."

"This one is," Morton declared. "We just need like-minded individuals who are willing to do whatever it takes to make their voices heard."

"Which is?"

Morton chuckled. "We aren't ready to tell you everything yet," he said. "I just need to know if you are interested or not."

"Let's say I do get caught on this special assignment," Baldwin started, "is it punishable by death?"

"Isn't every crime that is worth doing?" Morton asked, putting his hands out wide. "After all, the American colonists fought for freedom, at the expense of their own lives."

Baldwin frowned. "I'm not entirely sure I want a noose around my neck any time soon."

Morton tsked. "That is only if you get caught, and that isn't likely to happen."

"How can you be so sure about that?"

A door slammed above them, and Morton glanced up towards the ceiling before saying, "We have someone who is going to help us."

"Who?"

"Someone who knows our plight and has offered to help," Morton declared. "Our numbers are constantly growing, and we have factions all over London that are continuing to meet underground. But the time is coming when we will rise up and start a revolution." Morton stepped closer to him and placed a hand on his shoulder. "We are just waiting for a sign that will light the flame of rebellion."

"What is the sign?"

Watching him intently, Morton dropped his hand to his side and said, "That is what I want you to be a part of. You can make history happen."

Baldwin squared his shoulders. "I will do it, whatever it takes."

Morton smiled broadly. "I knew I could count on you." He walked over to the door. "I'll be in contact, but don't tell anyone. Not even your cousin. We don't want to risk our plans being uncovered."

"I understand."

After Morton closed the door behind him, Baldwin sat back down on the straw mattress and pondered what he had just uncovered. Was the person who was going to help with the rebellion the French spy that he had been tracking? And what job was Morton recruiting him to do?

The door opened, and Oliver stepped into the room with some bread in his hand. "I just saw Morton leave the building," he said as he closed the door. "What did he want?"

"He was recruiting me for a special assignment."

"Which was?" Oliver asked eagerly.

"He didn't say."

Oliver groaned. "Does that mean we have to stay in this dilapidated building for another night?"

"Possibly two."

"I am so displeased by your remark that I might not share this bread with you," Oliver replied, shaking his head.

"You are free to leave," Baldwin encouraged. "I told Morton that you were off chasing women."

Oliver broke the bread and extended half towards him. "I can't possibly leave you here alone."

"Why is that?"

"Because you will get yourself killed," Oliver teased. "After all, I left you alone for only a few hours and Miss Dowding broke your nose."

"She did not break my nose."

Oliver chuckled. "It looks pretty swollen from where I stand, and Mother would be furious if it is still swollen for the ball in your honor."

"That is in three days' time," Baldwin said. "I have no doubt that the swelling will go down before then."

"Let's hope for your sake it does," Oliver joked as he sat down on his mattress. "Did Morton give you any hints on the type of assignment that he was recruiting you for?"

"I do know that the crime is punishable by death."

"That could be a host of things," Oliver remarked. "Any treasonous activity is punishable by death."

Baldwin leaned his back against the wall. "He indicated that someone was going to help with the plan."

Oliver swallowed the bite in his mouth. "Do you think Morton was referring to the French spy?" he asked.

"I don't know, but it is a promising lead."

"That it is," Oliver agreed. "When do you intend to report your findings to Corbyn?"

"I will go later tonight."

"It's a good thing Corbyn doesn't sleep."

Baldwin rubbed the back of his neck with his hand. "I'm getting tired of sleeping on these mattresses."

"Do you suppose there are more fleas or straw in them?" Oliver asked.

"Fleas, definitely."

Glancing over at him, Oliver asked, "Do you miss working in France?"

"I resided on Jersey Island, but I traveled back and forth constantly," Baldwin shared. "I miss the crashing of waves outside my window and the smell of fish on my hands and clothes."

"The smell of fish?"

"I worked beside a fisherman as my cover," Baldwin explained.

"That is how I traveled to France without being detected."

Oliver looked at him in amazement. "You failed to mention that in any of your letters."

"Coded letters do not allow room for trivial information."

"True, but I must admit that I am having a hard time imagining my brother as a fisherman," Oliver joked.

Baldwin smiled. "I never said I was good at it."

The sound of someone dumping the contents of a bucket out the window and into the alleyway caused Baldwin to grimace. "Between the smell wafting up from the alleyway, the thin walls, and the constant cries of children, I don't know how anyone can get any sleep around here."

As if on cue, a baby started crying from the floor above them.

Oliver laid his head on the mattress. "The noise doesn't bother me," he admitted. "It is the silence that I can't handle."

"The silence?"

"That is when I am alone with my thoughts," Oliver said.

"Is that a bad thing?"

Oliver grew quiet, and Baldwin didn't press him for a response. Finally, Oliver spoke. "It is for me, when I have to account for all the wrongs that I have done," he said before rolling onto his side, placing his back towards Baldwin.

Baldwin laid down and stared up at the ceiling. It's going to be a long night, he thought to himself.

CHAPTER TEN

M ADALENE HURRIED DOWN the steps of her townhouse with a burst of newfound energy. She found herself growing increasingly anxious to see Lord Hawthorne today. She wasn't entirely sure why, but it most likely had to do with the fact that he was going to teach her how to use a muff pistol. That had to be it. It wasn't as if she were excited to see *him*. Heavens, no. The man was insufferable.

Stopping at the mirror in the entry hall, she took a moment to peruse her reflection. She was dressed in a simple white cotton gown with a round neckline, and her hair was pulled back into a tight chignon. She hoped she was properly prepared for the meeting with Lord Hawthorne.

The smell of food wafted out of the breakfast parlor, and Madalene felt her stomach growl in response. It took only a few moments for her to walk into the parlor and step over to the buffet table. She piled her plate high with food and went to sit across from her companion.

Mrs. Foster lowered the newspaper in her hands and greeted her. "Good morning."

"Good morning," she replied. "Is there anything of worth in the newspaper today?"

Laying the paper on the table, her companion said, "Not particularly. It is just the same articles, day in and day out."

"What, no noteworthy gossip on the Society page?"

"Lord Hawthorne's ball is mentioned," Mrs. Foster shared. "It is to be the event of the Season."

"Truly?" Madalene asked as she laid her napkin on her lap.

Mrs. Foster nodded. "I must admit that I am looking forward to it."

"Why?"

"Lady Hawthorne always hosts the most elaborate social events," Mrs. Foster expressed. "I can't imagine the ball will be any different."

"Personally, I am dreading the ball."

Mrs. Foster gave her a curious look. "Why is that, dear?"

"No doubt I will be forced to dance nearly every set with gentlemen that are far too eager to please me," Madalene explained.

"Oh, you poor thing," Mrs. Foster teased. "What a terrible plight you have. You are rich, handsome, and clever. Not to mention, unmarried."

Madalene leaned to the side as a footman placed a cup of chocolate in front of her. "It is quite the burden to deal with the scheming matchmaking mothers."

"I can only imagine," Mrs. Foster said as she reached for her teacup, "but that is why I will be keeping a watchful eye on you. We can't have a gentleman abscond with you to Gretna Green, now can we?"

"That isn't likely to happen."

"I'm afraid it is much more common than you think," Mrs. Foster remarked, frowning. "Some men are desperate to get their hands on a woman with a fortune."

"It is a good thing that Lord Hawthorne is teaching me how to use a muff pistol today, then," Madalene shared.

Mrs. Foster placed her teacup back on the saucer. "What did you discuss yesterday when he came to call?"

"Nothing of importance," Madalene said vaguely.

Mrs. Foster gave her a look that implied she didn't believe her. "Why don't I be the judge of that?"

"We spoke mostly of polite topics."

"Now I know you are lying to me," Mrs. Foster stated with a shake of her head. "You hate speaking to gentlemen about polite topics."

"It is different with Lord Hawthorne."

"In what respects?"

Madalene pressed her lips together as she attempted to come up with a believable lie. Finally, she settled on the truth. "We are such vastly different people."

"That you are, but I urge you to use restraint around Lord Hawthorne."

"Restraint?"

Mrs. Foster gave her a knowing smile. "Lord Hawthorne is a handsome man with a sizeable fortune, but there is something dark about him that I can't explain. I just don't want you to become enamored with him—"

"No, no, no," Madalene spoke over her companion. "I have no interest in Lord Hawthorne."

"No?"

Madalene shook her head. "Good heavens, no. Whatever gave you that impression?"

"He did come to call on you yesterday," Mrs. Foster pointed out.

"Lord Hawthorne wanted to discuss something with me privately."

Mrs. Foster lifted her brow. "What could he possibly want to discuss with you privately? You two are barely acquaintances."

"It matters not."

"I don't like you keeping secrets from me," Mrs. Foster said, frowning. "It makes me wonder what you are up to."

"You don't need to worry," Madalene assured her. "It is nothing that I am unable to handle on my own."

"It is my job to worry about you, and I do—incessantly."

Madalene gave her a reassuring smile. "You have been my favorite companion, and I don't know what I would have done without you these past six months."

Mrs. Foster huffed. "I have been your *only* companion."

"That makes my statement no less true."

Graham stepped into the room and met her gaze. "Lord Hawthorne is here to call upon you, Miss. Are you available for callers?"

"I am," Madalene replied as she reached for her cup of chocolate. "Will you show him to the lawn and inform him that I will be along shortly?"

"Yes, Miss," Graham said, tipping his head.

After her butler departed, Madalene took a long sip of her chocolate. She returned the empty cup to the table and put her napkin on her plate.

Mrs. Foster leaned back in her chair. "I will be watching you both from the window. Try to avoid doing anything too scandalous."

Madalene smiled. "I would expect no less from you."

As she made her way towards the rear of the townhouse, Madalene wasn't entirely sure which Lord Hawthorne she was going to see today. Would it be the unapproachable side of him, or would it be the pleasant side that she had seen a glimpse of in the drawing room yesterday? She found she rather liked seeing him smile, even if it was only for a moment.

She stepped outside and saw Lord Hawthorne standing on the lawn. He acknowledged her with a tip of his head.

As she came closer, Lord Hawthorne didn't exactly smile at her, but he didn't frown at her either. Rather, his expression held an emotion she couldn't quite decipher. How is he able to mask his emotions so efficiently, she wondered.

"Miss Dowding," Lord Hawthorne greeted.

She came to a stop in front of him. "Good morning, my lord," she said. "May I ask how your nose is faring?"

"Tender," he remarked. "I apologize for calling upon you at such an early hour, but I'm afraid my presence is required at Parliament this afternoon."

Madalene smiled at him. "I am so pleased that you did," she replied. "It is no imposition, as I am typically an early riser."

"You are?"

She nodded. "I prefer riding in the morning, just as the sun comes up. It is peaceful and gives me time to reflect on what I truly want most out of life."

"Which is?"

"I suppose I want what most people want," she said, "to find happiness in my life."

Lord Hawthorne visibly stiffened. "Not everyone is entitled to happiness," he remarked, his voice gruff.

"I don't believe that to be true."

"Then you are incredibly naïve."

"Perhaps, but I choose to be."

"There are bad people in this world," Lord Hawthorne said with a shake of his head, "people that rejoice in others' misery. Do you suppose they are entitled to happiness?"

"I'm afraid I haven't had a chance to consider that," she admitted truthfully.

Lord Hawthorne gestured towards her townhouse and remarked dryly, "You live in a gilded cage, one that keeps you safe from the horrible atrocities of the world. But you have no idea the level of corruption, death, and hatred that spews from every corner of this earth. It is everywhere, and you don't even have to seek it to find it."

Hearing the undeniable pain in his words, Madalene asked, "Have you seen this hatred in the world?"

"I have," he admitted softly. "I have been in the midst of it, and I have seen the devastating effects of it."

"I'm so sorry to hear that," Madalene murmured, taking a step closer to him.

Lord Hawthorne watched her with anguish in his eyes, but then he blinked, and his emotions retreated.

He reached behind his back and retrieved a small pistol. "I want to give you this muff pistol," he said.

Madalene eagerly put her hand out to accept it, but Lord Hawthorne didn't place it in her hand as she had expected. "There are a few things we need to discuss before you can handle a pistol," he remarked instead.

"Which are?" she asked, dropping her hand to her side.

"You never point a pistol at anyone unless you have no other option," Lord Hawthorne stated. "Taking someone's life is not something you should regard lightly."

"I understand."

"I don't think you do," Lord Hawthorne responded, a solemn look on his face. "Watching the life draining out of a person's body will forever remain with you. It will haunt you every time you close your eyes."

Madalene looked at him curiously and was a bit fearful. Lord Hawthorne spoke with such conviction that she had no doubt he had experienced this firsthand.

An image of her mother came to her mind, and Madalene grew solemn. "I understand more than you can possibly know," she breathed.

Lord Hawthorne gave her a look that implied he didn't believe her but, thankfully, he didn't press her. He glanced over at the townhouse and remarked, "I see that Mrs. Foster is watching us rather dutifully."

Following his gaze, she saw Mrs. Foster standing by the window with her arms crossed over her chest.

"She is rather intense for a companion, is she not?" he continued.

Madalene smiled and waved at Mrs. Foster. "She may be, but she is all that I have left."

"Oh?"

"Mrs. Foster and my mother grew up in the same village and were dear friends," Madalene explained. "After her husband died, Mrs. Foster came to live with us and became a second mother to me. Sadly, after a few years, my mother grew sick, and she made Mrs. Foster promise to look after me."

"That must have been nice, to have someone who could help you navigate through your grief," Lord Hawthorne remarked.

"It was," she admitted, "but not a day goes by that I don't miss my mother."

"That is to be expected."

Madalene pressed her lips together as she tried to quell her suddenly raging emotions. She let out a shaky breath before saying, "It has only been six months since my mother died, but I can still remember watching her take her last breath. Her breathing started to become more labored, and then it... stopped." She blinked back her tears. "And just like that, my mother was gone."

"You do understand, then," Lord Hawthorne remarked compassionately.

She offered him a sad smile. "I do, and I hope to never watch another person pass away. It was nearly too much for me to handle."

"Life is fragile, and people can die within a blink of an eye."

Boldly, she asked, "How is it that you are so acquainted with death?"

Lord Hawthorne looked off into the distance. "I have done some terrible things in my life, things that I don't dare to ever admit out loud," he admitted.

"Surely they can't be that bad."

Bringing his gaze back to meet hers, Lord Hawthorne spoke firmly. "I assure you that they are. Frankly, you should fear me."

"Do you want me to fear you?" she asked, cocking her head.

Lord Hawthorne stared at her for a moment. "No, I find that I don't want you to."

"That is good, because I don't."

"That is because you are foolish and naïve."

Madalene sighed dramatically. "We are back to name calling, I see," she teased. "I thought we had grown past that."

Lord Hawthorne's lips twitched as he extended the muff pistol towards her. "I have taken the liberty of loading the pistol, so I urge you to use caution when handling it."

Accepting the gun, Madalene ran her hand over the metal frame as she adjusted to the weight in her hand. "It is heavier than I imagined."

"You will soon become accustomed to its weight," Lord Hawthorne said. "Furthermore, the recoil is minimal."

Madalene held the pistol down at her side. "When do you plan to abduct me?"

"Would tomorrow be acceptable?"

"I suppose I could move some things around," she joked.

Lord Hawthorne chuckled. "I will call on you tomorrow under the ruse of taking you on a carriage ride through Hyde Park."

"I must admit that being abducted sounds much more appealing than a carriage ride."

"I find that your responses intrigue me," Lord Hawthorne said as he stepped back. "I never seem to know what you will say next."

Unsure of how to reply to his remark, Madalene remained quiet.

Lord Hawthorne broke the silence, gesturing towards the gun in her hand. "Allow me to show you how to use the pistol now."

"Thank you," she said, gladly accepting the turn of the conversation.

***

BALDWIN SAT IN the coach as it traveled on the busy streets to the

House of Lords. He had just left Miss Dowding's townhouse, and he found that he had lingered for far too long with her. There was just something about her that gave him pause.

She had a vulnerable quality about her that seemed to mask a strength even she didn't know existed. He had no doubt that she was clever, but she always said the most outlandish things. Furthermore, she believed in hope, which was ridiculous. Hope isn't a tangible thing, he thought. Miss Dowding couldn't possibly understand the torment that he endured every single day. No. No one could. He was battling his demons on his own, and he was failing. *Miserably.*

The coach came to a stop on the street, and Baldwin glanced out the window. Street urchins were running through the traffic, without any heed to the dangers surrounding them.

Unexpectedly, the door to the coach opened and Corbyn stepped in. "Good," he said as he came to sit across from him. "I see that you are alone."

"Did you need a ride?"

Corbyn shook his head. "I was meeting with my informant and saw your coach passing by. I thought it was a good time to speak to you about your plan with Miss Dowding."

"I spoke with Miss Dowding today."

"And she is still allowing you to abduct her?"

Baldwin nodded. "Yes," he replied. "As a precaution, I gave her a muff pistol to carry on her person."

"Oh, good," Corbyn remarked dryly. "Another woman is walking around the streets of London with a muff pistol."

Ignoring his friend's snide comment, Baldwin continued. "Have you spoken to the Bow Street magistrate?"

"I have."

"And?"

"I informed him of the location of the missing girls, and the Runners intend to raid the Flailing Duck tomorrow at two."

"That should give us enough time."

"I hope so, because I don't want to have to bail you out of prison."

Baldwin huffed. "Why do you assume I will get caught?"

"Call it a hunch," Corbyn joked.

"If I can hide in plain sight under the French's noses, I can escape from a pub," Baldwin asserted.

"We shall see," Corbyn replied. "The magistrate also assured me that the girls' names will not be in the paper. They will just announce that the missing girls have been found and freed."

"Excellent."

"I just hope you know what you are doing. I don't like involving innocent civilians in covert operations."

The coach lurched forward as Baldwin said, "I just need to convince Morton that I didn't tip off the Runners."

"Have you figured out a way to accomplish that feat?"

"No, but it will come to me."

Corbyn stared at him. "Sometimes your arrogance astounds me."

"Thank you."

"This plan of yours better work," Corbyn warned. "If not, I will have no choice but to personally round up all these rebels and put them in jail."

"If my plan doesn't work, then I will help you round up the rebels myself."

Corbyn placed his hand on the door handle. "I shall hold you to that," he said as the coach began to slow down. "This is where I shall leave you." He opened the door, stepped down and closed it behind him.

Baldwin sat back in his seat and enjoyed the rest of the trip to the House of Lords in silence. The coach came to a stop, and he waited for the footman to put the step down and open the door. As he stepped down, he heard Lord Desmond calling to him from across the yard.

"Lord Hawthorne, a word."

Baldwin turned towards Lord Desmond and watched him cross the busy yard. "What is it that you wish to discuss, Lord Desmond?"

Lord Desmond stopped in front of him and smiled. "I need your support on my bill," he said plainly. "With your support, I believe we could turn the tides on it."

Baldwin chuckled. "I'm afraid that won't happen."

"Why not?"

Growing serious, Baldwin said, "I am not opposed to building workhouses, but I don't believe the Home Office should oversee them."

"Ah, yes," Lord Desmond mocked. "And how exactly do you propose we finance them?"

"I am not sure, but the Home Office has other responsibilities and obligations."

"The parishes cannot handle the influx of the poor," Lord Desmond argued. "We need to change the Poor Laws."

"That may be the case, but I can't in good conscience have you cut funding to agencies within the Home Office."

"Have you at least read my bill?"

"I attempted to, but it is much too long and convoluted for me to wade through."

Lord Desmond looked displeased by his admission. "We are in a position to make real changes here, Hawthorne. If we place the workhouses around the rookeries then we can save hundreds, if not thousands, of people's lives."

"I can respect that, but you need to find another way to fund it."

"There is *no* other way. Currently, the parishes support the workhouses, but many can't afford the cost of one. *We* need to oversee the poor and not just leave it to the parishes anymore."

"I'm afraid I can't support your bill."

"I don't have the faintest idea why," Lord Desmond said, "but the Tory party is looking to you while deciding how they intend to vote on this bill."

"You flatter me, but I daresay that is not true," Baldwin dismissed the argument, brushing past him.

Lord Desmond's voice came from behind him. "When will you stand for something that is greater than yourself, Hawthorne?"

Baldwin slowly turned around. "How dare you presume to know what I stand for?"

Lord Desmond took a step closer to him, his voice accusing. "You cry off your responsibilities for three years, and then you stand here and deny poor men and women an opportunity to survive."

"I am doing no such thing," Baldwin argued.

"I have been contracted to run many of these workhouses in London, and I have seen them change lives for the better," Lord Desmond contended.

"I don't dispute what you are saying is true."

"But you won't help me."

"Not at the expense of the Home Office."

Lord Desmond shook his head. "Why are you so protective of the Home Office?"

"Why aren't you?" Baldwin asked. "They are warding off potential threats."

"The people are rioting because they don't have enough to eat. If we give them hope, then the people will disperse."

"You can't possibly be as naïve as that!" Baldwin declared.

Lord Desmond tugged down on the lapels of his jacket. "I thought if I appealed to your common decency that you would come around, but I see that I was wrong."

"Withdraw your bill. If you can find another way to finance the workhouses, I will support it," Baldwin said firmly.

"I will not."

"Then I look forward to having your bill defeated."

Lord Desmond narrowed his eyes. "You have just made a dangerous enemy in me, Hawthorne," he warned.

"I assure you that I won't lose any sleep over it," Baldwin smirked in reply.

"You are just as much of a blackguard as your father was," Lord Desmond growled as he brushed past him.

Baldwin turned to watch the man's retreating figure. He didn't understand why Desmond was attempting to push his bill through the House of Lords at such a quick pace. It was fundamentally flawed.

Lord Brinton came to stand next to him. "That was rather painful to watch," he said.

"Percy," Baldwin greeted. "You saw that?"

"I did," Percy admitted. "It wasn't as if you two were keeping your voices down."

Baldwin turned to face Percy. "Why is Desmond so determined to have the Home Office oversee the workhouses?"

"I suppose it is the quickest way to get funding," Percy suggested.

"It is a foolhardy thing to do."

Percy nodded. "Desmond is hoping to have us overlook that by tugging at our heartstrings."

"I heard that Lord Liverpool is against the bill, as well," Baldwin said.

"That doesn't surprise me in the least," Percy acknowledged. "I am sure the cabinet members are complaining to the Prime Minister about this bill at great length."

Baldwin reached into the pocket of his waistcoat and pulled out his pocket watch. "It is almost time for the session to begin."

"Shall we?" Percy asked, gesturing towards the building.

CHAPTER ELEVEN

"I MUST ADMIT that I am rather nervous about being abducted," Madalene shared as she rode in an open carriage with Lord Hawthorne.

"It is technically not an abduction, since you are going along willingly," he pointed out.

Madalene smiled playfully. "I know, but it sounds much more exciting to call it that."

Lord Hawthorne looked at her with mild amusement. "Regardless, you need not fear for your safety."

"What if something terrible goes wrong?"

"It won't."

"How can you be so sure?" she asked, hands clasped in her lap.

"Because I have planned for any situation," he explained. "There are times when I have to go into a situation unprepared, but that is not the case here."

"What kind of situations?"

Lord Hawthorne arched an eyebrow. "Are you always this much of a busybody?"

"I am," she replied, unabashed.

"It is not very becoming."

"I just can't help but notice you are shrouded in a cloud of secrecy," she said with a half-shrug, "and I find it fascinating."

"My life is rather dull."

"It doesn't appear that way to me."

"You would be wrong, then," he remarked dismissively. "Do you have the muff pistol on your person?"

She nodded. "I do."

"Good."

Lord Hawthorne turned the carriage down a road that she was unfamiliar with. "Where are we going?"

"We need to get rid of the open carriage and travel the rest of the way in a closed carriage," he explained.

"But I can't ride in a closed carriage with you," she declared, her voice taking on a hint of unease. "What if someone saw us? I would be ruined."

"That is why the closed carriage is parked under a bridge. No one will see us get in, I'm sure of it."

"And if you are wrong?"

Lord Hawthorne met her gaze, his eyes growing intense. "Then I will have no choice but to marry you."

Her brow shot up. "You cannot be in earnest!"

"I wouldn't let your reputation suffer on my behalf," he stated. "I refuse to have that on my conscience."

"You would willingly enter into a marriage of convenience with a woman that you hardly know?"

Adjusting the reins in his hand, he commented, "There are worse things."

"Such as?"

"Death," he replied curtly.

Madalene shifted on the bench as she turned to face him. "That is a wonderful endorsement of matrimony."

"I only speak the truth."

"Do you not intend to marry for love?"

Lord Hawthorne kept his gaze straight ahead. "Frankly, I do not intend to marry," he replied.

"But don't you require an heir?"

"My brother is my heir."

Madalene found herself smiling at his admission. "I can only imagine the matchmaking mothers and their attempts to ensnare you into matrimony. I wonder what their reaction to seeing you now would be, dressed in your pauper's clothes."

"I can avoid them easily," he said, ignoring the comment about his appearance.

"They can be quite crafty," she warned.

Lord Hawthorne spared her a glance. "And do you wish to marry for love?" he asked.

She shook her head. "Like you, I wish to avoid the marital noose."

"But you are a woman."

A disbelieving puff of air left her lips. "Thank you for noticing, my lord."

"I did not mean to insult you, but I thought all women wished to be wed."

"Not I," she admitted. "I have my own sizeable fortune, and I do not wish to be tied down to any man."

"What if you fell in love?"

She considered his words carefully before responding. "I would have to fall indisputably in love with him, much like my father and mother were."

"Were they a love match?"

"They were, and after my father passed away, my mother couldn't bring herself to ever marry again."

"I find that admirable."

With a curious glance at him, Madalene asked, "Were your parents a love match?"

Lord Hawthorne nodded. "It started off as an arranged marriage, but my parents grew to love each other deeply," he shared as he pulled back on the reins, bringing the carriage to a stop. "We will just need to walk a short distance to the bridge."

After Lord Hawthorne set the brake, he came around and assisted her off the carriage. The bridge was ahead of them, a closed carriage parked under it. A driver and a footman were standing guard as they approached.

The footman opened the door and assisted Madalene as she stepped inside. Lord Hawthorne ducked inside the coach and sat across from her.

They didn't speak until the coach started rolling down the street. "That was the easy part. Now comes the hard part," Lord Hawthorne said, breaking the silence.

"Which is?" Madalene asked nervously.

Reaching under the bench, he pulled out a large sack. "You will need to get inside the gunnysack, and I am going to tie the top with rope."

"You want me to get inside that?" she repeated in disbelief.

"Yes, but not right now."

"And you are just going to throw me over your shoulder?"

He looked at her blankly. "Will that be an issue?"

"I suppose not."

Lord Hawthorne held up the gunnysack and placed a finger inside one of the many holes. "I took the liberty of cutting small holes into the material so you can breathe."

"How thoughtful of you," she muttered. "How long am I required to be in there?"

"At least until we arrive at the pub."

Madalene nibbled her lower lip, wondering why she had agreed to this madness in the first place. "What happens after we arrive at the pub?"

"Most likely, I will take you to where the other missing girls are being held; hopefully that includes Miss Hardy."

"I hope so," she murmured.

Lord Hawthorne moved the drape that covered the window and glanced out. "I have no doubt that my brother is trailing us at this moment."

"How can you be so sure?"

"Because I know my brother," he replied, bringing his gaze to meet hers.

"It must be nice to have a brother that you can rely on."

"It is."

Madalene grew silent as her eyes strayed to the sack. She had no doubt that traveling in that gunnysack was going to be deucedly uncomfortable.

Lord Hawthorne's voice broke her out of her musings. "You need to do something with your hair."

"Pardon?" Her hand flew up to touch her neatly coiffed hair. What's wrong with my hair, she wondered.

He leaned forward in his seat. "May I?" he asked.

She nodded, unsure of his intent.

His hand reached out and started removing strands of her hair from the chignon in a haphazard fashion. "Much better," he declared, his eyes sparking with approval. "Now your gown needs some work."

She swatted away his hand as he reached for the sleeve of her blue cotton gown. "I think not," she proclaimed haughtily.

"You need to appear as if you fought while being abducted," he pointed out.

"I am sure that spending time in a gunnysack, slung over your shoulder, will do the trick," Madalene responded.

Lord Hawthorne put his hands up in surrender. "As you wish," he muttered as he sat back on the bench.

"You mentioned the Bow Street Runners will raid the pub and rescue me," she started, "but you failed to mention how I will return home."

"My brother will see to that."

"Where will you be?"

Lord Hawthorne smirked. "Hiding from the Bow Street Runners."

"I see," she mumbled, even though she didn't see.

A silence descended over the coach as they both retreated to their own thoughts. After a long moment, Lord Hawthorne spoke up. "These men who have abducted the girls are dangerous and need to be stopped, and your cooperation will go a long way in helping to do that."

"I am glad to be of assistance, then."

"And I'm truly hoping that Miss Hardy is among the missing women."

"As am I."

Lord Hawthorne grew solemn. "But if she isn't, I promise you that I will keep looking for her."

"You would do that for me?"

His face softened. "I would," he replied, "especially since you have done me a great favor by allowing me to abduct you."

She attempted to muster up a smile but failed miserably. "It will be an adventure."

"You will be safe; I assure you of that."

She nodded. "I believe you."

"Why is that?" he asked, his eyes searching hers.

"I don't rightly know," she replied.

The coach came to a creaking stop. "Get into the sack," Lord Hawthorne ordered.

He placed the gunnysack on the floor and Madalene stepped into it. As she crouched down, he pulled the bag over her head and she could feel him securing the top with the rope.

The door opened and she felt the coach dip as Lord Hawthorne exited first. He reached back in and grabbed her. She stifled a gasp as he flung her over his shoulder, which he did as if she weighed no more than a bag of feathers.

The inside of the gunnysack became stifling hot, and Madalene sought out one of the many holes to feel the cool air on her skin. She could hear men's muffled voices as they passed them on the street, appearing to be unaware, or unconcerned, that she was being abducted.

"We are almost there," Lord Hawthorne whispered.

A few moments later, she heard him pound on a door, then say, "Where should I put the girl?"

She didn't hear a response, but Lord Hawthorne started walking again. He carried her up a flight of stairs and down what she imagined was a hall.

He pounded on another door, and she heard it creak open. "I have the girl."

"Bring her in," came the reply.

Lord Hawthorne took another five steps before he lifted her off his shoulder and lowered her to the ground.

"Want to look at her?" Lord Hawthorne asked.

"Why not?"

Madalene could feel Lord Hawthorne untying the rope and then the gunnysack fell to the ground around her. She blinked a few times as her eyes adjusted to the dimly lit room, and she was vaguely aware of other women somewhere behind her. Being carried with her head downward had made her dizzy, though she supposed her dazed appearance was helpful in this circumstance.

A brawny man crouched down in front of her and grabbed her chin. "She will do quite nicely," he declared, his eyes lewdly roaming her face. "She's a pretty little thing."

Lord Hawthorne's face was expressionless as he replied, "That she is."

"Where did you find her?"

"She must've lost her chaperone, because she was walking alone on the street. I grabbed her when no one was looking," Lord Hawthorne said.

The man tugged down on her jaw, causing her mouth to open. "She has some nice teeth. She will be a fine prize for any man."

Madalene jerked her head back and the man's hand dropped. "I will belong to no man," she declared forcefully.

The brawny man chuckled. "This one is feisty."

"Did I earn my five pounds?" Lord Hawthorne asked.

"That you did," the man replied as he rose. "You did good, Baldwin."

Madalene turned her head, and her eyes sought out the five other young women sitting on the floor near the wall. They had their hands bound in front of them, and all stared back at her with fearful eyes. Her heart dropped when she realized that Edith was not among them.

The brawny man reached behind him for some rope and brought it in front of him. "We should celebrate over a drink."

"That would be nice," Lord Hawthorne replied as he turned his gaze towards her, and a shiver of fear ran down her spine. His eyes had turned cold, dark. Any trace of the man she thought she knew was gone.

Roughly, the brawny man grabbed her hands and tied them securely with the rope. "This will do nicely until it is time for them to depart," he stated as he stepped back.

"When is that?" Lord Hawthorne asked.

"In a few hours."

"This was the easiest money I ever made," he said.

"That is the point, and you have helped advanced the revolution, as well," the man replied, clapping his hand on Lord Hawthorne's shoulder.

Together, they walked over to the door and departed from the room without even sparing the women a glance. The sound of a key locking them in could be heard.

Without waiting another moment, Madalene rose and walked swiftly over to the girls. "You need not fear. The Bow Street Runners will be rescuing us shortly."

She could see the disbelief in the young women's eyes. Their hair was matted to their heads, tear lines could be seen running down their dirtied faces, and their dresses were terribly wrinkled.

"It is true," she asserted.

A brunette girl spoke up in a timid voice. "How do you know for certain?"

"The man that brought me here has planned the whole thing," she explained. "He said he tipped off the Bow Street Runners."

The girl shook her head. "You have been tricked. I was lured here, as well."

"I haven't been." Madalene tried to loosen her bands, but to no avail. "I assure you that it is all true."

"Then we shall wait and see, won't we?" the girl replied as she rested the back of her head against the wall. "But I wouldn't get your hopes up."

Madalene turned towards the door and declared, "The Bow Street Runners will be here any moment, I am sure of it."

She began searching the room, looking for anything sharp that might help in removing her bonds. But there was nothing that could help her. She walked towards the window and opened the dusty drapes. The sunlight poured into the room, and the other young women seemed to shrink back from it.

Madalene attempted to open the window but discovered that it was nailed shut. Drat! She realized there was no way for her to aid in her own rescue.

After some time, Madalene found her legs growing weak and she sat down. Why is it taking so long for the Bow Street Runners to arrive, she wondered. She glanced over at the girls, and they each gave her a look of pity. They truly believed that she had been deceived. But she hadn't been. Lord Hawthorne wouldn't have betrayed her like this.

But doubt crept in, and she began to wonder if she would be rescued after all.

BALDWIN STARED AT the door and wondered where the blasted Runners were. They had one simple task—to raid the pub and rescue the women—and they would be rewarded with accolades. Instead, they were botching it. Horribly.

He cast a glance towards Corbyn, who was sitting at a crowded table on the other side of the room. He had a smile on his face, but Baldwin wasn't fooled by his act. He knew his friend was alert, preparing for a fight and just biding his time.

"Don't you agree?"

Baldwin turned his attention back to Morton. "About what?"

Morton chuckled and held up his tankard in the air. "I think you have had one too many to drink, mate."

"Why do you say that?"

"I have been trying to get your attention for the past few minutes."

Baldwin placed his nearly-full tankard down on the table. "I was thinking about how I intend to spend my money."

"It is rather a large sum for a man like you."

"I would agree."

The serving wench approached the table and asked, "Can I get ye another round?"

Baldwin shook his head. "Not for me," he said. "We have been drinking for hours, and I'm afraid I have met my limit."

Morton waved the serving wench off with a flick of his hand. "I have been meaning to ask you if you have any experience with explosives."

"Minimal," he replied.

"That is good."

"Why do you ask?"

Morton leaned closer and lowered his voice. "We are going to do something that will incite a revolution."

Baldwin looked at him expectantly. "Which is?"

"We are going to assassinate Lord Liverpool, Lord Sidmouth, and Lord Desmond," Morton revealed, his eyes growing dark.

With a baffled expression, Baldwin asked, "I understand killing the Prime Minister and the Home Secretary, but I don't understand why you wish to kill Lord Desmond. After all, isn't he a champion for the people?"

Morton scoffed loudly. "I'm afraid not," he said. "He has been stealing money from the workhouses for years."

Baldwin frowned. "How do you know that?"

"I know a man who works as a solicitor for Lord Desmond, and he informed me that Desmond is contracted to run ten workhouses in London," Morton shared. "He intentionally inflates the number of the poor inmates to get additional funding for the workhouse, then he takes the money and lines his own pocket."

Baldwin clenched his jaw. "That is despicable. We must stop him."

"How?" Morton huffed. "It isn't as if anyone would believe a solicitor over an earl. It would take a duke to level charges against him before anyone takes them seriously."

"Or a marquess," Baldwin muttered.

"That, too, but I don't run in those type of circles."

"Nor I," Baldwin said, "but we can't keep letting Desmond get away with it."

Morton pushed his empty tankard to the side. "Don't worry," he assured him. "Desmond will get what he deserves."

"How do you intend to do that?"

Morton's eyes darted around the room. "Are you familiar with how the French royalists attempted to assassinate Napoleon in 1800?"

"I am," Baldwin replied. "The conspirators attached a large wine cask to a cart and loaded it with a bomb. They laid in wait for Napoleon's carriage, but they were too late, and they failed in their attempt."

Morton nodded in approval. "Their plan was brilliant, but they lit it too late, and the gunpowder they used was bad, causing a few more seconds of delay."

"If I recall correctly, they caught most of the conspirators, but one was able to flee to the Americas."

A smile came to Morton's lips. "They didn't catch all the conspirators."

"They didn't?"

Morton shook his head. "Carbon was the one who made the bomb, and he was killed for his crime."

"But that was only after he confessed the names of his fellow conspirators."

"Not all of them," Morton said in a low voice. "He protected his fifteen-year-old daughter, who helped him make the bomb."

Baldwin gave him a skeptical look. "Are you truly insinuating that a girl could assist in making a bomb that killed a dozen people and wounded nearly forty others?"

"I am."

"Then you are mad."

Morton put his hands up. "Hear me out," he said. "Carbon's daughter, Marie, has come to England to help us execute our plan."

"Why would she do that?" he asked.

"The royalist group that Carbon belonged to was connected to Chouan leader Georges Cadoudal, who was in England's pocket," Morton shared. "Cadoudal had assured Carbon and his fellow conspirators that England was supportive of the assassination attempt and would help them escape France after they executed their plan. However, when the plan failed, the English turned their backs on the conspirators, leaving them to their fates."

"How awful," Baldwin murmured.

"Now Marie wants revenge, and I want a revolution," Morton said, leaning slowly back in his chair. "It is a perfect partnership."

"How do you intend to blow..." Baldwin's voice trailed off as he saw three men with red waistcoats passing by the window.

"Runners," he uttered.

Morton looked at him curiously. "Pardon?"

"We need to leave now!" Baldwin proclaimed, shoving back his chair.

"Why?"

"I just saw three Runners outside the window," he explained. "We need to leave through the back."

Morton jumped up from his chair. "Follow me," he ordered with a tremor in his voice.

Baldwin followed Morton towards the door in the back of the room. Just as he reached for the handle, the main door was thrown open and someone ordered, "Stay where you are!"

Ignoring the command, Morton threw the back door open and raced out into the alley with Baldwin close behind.

"Hey, you there!" a Runner shouted at the end of the alley. "Stop where you are!"

They both ran out of the alley and Morton turned left. Baldwin turned right. Unfortunately, the Runner decided to chase after him.

Baldwin dodged in and out of the men and women he passed on the narrow street. He kept running until he turned down an alley with a low brick wall. He effortlessly jumped over it, but the Runner hadn't been able to do so with the same ease, giving him a slight advantage.

Removing his ragged jacket, Baldwin handed it to a man who was begging on the street, then kept running until he was sure the Runner wasn't following him anymore.

The sun was starting to set as he headed towards his room on Draper Street. When he opened his door, he was surprised to see Morton standing there, his eyes sparking with fury.

"Morton," Baldwin acknowledged as he closed the door. "What are you doing here?"

"Where have you been?" Morton shouted.

Baldwin huffed as he went and dropped down onto his mattress. "I have been racing through the rookeries to make sure I lost the Runner who was following me."

"How do I know it wasn't you that ratted me out to the Bow Street Runners?" Morton accused, crossing his arms over his chest.

"For what purpose?" Baldwin asked defiantly.

Morton's eyes narrowed. "You could have brokered a deal with the Bow Street Runners to ensure your freedom."

"We both know that Bow Street Runners are not to be trusted, and I can assure you that I would never intentionally seek them out," Baldwin assured him. "Furthermore, it would have been foolhardy to tip them off *before* I got paid for abducting the girl."

"What about your cousin?" Morton asked. "Could he have tipped off the Bow Street Runners?"

Baldwin shook his head. "That is impossible."

"How can you be so sure?"

"It is simple," Baldwin replied. "I never told him that I intended to abduct a girl in the first place."

Some of the anger in Morton's expression dissipated at his words. "I do apologize for being suspicious but there is so much at stake here."

"I understand."

"I must assume that Oliver is with some woman," Morton commented as he looked at Oliver's empty mattress.

Baldwin shrugged. "Where else would he be?"

Morton walked over and sat down on the mattress. "Thank you for what you did back at the pub."

"I didn't do much."

"If you hadn't seen those Runners, then we both would have ended up in jail. You saved me."

"I suppose that is true," Baldwin agreed as he leaned his back against the wall.

Running a hand through his tousled hair, Morton sighed. "That was a close call. Too close."

Baldwin chuckled. "You get used to those," he said. "It's what keeps you alert for the next time."

"We were so close to a payday," Morton declared, clenching his fists. "Why did the Runners have to raid the pub when they did?"

"Someone must have tipped them off."

"Perhaps, or they just got lucky."

Baldwin scoffed. "You are giving Runners entirely too much credit."

"Who do you think could have tipped them off, then?"

"It could have been someone who worked at the pub," Baldwin suggested with a shrug.

Morton's expression grew hard. "I won't rest until I discover who betrayed me," he growled, "and then I will kill them."

"Smart plan," Baldwin said. "Make sure their death is especially painful."

"That is a given." Morton paused. "At least I can safely rule you out."

"I appreciate that. Besides, I know my fate if I ever get caught." Baldwin reached under his pillow and pulled out a stale piece of bread. "Are you hungry?" he asked, holding it up.

Morton stuck up his nose at the offering. "That is what you are eating for dinner?" he asked in disbelief.

"It looks worse than it tastes."

"I can only imagine," Morton muttered.

Baldwin took a bite of the foul-tasting bread and slowly chewed it. "Where do we go from here?"

"We may have lost the opportunity to make some quick money by selling those girls, but we still have collected a large amount from the other rebels," Morton shared. "We will continue to implement our plans for the assassinations."

"Before I go along with this plan, I want to meet Marie," Baldwin insisted.

Morton rose awkwardly from his seat. "I can arrange that," he said. "We need to meet regardless to go over the specifics."

"This mission won't cause me to end up dead, will it?" Baldwin asked.

Morton shook his head. "If all goes well, you will be on a ship bound for America by the time England recovers from the shock of losing their Prime Minister, Home Secretary, and their beloved crook."

"What about the other conspirators?"

"You need not concern yourself with them."

"Why not?"

Morton walked over to the door. "It matters not," he remarked. "Has anyone ever told you that you worry too much?"

Baldwin studied Morton. "What is it that you are not telling me?"

"Get a good night's sleep and I will be in touch," Morton said dismissively as he opened the door.

After Morton closed the door, Baldwin tossed the bread down and wiped the crumbs off his hands. He would wait for a moment before traveling to Hawthorne House for the rest of the evening. He needed a good soak and a proper meal.

CHAPTER TWELVE

THE FOLLOWING MORNING, Baldwin walked purposefully along the pavement as he covered the short distance to Miss Dowding's townhouse. He found that he needed to reassure himself that she was safe after the staged abduction, even though Oliver had assured him that she was. But for some inexplicable reason that didn't ease his mind. He wanted to see Miss Dowding for himself.

Unexpectedly, Corbyn appeared by his side, matching his stride. "I received your missive last night."

Baldwin glanced over at him in surprise. "Where did you come from?"

Corbyn tsked. "I had correctly assumed you would be on your way to visit Miss Dowding this morning, so I just waited for the chance to speak to you."

"Why would you have assumed that?"

"Call it a hunch," Corbyn remarked.

Baldwin tipped his head politely at a gentleman passing him on the street before saying, "I can't help but think that Morton believes me to be expendable."

"Why do you think that?"

"He keeps promising to give me a new life in the Americas, but I believe that to be an empty promise."

"It wouldn't be the first time that someone used a scapegoat for their scheme."

Baldwin nodded. "Regardless, I intend to see this through and stop their plan before it comes to fruition."

"Do you have any leads on where Marie is?"

"Not at this time."

Corbyn kept his gaze straight ahead as he remarked, "Until we get more information, I will hold off on warning Lord Liverpool, Lord Sidmouth, and Lord Desmond of the impending threat."

"I think that is wise," Baldwin agreed. "Furthermore, if what Morton said was true last night, then we need to start an investigation into Lord Desmond."

"I agree, and I will assign an agent to the case."

With a side glance at his friend, Baldwin remarked, "Thank you for your assistance yesterday at the pub."

"You need not thank me," Corbyn said. "I met a new group of friends."

"You did?"

Corbyn chuckled. "They were all deeply in their cups, but they were a jovial group of men."

"Did you discover why the blasted Runners took so long to raid the pub?"

"No, but I expected as much from them," Corbyn muttered. "You can't trust a Runner with even the simplest task."

As they approached Miss Dowding's townhouse, Baldwin reached up and adjusted his white cravat. "I did notice that the morning newspaper reported their heroics in rescuing those missing girls."

"That should please the Bow Street magistrate."

"I should hope so."

Baldwin stopped outside of the black iron fence that surrounded the townhouse. "Would you care to call upon Miss Dowding with me?"

"Not in the least," Corbyn said as he continued walking down the pavement.

Chuckling, Baldwin opened the gate and walked up to the door. He knocked on it and took a step back.

The door was opened, and the butler politely smiled at him. "Good morning, Lord Hawthorne," he greeted, opening the door wide. "Please come in."

"Is Miss Dowding available for callers this morning?"

The butler closed the door. "I shall inquire, milord."

Baldwin watched as the butler walked across the entry hall and stepped into a side room. He turned his attention towards the blue wallpaper and ornate woodwork that ran the length of the hall.

The clip of the butler's heel on the tile alerted Baldwin to his return. Stopping in front of him, the butler revealed, "I apologize, but Miss Dowding is not available for callers at the moment."

"Will you kindly inform Miss Dowding that I will not leave until I have the opportunity to speak to her?" Baldwin pressed, not deterred by her rejection.

The butler's face remained expressionless as he replied, "Yes, milord."

Baldwin watched the butler walk across the entry hall again and disappear into the same room. After a moment, he reemerged and approached.

"Miss Dowding will see you. Please follow me to the drawing room."

After Baldwin stepped into the drawing room, he walked over to the mantel that sat over the fireplace and admired the vases on display.

It was a long moment later when Miss Dowding stepped into the room, wearing a white gown with a green sash tied around her waist.

"Good morning, Lord Hawthorne," she said, her words uncharacteristically soft.

He turned to face her, and he was surprised to see that she appeared tense. "Good morning, Miss Dowding," he greeted. "Thank you for agreeing to see me."

"I'm afraid you left me very little choice in the matter."

"That may be true, but I wanted to see how you are faring after yesterday's ordeal."

She smiled, but it didn't reach her eyes. "As you can see, I am well."

"Are you?"

Her smile dimmed. "Why do you ask?"

"Pardon me, but I can't help but notice that you seem rather out of sorts."

Miss Dowding walked over to the settee and placed her hands on the back, creating more distance between them. She refused to meet his gaze. "I'm afraid yesterday was rather taxing, and I will need time to recover," she said.

Liar.

Why is Miss Dowding lying to me, he wondered. He decided to pose another question. "Was Miss Hardy amongst the missing girls?"

She shook her head. "She was not."

"Then I will keep searching for her."

"I appreciate that," Miss Dowding responded as she played with the fringe of a pillow.

Baldwin frowned as he tried to make sense of Miss Dowding's odd behavior. "My brother informed me that he escorted you home last night," he attempted.

"That he did," Miss Dowding confirmed as she continued to avert her gaze from his. "I was most appreciative of that."

Taking a step closer to her, he was astonished when she took a step back and a panicked look came to her face.

What in the blazes?

"Miss Dowding," he started, "I must pose the question, were you harmed in any way yesterday?"

Her gaze snapped up to meet his. "I was not."

"Then I must have done something to upset you," he prodded

gently. "Whatever it is, I am truly sorry."

Baldwin could see the indecisiveness in Miss Dowding's expression as she watched him. Finally, she spoke in a timid voice. "I thought you had deceived me."

"Pardon?"

Miss Dowding remained stiff as she explained, "You informed me that the Bow Street Runners were going to rescue us right away, but it was hours before they finally saved us."

"I am not entirely sure why the Runners were delayed, but—"

She spoke over him. "My hands were bound tightly, and my wrists are still reddened. I had to put powder on them this morning to hide the marks."

"Again, I am sorry—"

"You did not prepare me adequately for being abducted."

He let out a disbelieving laugh. "That is generally what happens when someone is abducted."

Coming around the settee, she declared, "This is no laughing matter."

Baldwin saw the seriousness on her face, and he realized that he was being rather unfair to discount her feelings. "I'm sorry for being insensitive," he attempted.

Miss Dowding stopped in front of him, her eyes searching his. "And I watched as your eyes grew cold."

He furrowed his brows. "I'm afraid I don't understand."

"When you spoke to that man in the pub, I watched your demeanor change," she explained. "It was as if you became a whole different person."

Baldwin sighed. "I must apologize for that—"

She cut him off. "No more apologizing," she declared. "I was in that room for hours and I began to lose hope that I would ever be saved. I saw the other girls give me looks of pity as I tried to convince them that the Runners were coming to save us."

"The Runners were late, but you were in no real danger," he assured her.

Her eyes grew fiery. "It certainly felt like I was."

Baldwin put his hand up, and Miss Dowding flinched. He stared at her in bewilderment. "Did you think I was going to hit you?" he asked.

"I don't know what to think," she replied, and he could hear the sincerity in her voice. "I can't seem to determine who you truly are anymore."

"I am the same man that you knew before the abduction."

"You aren't," she said with a shake of her head. "I became frightened of you in that room in the pub."

"Please don't say that," he murmured.

"How is it that you can be such vastly different versions of yourself?"

"I'm afraid I cannot say."

"You can't or you won't?" she asked defiantly.

Baldwin ran a hand through his hair. "You don't even know what you are asking me to confess," he said.

"That may be true, but I can't seem to come to terms with what I saw in that room," she said. "Your cold eyes haunted me every time I closed my eyes last night."

"I know what you saw in that room was confusing, but that is not a reflection of who I truly am," he attempted.

Crossing her arms over her chest, she asked, "Why are you even associating with those types of people?"

"I am not at liberty to say."

"You are a marquess and should be above reproach. It looks suspect that you associate with such ruffians—"

He cut her off. "I am well aware of my responsibilities, and I don't need you to lecture me on it."

"Well, someone needs to."

Baldwin shook his head. "You know not what you are speaking

of."

"Then enlighten me."

"I'm afraid you don't understand the depravities of men, my dear," he mocked.

Madalene tensed at his remark, but she didn't back down. "I believe I experienced a taste of it yesterday when I was abducted by *you*."

Taking a step closer, he said, "Need I remind you that you willingly allowed yourself to be abducted in an attempt to save your friend?"

Madalene tilted her head to look up at him. "That is true, but—"

"Perhaps I misjudged you," he stated, speaking over her.

"I am asking myself if I have misjudged *you*," she declared.

Being this close to Miss Dowding, Baldwin had a sudden urge to gather her in his arms and kiss her until she came to her senses, which was ludicrous. The last thing he wanted to do was complicate his situation with Miss Dowding by kissing her.

Finding strength deep inside himself, Baldwin stepped back and bowed. "If you will excuse me, I am late for a meeting at the House of Lords."

As he brushed past her, Miss Dowding spoke up. "Out of curiosity, are you voting in favor of Lord Desmond's bill?"

"I am not."

She frowned, appearing displeased by his response. "Are you not in favor of additional workhouses in the rookeries?"

"I am, but I do not believe that the Home Office should be responsible for overseeing the workhouses."

"But the morning newspapers say—"

He cut her off. "I'm afraid I don't have the energy or the right mindset to continue debating with you, Miss Dowding," he said. "But you should be careful not to believe everything you read in the newspapers."

"I suppose you make a good point," she replied, albeit reluctantly.

"Good day, Miss Dowding."

She tipped her head politely. "Good day, Lord Hawthorne."

Baldwin continued to watch her for a moment before he departed from the room. He knew he shouldn't have spoken so harshly to her, but he found that Miss Dowding caused him to lose all rational thought. Something he hadn't thought was possible.

Blasted woman!

Miss Dowding was proving to be a distraction, and he didn't need any more distractions in his life.

"WILL YOU SEE that coach is brought out front?" Madalene asked Graham as she put her gloves on.

"Yes, Miss," Graham replied as he departed from the entry hall.

The butler had barely stepped out of the room when she heard her companion ask, "May I ask where you are going?"

Madalene turned around to face Mrs. Foster, who was descending the stairs. "I am going to call on Lady Jane."

"Would you like me to go with you?"

"No, I will be fine going alone."

Mrs. Foster came to stand in front of her. "Do you think that is a good idea?"

"Why do you ask?"

With a pointed look, Mrs. Foster replied, "You haven't seemed to be yourself since you came back from your extremely long carriage ride with Lord Hawthorne yesterday."

"It was rather long, wasn't it?"

Mrs. Foster didn't appear fooled by her response. "You are keeping secrets from me again, my dear, and I don't like it. Not one bit."

"Lord Hawthorne and I had much to discuss, and it took longer than we anticipated," she attempted.

"It appears that you and Lord Hawthorne are growing closer to one another."

Madalene huffed. "Heavens, no. We are merely acquaintances."

"I daresay that you are more than acquaintances if he is taking you on carriage rides through Hyde Park."

"Trust me," she started, "the more I learn about Lord Hawthorne, the more I realize that he is an insufferable man."

Mrs. Foster clasped her hands in front of her. "Pray tell, why do you keep spending time with him if he is so 'insufferable'?"

"If you recall, he offered to help find Edith."

"I do, but he hasn't been able to locate her yet."

"That is true," Madalene admitted, "but neither have the constable or the Bow Street Runner."

Mrs. Foster stepped forward and tucked a wisp of Madalene's brown hair behind her ear. "I just want you to be careful around men who use flowery words and offer promises they don't intend to keep."

"Lord Hawthorne isn't like that."

"Isn't he?" her companion asked, the concern evident in her voice. "He keeps promising to find Edith, but what can a marquess truly do?"

Graham stepped back into the room. "The coach is waiting for you out front, Miss," he announced, then approached the door and opened it.

Mrs. Foster placed a hand on her shoulder. "Just think about what I have said."

"You know I always do," Madalene replied before heading out the door.

After she was situated in the coach, Madalene rubbed her reddened wrists. They still continued to hurt, despite the lotion that she put on them when the powder had failed to help.

Her thoughts strayed back to earlier in the day when Lord Hawthorne had come to call. She recalled the hurt that was on his face when she flinched. She hadn't thought he was going to hit her, but she had simply reacted. Frankly, she wasn't entirely sure what Lord Hawthorne was capable of. All she knew was that he was so much more than he let on.

What concerned her the most was that he was associating with the miscreants of Society. Why was a marquess even associated with men who were abducting women? She was missing something, and it was driving her mad!

Which one is the real Lord Hawthorne, she wondered. The one who was starting to occupy her thoughts during the day, or the cold, unfeeling man from the pub who haunted her dreams at night? She wanted to believe the best of him, but she refused to be fooled.

The coach came to a stop in front of Hawthorne House, and the coach dipped as the footman stepped off his perch. He put the step down and then assisted Madalene out of the coach.

She approached the door and knocked. A moment later, it was opened by the butler, who had a kind smile on his lips. "Good afternoon, Miss Dowding," he greeted, opening the door wide. "Lady Jane has been expecting you and is in the drawing room."

As Madalene stepped into the entry hall, she asked, "Is Lord Hawthorne home?"

"He is not."

She let out a sigh of relief. "That is wonderful news."

The butler lifted his brow. "Miss?"

Realizing her blunder, Madalene turned and headed towards the drawing room. She stepped into the room, then closed the door behind her.

Jane gave her a curious look as she sat at the writing desk. "Is everything all right?"

"No," Madalene replied honestly.

Placing the quill down, Jane shifted in her chair to face Madalene. "Then you must tell me what is going on."

Madalene started pacing the small room. "Your brother is..." Her voice trailed off.

"Vexing!" Jane exclaimed. "Irritating!"

"Yes, to both of those things, but he is also..." Her voice stopped. Why couldn't she think of the right word to describe Lord Hawthorne?

"Bothersome?" Jane attempted.

"Yes, that, too. But I am thinking of a specific word."

Jane smiled mischievously. "I like this game," she said. "What about devil's spawn?"

"No, nothing that harsh."

"I know," Jane declared, her voice rising in excitement. "My brother is a nincompoop!"

Madalene giggled, bringing her hand up to cover her mouth. "You are terrible, but that is a good way to describe him."

"It feels good to call him names," Jane said, rising.

"I must admit that it does."

Jane walked over to the settee and sat down. She patted the seat next to her and asked, "Now, will you tell me what is going on with you and my brother?"

"Nothing is going on between us," Madalene replied.

"Heavens, you don't truly expect me to believe that, do you?"

"It is not what you are thinking."

"Good," Jane replied. "Why don't you start with why my brother called on you a few days ago?"

Madalene walked over and sat down on the seat next to her friend. "He had a lead on some missing girls, and he thought one of them might be Edith. Furthermore, he needed to ask a favor of me."

"Which was?"

"He needed to abduct me," she replied, holding her breath, "and use me as bait."

Jane jumped up from her seat. "And you allowed him to do this—*willingly?*"

"I did," Madalene said. "He took me to where the other missing girls were being held and a man tied my wrists together. Then, we were to wait for Bow Street Runners to rescue us."

"And?"

"The Bow Street Runners didn't raid the pub until much later, but they did rescue five girls that were about to be sold into slavery," she admitted.

"Was Edith among the missing girls?"

"Sadly, she was not."

Jane placed a hand on her hip. "And where was my brother during all of this?"

"He went to have a drink with the man who tied my hands together," Madalene revealed.

"Didn't he at least see you home?"

Madalene shook her head. "Lord Oliver saw to that," she said. "He arrived with a coach and ensured I returned home safely."

"What were you thinking, Madalene?" Jane asked. "You put your life in the hands of my brother. That was rather a stupid thing to do."

"I just wanted to find Edith."

"As do I, but not at the expense of losing you, as well," Jane said as she returned to her seat.

Madalene pressed her lips together before admitting, "I worry that your brother might be in danger."

"Why do you say that?"

"He is associating with disreputable people, and I couldn't help but see his demeanor change in front of my captor."

"In what way?"

"It was as if he became another person," Madalene muttered. "I know that sounds foolish, but it is true."

"That doesn't surprise me in the least," Jane said with a shake of her head, "especially since I don't recognize the man who came home."

Madalene shifted in her seat. "We must help him."

"How?"

"Will you talk to him?"

Jane huffed. "My brother and I aren't exactly on speaking terms right now."

"Why is that?"

"I'm afraid it is fairly complicated," Jane remarked dismissively.

Madalene blew out a puff of air. "I see."

"But," Jane hesitated, "I will see what I can do."

"Thank you," Madalene said. "You are the best…"

Her voice trailed off when the door to the drawing room opened and Lord Hawthorne stepped into the room. His eyes widened when they landed on her, and he rushed to say, "My apologies. I didn't mean to intrude."

"Nonsense," Madalene said, abruptly rising. "I was just leaving."

"You were?" Jane asked.

Madalene nodded. "I was, but would you like to meet for some lemon ice at Gunter's tomorrow?"

"I would."

"Wonderful," Madalene replied. "I shall see myself out, then."

As she walked towards the door, she offered Lord Hawthorne a polite smile. He acknowledged it with a tip of his head.

She stepped out of the drawing room and swiftly walked across the entry hall, hoping to create more distance between her and Lord Hawthorne.

A deep, baritone voice came from behind her. "A word, Miss Dowding."

Madalene stopped and closed her eyes in dread. The last thing she wanted to do right now was converse with him.

Slowly, she turned around and watched as he approached her. "Yes, Lord Hawthorne," she said, hoping her words were cordial enough.

He stopped in front of her, leaving more than enough distance to be considered proper. "I would like to apologize for my harsh words earlier this morning."

An apology? She had not been expecting that.

"Thank you for that, my lord," she replied, and started to turn away, but his next words stopped her.

"I hope we can remain friends."

"Friends?" she repeated back incredulously.

Lord Hawthorne was watching her with an intensity that she could not discern. "Am I being too presumptuous in assuming that we are friends?" he asked.

"No, you are not," she rushed to say. "I would be honored to call you my friend."

A smile came to his lips, making him devilishly handsome. Now where had that thought come from, she wondered.

He took a step closer to her and said, "I am happy to hear that, especially after everything we have been through."

"I agree," she responded, returning his smile.

They both remained rooted in their spots, smiling at one another, when Jane's voice came from behind her brother.

"You must not delay Madalene's departure any longer, Brother," Jane remarked tersely.

Lord Hawthorne blinked, and the smile dropped from his lips. "Of course," he replied. "My apologies... again."

Madalene shifted her gaze towards Jane. "I shall see you tomorrow, Jane," she said before turning to leave.

Once she had stepped onto the cobblestone courtyard, Madalene found her smile returning. Why did the thought of being Lord Hawthorne's friend have to be so intriguing? And how was it possible that she was this fickle about him? Hadn't she just been afraid of him?

Good heavens, she thought. She didn't know what to think about Lord Hawthorne anymore.

CHAPTER THIRTEEN

THE MOMENT MISS Dowding had departed from Hawthorne House, Jane exclaimed, *"You abducted my friend?!"*

Baldwin sighed before turning back towards his sister. "She shouldn't have told you that."

"Why?" Jane asked, placing a hand on her hip. "Is it because you want to keep up the pretense of being such an honorable lord?"

"If you would like to talk about this, I suggest that we adjourn to the privacy of my study," Baldwin said. His tone brooked no argument, and he started walking towards the rear of the townhouse.

Jane followed closely behind, and he could practically feel her piercing gaze on his back. He stopped in front of the open door and stood to the side. Once Jane had entered, he stepped inside and closed the door behind him. He walked over to the drink cart, knowing he would need something strong to drink to help him with this conversation.

As he removed the stopper from the decanter, he asked, "What is on your mind, dear sister?"

"You abducted my friend."

"To say that would imply she wasn't in on the ruse."

"Do you have no remorse?"

Baldwin poured himself a drink before he responded. "I do not," he replied. "Because of Miss Dowding's cooperation, we were able to rescue five girls who had gone missing and saved them from a life of slavery."

"Did you not concern yourself with Madalene's reputation in the least?"

"I care greatly," he replied, "which is why every care was taken to ensure no one discovered what we intended to do."

"Madalene said you left her alone with the girls while you went off to have a drink with the person who tied her hands together."

"That is true." He took a sip of his drink.

Jane eyed him suspiciously as she lowered her voice. "Why are you even associating with those types of people?"

"You do not need to concern yourself with that."

"You cannot possibly be in earnest!" she exclaimed in disbelief.

With his drink in his hand, Baldwin walked over to his desk and sat down. "Why do you say that?"

"Because if word ever got around Town that you were associating with those types of people, you would damage our family's reputation."

"No one will ever know," he gave her a pointed look, "unless you intend to tell them."

"Why would I intentionally ruin our reputation amongst the *ton*?"

Baldwin brought the glass up to his lips. "Frankly, I don't know what to think about you anymore."

"I feel the same way about you," she countered.

He considered his sister for a moment before saying, "We can't keep going on this way. We need to sort out our differences and move on."

"Move on?" she asked, arching an eyebrow. "You just want me to forgive you for abandoning our family and be done with it?"

"I understand your hostility—"

She cut him off. "No, you don't," she declared. "When Father died, I needed you here. I needed my brother, but you left, without an explanation."

"And I am sorry for that."

"Are you?" she asked.

"I am sorry for hurting you."

"But not for leaving?"

Placing his empty glass on the desk, Baldwin replied, "I had to leave."

"Why?" she asked, coming closer to the desk. "Why did you have to leave your family when we were all grieving Father's death?"

"It is a long story."

"I have time."

With a shake of his head, he asserted, "I'm afraid you wouldn't understand my reasons."

Jane sat down on a chair that faced the desk. "Perhaps not, but I am willing to try," she said, her voice softening.

"I was not prepared for Father's death," he murmured.

"None of us were."

Baldwin abruptly rose from his chair and walked over to the window. He continued to stare out at the gardens. "After I discovered Father had died, I knew I needed to leave Hawthorne House, to escape his memory," he shared.

"But what about us?"

Bringing his gaze back to meet his sister's, he admitted hesitantly, "I'm afraid I was only thinking of myself."

"Where did you go?"

"That is not important."

Jane looked displeased by his response. "Why are you keeping so many secrets?"

"I'm trying to protect you, Jane," he stated.

"I don't need your protection anymore."

Baldwin turned and leaned back against the windowsill. "You may not want my protection, but I will always extend it towards you," he said. "You may hate me, but I will always love you."

Jane paused. "I don't hate you, but I am angry with you."

"That is a start, at least."

Glancing down at her lap, Jane said, "We used to be so close before Father died. Why don't you trust me anymore?"

"I do trust you."

Jane gave him a disbelieving look. "No, you won't even tell me where you have spent the last three years of your life."

Baldwin knew he needed to share some aspects of where he had been to appease his sister, but he needed to be careful as he skirted around the truth. "If you must know, I spent a portion of my time on Jersey Island."

"Jersey Island?" she asked. "Why would you wish to be so close to France?"

"The island was perfectly safe since the harbors were fortified with cannons and our naval ships were constantly docking there. Furthermore, the local militia was well trained and could assemble nearly three thousand men in a day's time."

"Where did you stay?"

"I rented a room at a coaching inn."

Jane frowned. "I am not entirely sure if I believe you."

"I assure you that it is all true."

"Why would you give up all that you have to rent a room on an island in the Channel?"

Crossing his arms over his chest, Baldwin replied, "Because I wanted to be anywhere else but here."

"Why didn't you go to our Scottish manor?"

"It still held memories of our father."

Jane's voice was soft as she asked, "Why do you wish to forget Father?"

"I'm not ready to accept his death."

"It has been three years."

"I know, but the pain is still raw. It gnaws at me," he admitted.

Tears came to Jane's eyes. "I feel the same way," she shared. "I think of Father every single day. I miss his smile, his laugh, and how he used to let me help him balance the ledgers."

"That was quite scandalous of him," Baldwin joked.

"But Father didn't care," Jane remarked. "He was patient, and he always made me feel loved and protected."

Baldwin grew solemn. "I am sorry I failed you by leaving."

"When you left, I was forced to grieve two men that I loved dearly," she confessed as she wiped away the tears from her eyes. "I didn't know if you were ever coming back."

"I should have sent word."

"Yes, you should have," Jane remarked firmly.

Uncrossing his arms, Baldwin said, "I think we both can agree I didn't handle the situation very well."

"No, you did not."

"But I don't want it to ruin our relationship."

Jane grew silent as she watched him. Finally, she spoke. "Neither do I," she replied. "But I still need some time."

"Take all the time that you need. I am not going anywhere."

"I am relieved to hear that," she said, rising.

"As am I."

Baldwin watched as his sister walked over to the door. Just as she reached to open it, she stopped and spun back around.

"What are your intentions towards Madalene?"

His brow shot up at that unexpected question. "My intentions?" he repeated. "I have no intentions towards Madalene."

"None?"

"If you must know, we are merely friends."

Jane gave him a look that implied she didn't believe him, but she didn't respond to his remark. Instead, she said, "Please don't abduct any more of my friends."

"I can promise you that."

"Thank you," she replied with a smile. "Although, I am slightly envious that Madalene had such a fun adventure."

"I don't think Miss Dowding would consider it an adventure."

"How could she not?" Jane asked as she opened the door.

After Jane departed from the room, Baldwin straightened from the windowsill and went to sit down at his desk. He might as well attempt to review the ledgers before he had to leave for the rookeries.

He had just reached for a ledger when Oliver stepped into the room, closing the door behind him.

"That went well," Oliver remarked.

Baldwin leaned back in his chair. "I see that you were spying on my conversation with Jane," he said.

"Well, I am a spy," Oliver joked.

"That you are." Baldwin grinned. "What is it that you want?"

"Do you need me to accompany you to the rookeries tonight?"

Baldwin shook his head. "I do not. Morton has come to accept that you are always chasing after women so your presence will not be missed."

"That is good," Oliver replied. "That is one less thing for you to have to worry about."

"How will you spend your evening?"

Oliver sat down in a chair. "I intend to go to the gambling halls. After all, I have a cover that I need to protect."

"I do not envy you," Baldwin said. "Besides, I am terrible at cards."

Oliver chuckled. "Then I would stay far away from the gambling halls if I were you. The men in those clubs would have no hesitation in taking you to the poorhouse."

Baldwin glanced at the closed door before asking, "What do you make of our sister?"

Oliver grew serious. "She is rather clever, and I think it is only a matter of time before she suspects that you are a spy."

"But not you?"

Oliver shook his head. "Sadly, Jane looks at me with disapproval in her eyes, just as Mother does."

"I'm sorry."

"That is generally what happens when you are labeled a rakehell amongst the *ton*," Oliver said despairingly.

"But that is not who you truly are."

Oliver sighed. "No, but it is for the good of England. My cover helps me root out the radicals amongst the members of Society."

"We must put our duty ahead of our own wants," Baldwin stated.

"Father used to say that."

Baldwin grew nostalgic at that thought. "That he did."

Rising from his chair, Oliver said, "If you need me for any reason, you know where to find me."

"Thank you for escorting Miss Dowding home safely last night," Baldwin said, leaning forward in his seat and opening the ledger.

"It was my privilege," Oliver remarked. "She was even astute enough to give the Runners a false name."

"She is no simpleton."

Oliver smiled. "No, she is not," he agreed. "But I can't help but wonder what your intentions are towards her?"

Baldwin shot his brother an exasperated look. "Not you, too."

Oliver chuckled. "I was only teasing," he replied.

"Thank you."

"But in all seriousness," Oliver started, "you would be a fool to pass on a woman like Miss Dowding."

"Why do you say that?"

"Because I have never met another woman like her, and I doubt you will either."

"That may be true, but I have no thoughts of matrimony at this time."

Oliver stepped closer to the desk and asked, "Do you mind if I try for Miss Dowding?"

Baldwin stiffened, and an adamant refusal was on the tip of his tongue. But he didn't want to admit that he was harboring some feelings for Miss Dowding, albeit unrequited.

"By all means," he said with a clenched jaw.

Oliver smirked. "That is generous of you, Brother." He walked over to the door and opened it. "I wish you luck tonight."

Baldwin huffed as he watched Oliver depart from the room. It might be best if his brother attempted to woo Miss Dowding, he decided. Then, he might finally be able to stop thinking about her constantly.

IN THE DARKENED coach, Madalene fidgeted with the strand of pearls around her neck as they headed towards Hawthorne House. She found she was rather nervous to see Lord Hawthorne again, but that made no logical sense. Why would I be anxious to see him, she thought. He was a friend, nothing more. So why did he occupy so much of her thoughts?

"Good heavens," Mrs. Foster proclaimed, "whatever is the matter?"

Her fingers stilled on the pearls. "Nothing," Madalene replied. "Why do you ask?"

Mrs. Foster gave her a knowing look. "Whenever you get anxious, you start fidgeting."

"I do?"

"It is a very telling sign, at least for me."

Dropping her hand to her lap, Madalene admitted, "I find that I am anxious about seeing Lord Hawthorne again."

Mrs. Foster looked displeased by her admission. "You know how I feel about Lord Hawthorne."

"I do, and you do not need to worry yourself on that account," Madalene said. "We are only friends."

"You seem to have started keeping secrets from me the moment that you two met, and that concerns me greatly."

"You have nothing to worry about."

Mrs. Foster reached forward and patted her on her knee. "I will always worry about you. I couldn't love you more even if you were my own child."

"I know, and I feel the same way about you."

"Then I urge you to be cautious around Lord Hawthorne," Mrs. Foster said, leaning back, "and his brother."

"Lord Oliver has only ever behaved as a perfect gentleman to me."

Mrs. Foster gave a disbelieving huff. "He is a rakehell."

"He is harmless," Madalene countered.

With a shake of her head, Mrs. Foster replied, "You are entirely too trusting when it comes to men, my dear. They will take advantage of your innocence."

"I can handle myself."

The coach came to a stop, and it was only a moment before the door was opened. After they exited the coach, they started following the line of people into Hawthorne House as they made their way towards the ballroom.

Stepping into the rectangular room, they were immediately greeted by Jane. She went to embrace Madalene and whispered next to her ear, "I am so glad that you are finally here."

Madalene laughed and replied in a hushed voice, "I can only imagine how much you hate standing here to greet people."

"You have no idea," Jane said, taking a step back.

Mrs. Foster spoke up. "You are looking lovely this evening, Lady Jane."

"Thank you, Mrs. Foster," Jane responded, running a hand down her pink ballgown.

"I am so glad that you could accompany Madalene this evening, Leah," Lady Hawthorne interjected.

"Someone needs to keep her out of trouble," Mrs. Foster joked, earning a laugh from Lady Hawthorne.

Madalene looked over and saw Lord Hawthorne standing rigidly next to his mother. He was speaking to one of their guests, but he didn't appear to be enjoying himself. He shifted his gaze towards her, and she realized that she had been caught staring, causing her cheeks to grow increasingly warm.

"Madalene, you are holding up the line," Mrs. Foster murmured before she gently nudged her down the line and closer towards Lord Hawthorne. Their gazes met and, for the briefest of moments, she felt as if they were the only two in the room. However, it was evident that he didn't feel the same because he dropped into a stiff bow.

"It is a pleasure to see you again, Miss Dowding."

She curtsied. "You are too kind, Lord Hawthorne."

Lord Hawthorne turned his head towards Mrs. Foster and said, "Thank you for coming to my ball." She couldn't help but notice the terseness in his voice.

After Mrs. Foster responded politely, they left the line and stepped further into the ballroom. An ostentatious golden chandelier hung from the painted ceiling, and the ivory papered walls were embellished with golden accents. In the rear, there were a set of French doors that opened to the gardens.

A half-orchestra was warming up in the corner, and guests lined the walls, leaving the chalked dance floor open.

They had barely advanced further into the room when Madalene was approached by Mr. Ridley and his mother.

"What a pleasant surprise!" Mrs. Ridley exclaimed. "I hadn't expected to see you in Town, Miss Dowding."

Madalene smiled politely. "I'm afraid my departure has been delayed."

"I am sorry to hear that, but happy that we are able to enjoy your company a little longer," Mrs. Ridley said, giving her son a pointed look. "Aren't you?"

A line of sweat was forming on Mr. Ridley's brow as he replied, "I am. I hope this means that you will be willing to save me a dance?" His tone was hopeful.

"I would be happy to."

Mr. Ridley let out a relieved sigh. "I thought you would say no," he said before his face grew splotchy.

Madalene suspected that Mr. Ridley had not intended to say his last words out loud. Poor man, she thought.

"Why would I say no?" she asked. "You have been an excellent dance partner on multiple occasions."

Mr. Ridley puffed out his chest in pride at her praise. "I am happy to hear you say that, Miss Dowding."

Mrs. Ridley must have liked her response as well, because an approving smile was on her lips. "My son will be by later to collect his dance."

As they walked off, Mrs. Foster whispered, "I wish you wouldn't give that man false hope."

"Frankly, I feel bad for him."

"Just don't feel too bad for him, because I don't think you would enjoy having Mrs. Ridley as your mother-in-law," Mrs. Foster teased.

Madalene shook her head vehemently, causing the brown curls that framed her face to sway back and forth. "I would resign myself to being a spinster before I ever agreed to marry Mr. Ridley."

They came to a stop next to an opening by the wall, and Mrs. Foster said, "Your presence here is causing quite a sensation."

"Why do you say that?"

"Because you rarely attend social events, and I can't help but notice that the gentlemen are eyeing you with interest."

Madalene stifled a groan as she adjusted the sleeve of her ivory muslin ballgown. "I just hope I don't have to deal with scheming mothers this evening."

Her words had barely left her lips when a man's chuckle came from behind her.

Madalene turned around and saw Lord Oliver, his eyes holding amusement.

"I have complained about the same thing on multiple occasions," he said. "The scheming mothers can be quite relentless, can they not?"

Smiling, Madalene replied, "I wonder if they have any shame at all."

"Not when it comes to securing a suitable match for their child." Oliver's lips quirked slightly. "How are you this evening, Miss Dowding?"

"I am well."

"It pleases me immensely to hear that," he said. "Apparently, others are happy that you are here, as well. One cannot help but notice the attention that you have garnered since you first stepped foot into the ballroom."

"Unfortunately, I find that I have grown accustomed to the stares and whispers."

"As have I," Oliver shared. "I'm afraid it doesn't make it any easier though."

"No, it does not," Madalene agreed.

Oliver took a step closer to her and said, "I was hoping to secure you for the first set of the evening."

Madalene tipped her head. "I would be delighted, my lord."

"Wonderful," Oliver declared as he extended his hand towards her. "Shall I escort you to the dance floor?"

She accepted his hand and he led her towards the middle of the room. Once they arrived, he placed his hand over hers to secure it in place.

"The dance hasn't begun yet," Oliver said as other couples started making their way towards them, "but it should start shortly."

Madalene took a moment to study Lord Oliver. He was definitely a handsome man, sharing many of the same physical attributes as his brother. She had no doubt that he was aware of that fact, because his words always seemed too smooth, too rehearsed. But his eyes told her a different story. They held a great sadness in them, despite his cocky demeanor.

"May I ask what has you so preoccupied?" he asked, leaning closer.

"I was just woolgathering, I'm afraid."

Oliver chuckled. "Which is a polite way of calling someone boring."

"That is not what I meant, my lord," she rushed to say. "Please do not take offense when there was none intended."

He patted her hand. "I am only teasing you, Miss Dowding," he said. "What occupies your time?"

"The usual pursuits, I suppose."

"Such as?"

"Would you care to hear the polite answers or the truth?"

Oliver gave her an amused look. "The truth, if you don't mind."

"I enjoy riding at my country estate, and I recently opened an orphanage."

"Yes, the Elizabeth Dowding School for Orphan Girls," Oliver replied. "I remember my mother and sister telling me about that. What a tremendous accomplishment."

"Thank you." Madalene glanced over her shoulder to ensure no one would be privy to what she was about to ask. "May I ask you a question?"

Oliver smiled flirtatiously. "You may ask me anything that you want, my dear."

Ignoring his tone, she asked, "We didn't speak of it in the coach, but why were you in the rookeries that day your brother pretended to abduct me?"

His smile dimmed. "Why would you care to know that?"

"Lord Hawthorne also said you were following us to ensure my protection," she pressed. "Why was that?"

His eyes grew guarded. "You will have to ask my brother."

"Why is that exactly?" she questioned.

"I know it may sound confusing, but there was a perfectly rational explanation for why I was in the rookeries."

She looked at him expectantly. "Which was?"

"I am not at liberty to say," he murmured as his eyes scanned the room. "Furthermore, this is not the place to discuss such things."

"I apologize, but I have so many questions that remain unanswered."

Lord Oliver kept a smile on his lips, but she could hear the warning in his tone. "A ball is generally a place where you discuss things that are much more pleasant."

Madalene frowned, ever so slightly, and asked, "You aren't going to tell me anything, are you?"

"No, but I would like to hear more about your orphanage," Oliver said, glancing over at her. "That sounds more interesting."

It was maddening that Oliver refused to answer her questions, but before she could press him any further, the music started up and he led her to where she was to line up. He dropped her arm and went to stand across from her.

As Madalene began to dance to the music, she couldn't help but wonder what kind of illicit activities Lord Hawthorne and his brother were entangled with.

CHAPTER FOURTEEN

WITH A DRINK in his hand, Baldwin knew he was scowling as he watched Miss Dowding dance a set with that blond dandy, Lord Whitmore, but he didn't care. The poor man was making a fool of himself as he tried to win Miss Dowding's favor. He hoped that she wasn't foolish enough to fall for his pathetic attempts to woo her.

Miss Dowding looked especially lovely tonight in a gown that hugged her curves perfectly. Her hair was piled high atop her head, showing off the elegant curvature of her neck. Blast it! Those were things he most definitely should not be noticing about her, especially since he had no intention of pursuing her.

What a waste of an evening, he thought, as he tightened his hold on his glass. His mother had made him dance the first set with Jane, but he refused to dance with anyone else. He would rather be anywhere but here, including his filthy rented room on Draper Street, but his mother would have been devastated if he hadn't attended his own ball.

His brother's voice broke through his musings. "Why aren't you dancing?" he asked, coming to stand next to him.

"Not interested."

"Ah," Oliver replied, following his gaze. "Then, may I ask why you are staring at the lovely Miss Dowding?"

Bringing the glass up to his lips, Baldwin responded, "I'm not."

"You are a terrible liar, you know," Oliver joked as he turned to face him. "You have been scowling at Miss Dowding since the first set."

"I have not."

Oliver smirked. "You might want to turn your attention to another young woman for the rest of the evening or people may start talking."

Baldwin placed his empty drink on the tray of a servant passing by. "What are you even doing in the ballroom?" he asked. "I thought you had adjourned to the card room."

"I did, but I was thinking about asking Miss Dowding for another dance."

Now Oliver had his full attention. "You want to dance two sets with Miss Dowding?" Baldwin asked in disbelief.

"Why not?"

"In case you haven't noticed, Miss Dowding doesn't appear to have a shortage of dance partners," Baldwin said. "Men have been lining up to speak to her."

"That doesn't surprise me," Oliver replied, "but I assume most of them are fortune hunters and rakes."

"Why do you say that?"

Oliver gave him a surprised look. "Because Miss Dowding is one of the richest young women in all of England."

"She is?"

"How is it that you weren't aware of that?"

Baldwin ran a hand over his chin. "I had no idea," he replied. "She doesn't appear entitled or pretentious."

"No, she does not." Oliver accepted a drink from a servant before growing serious. "You should know that she was asking me questions about the night at the Flailing Duck."

"What did she ask?" he questioned, furrowing his brows.

Oliver lowered his voice and shared, "She wanted to know why I was in the rookeries on the night you abducted her."

"What did you say?"

"I told her to ask you." Oliver took a drink from his glass.

"Thank you for that," Baldwin remarked dryly.

Oliver lowered the glass to his side. "What would you have me say?" he asked. "I couldn't very well tell her the truth."

"No, you are right, of course," Baldwin replied.

"You will need to think of something to say to Miss Dowding, because she can't keep asking questions," Oliver warned. "It could jeopardize both of our covers."

"I am well aware of that fact."

With a concerned look, Oliver said, "We both know what Corbyn would say about this."

"I do," Baldwin replied, frowning. "He would say 'deal with it, or I will deal with it for you'."

Baldwin watched as Miss Dowding was escorted back to her companion by Lord Whitmore. A group of gentlemen were already waiting to speak to her, and she politely acknowledged them with a smile. But he could tell it wasn't genuine.

"The next dance is the waltz, you know," Oliver revealed.

"I hadn't realized that."

Oliver placed a hand on his shoulder and said, "You might want to ask her to dance before someone else does."

"I hate dancing," Baldwin muttered.

"True, but ladies generally enjoy it," Oliver teased.

Miss Dowding glanced his way, and their eyes met. He watched, transfixed, as her green eyes sparkled under the candlelight. In the next moment, he found himself walking purposefully as he made his way over to her.

Stopping in front of her, he extended his gloved hand and asked, "Would you care to dance, Miss Dowding?"

She glanced down at his proffered hand before saying, "I apologize, but this set is taken."

"By whom?" he growled.

"Mr. Thatcher has requested this set," she replied, gesturing towards a lanky young man standing nearby.

Turning his gaze towards Mr. Thatcher, Baldwin remarked in a stern voice, "I am sure that Mr. Thatcher will graciously step aside until the next dance. Won't you?"

A flicker of fear came to Mr. Thatcher's eyes. "I do not mind, my lord," he replied, his voice trembling slightly.

"Excellent," Baldwin replied as he returned his attention to Miss Dowding. "Shall we?"

As he led them towards the dance floor, Miss Dowding murmured, "Poor Mr. Thatcher. That was poorly done on your part."

"I asked, and he offered to dance the next set with you."

She huffed. "You practically threatened the poor man."

"I did not," he argued, glancing over at her. "Trust me when I say that when I threaten someone, you will most assuredly know."

Baldwin stopped in the middle of the dance floor, brought her left arm up, and slid his hand around her waist. He heard her slight intake of breath at his touch, which pleased him immensely. Perhaps she wasn't as immune to his charms as he had led himself to believe.

The music began, and Baldwin started leading her around the floor. "You dance superbly," he praised.

"Thank you," she replied as her gaze darted around the room.

"I must admit that I haven't danced the waltz in over three years."

"Well, it doesn't show, my lord."

Baldwin frowned. Why in the blazes is she avoiding my gaze, he wondered. He cleared his throat. "My brother mentioned that you might have some questions for me."

Her eyes snapped towards his. "I do."

"By all means, ask away," he replied, finding himself pleased that she was now looking at him.

"Do you truly mean that?"

"I do."

Miss Dowding pressed her lips together before asking, "Why are you associating with disreputable people in the rookeries?"

"There is a very simple explanation, but I didn't want to tell you until now."

"Which is?"

Baldwin leaned closer to her and said, "I was scouting locations for the workhouses in the rookeries, and I happened upon men who informed me about the missing girls. I befriended them only in the hopes of discovering the girls' location."

Miss Dowding eyed him critically. "I thought you weren't in support of Lord Desmond's bill."

"I'm not, but I am in support of building workhouses for the poor," he explained. "Insomuch that I plan to fund a portion of the project myself."

"Are you in earnest?"

Baldwin nodded, knowing that Miss Dowding was easily falling for his lies. A part of him almost felt bad for lying to her. *Almost.* "I am."

Her eyes softened as she watched him. "I believe I misjudged you, Lord Hawthorne," she hesitated before adding, "again."

Smiling, he said, "I believe we are both guilty of that."

"Why didn't you say anything before?"

"We couldn't take a chance that it would be leaked to the newspapers," he shared. "After all, a marquess doesn't typically stroll around the rookeries with his brother and friend."

A small smile caused Miss Dowding's perfectly formed lips to curve delightfully. He found his eyes lingering on them as she said, "I find what you are doing admirable."

"You mustn't tell anyone," Baldwin insisted. "We still haven't found a way to fund the rest of the workhouses."

"I would like to match whatever donation it is that you are contributing."

"You would?"

Miss Dowding tilted her head and commented, "You sound surprised."

"I am," he replied. "I hadn't even considered you would be willing to donate to the workhouses."

"And why wouldn't I?" she questioned. "I find building workhouses in the rookeries to be an exemplary thing, and I have more money than I can spend in two lifetimes."

Baldwin had to admit that his opinion of Miss Dowding rose significantly. He hadn't met a more charitable person before, nor did he think he ever would again.

"You are a formidable woman," he said softly.

"That is kind of you to say, my lord, but I am only doing what my conscience dictates."

The music stopped, and Baldwin found that he was not finished conversing with Miss Dowding. He took her left hand and placed it in the crook of his arm.

"Would you care to go walking in the gardens?" he asked.

"That sounds lovely."

As he led her towards the French doors, he noticed that Mrs. Foster followed discreetly behind them. They started down a footpath leading to the center of the gardens, where a pool glistened in the moonlight.

"Would you care to sit?" he asked, stopping near one of the iron benches encircling the water.

"I would," she replied, and gracefully lowered herself onto the bench.

Claiming the seat next to her, Baldwin shifted to face her and found himself rendered speechless at the way the moonlight lit up her enchanting face, forcing him to recognize that he had never met a more beautiful woman than Miss Dowding.

He had a sudden desire to learn everything he could about her.

Before he could stop himself, he said, "Tell me about your childhood."

"I had a happy childhood," she shared. "My mother made sure of that. Before I was sent to boarding school, we spent our days riding on our estate and visiting people in the village. We were always bringing a basket of food to someone in need."

"Your mother sounds like a wonderful person."

Miss Dowding grew silent. "She was," she finally said. "I was lucky to have her for as long as I did."

"Why do you say that?"

"We were in London when my mother grew sick, and the doctor recommended that we adjourn to the country for the fresh air," Miss Dowding explained. "But, for the next four months, I watched my mother wither away."

"That must have been hard."

"It was, but it was harder on my mother."

Baldwin looked at her curiously. "Why do you say that?"

"She hated being trapped in bed with her weak heart, and she hated that I had to care for her," Miss Dowding shared. "She felt that she was a burden to me."

"Was she?"

Miss Dowding huffed. "Heavens, no. Every moment I spent with my mother was a gift. But she couldn't see that, and she grew more and more despondent."

"That must have been hard to watch."

Tears came to her eyes, but Miss Dowding blinked them back. "I tried to stop her..." Her words trailed off as her face paled.

"What did you try to stop?"

"Nothing," she replied with a shake of her head. "Forget that I said anything."

Baldwin leaned closer to her and said, "You can trust me, Miss Dowding."

Miss Dowding dropped her gaze to her lap. "I do not wish to burden you with my shame," she murmured.

Reaching over, he picked up her hand and brought it to his lips. As her hand hovered near his mouth, he said, "Nothing that you say will ever frighten me away from being your friend."

"This might," she said, her eyes filled with sadness. "I haven't been able to speak of it with anyone else."

"Not even Mrs. Foster?"

She shook her head. "No."

"Then you must relieve yourself of your burden," he said. "Let me help you."

Uncertainty crossed her delicate features as she asserted, "You must promise not to tell another soul."

"You have my word." Baldwin lowered her hand, but he didn't release it.

Miss Dowding glanced down at their entwined hands. "My mother was tired of being sick, and she told me that she intended to overdose on laudanum that evening." She swallowed slowly. "I tried to talk her out of it, but she was adamant that it was time for her to die."

"I am so sorry," he said, knowing his words were wholly inadequate.

A tear rolled down her cheek, and Miss Dowding reached up to swipe it away. "I stayed with her the entire evening, and even after she was gone. What my mother did was incredibly selfish and..." Her words trailed off as it turned into a sob. "I just wasn't ready to say goodbye."

Baldwin had an overwhelming desire to pull Miss Dowding into his arms, but he knew it was not the place to do so. He didn't dare put her into a compromising position, no matter how much he wished to console her.

"Why haven't you told Mrs. Foster the truth about your mother?" he prodded.

"I don't want anyone to think less of her."

Baldwin looked at her incredulously. "Instead you shouldered this burden alone?"

She nodded slowly. "I thought I was strong enough."

"My dear," he started, "there is no shame in asking for help."

"If anyone discovers the truth, then my mother's legacy will be tarnished," Miss Dowding declared. "And I'm not willing to risk that."

"Then I shall keep your secret."

Miss Dowding offered him a timid smile. "Thank you, my lord. I must admit I find some relief in confiding my secret to you."

"I had no idea that you were carrying such a heavy burden," he admitted. "You hide it remarkably well."

"I believe everyone hides a part of themselves from others."

Baldwin heard the music start back up again. Rising from the bench, he said, "I should return you to the ball."

"Must you?" she asked as she rose.

He chuckled. "Do not tempt me. I would much rather stay out in the gardens with you than be in that stuffy ballroom. But I believe Mr. Thatcher, kind as he was to allow me the set, would still like to dance with you."

As they started walking along the footpath, Miss Dowding remarked, "I have noticed that you have sat many of the sets out."

Baldwin lifted his brow. "Have you been watching me, Miss Dowding?"

"I have not," she asserted as an adorable blush crept up onto her cheeks.

Taking pity on her, he replied, "Frankly, I detest dancing."

"That is a shame, my lord, because you are quite good at it," she said, sparing a glance in his direction.

Baldwin smiled at her remark. "Perhaps all I need is the right dance partner."

"In my experience, I have found that usually makes all the difference," Miss Dowding remarked.

BALDWIN SAT AT the head of the table as he read the morning newspaper. He reached for his cup of tea and took a long sip before returning it to the saucer on the table.

Pratt stepped into the room and asked, "May I have a moment of your time, milord?"

"You may," Baldwin replied as he lowered the paper.

The butler gestured towards the door and a familiar lanky man walked into the parlor, his eyes darting nervously around the room. He was wearing a tattered brown jacket and matching trousers and his dark hair was slicked to the side.

"You may remember Mr. John Harvey," Pratt said. "He shared that you two met briefly in the rookeries."

Baldwin tipped his head in acknowledgement. "That we did."

"We have hired John on as a gardener, and we reimbursed his travel expenses as you ordered," Pratt revealed.

"That is wonderful news." Baldwin turned his attention towards Mr. Harvey. "How have you settled in at Hawthorne House?"

"Very well, milord," Mr. Harvey replied. "And I wanted to humbly thank ye for this opportunity. It will go a long way to feed my family."

"I am pleased to hear that."

Mr. Harvey's eyes darted towards Pratt before saying, "I would like to apologize for attempting to rob ye."

"A man will do just about anything to care for his family," Baldwin stated.

"Aye, milord."

Baldwin gave him a pointed look. "However, I would strongly encourage you not to squander this opportunity by doing something so foolhardy again."

"I will not," Mr. Harvey asserted.

"I am pleased to hear that," Baldwin said.

Pratt spoke up. "If you will excuse us, John is set to meet with the head gardener to begin work for the day."

Baldwin watched as they departed from the room before he brought the newspaper back up. He had just finished reading an article when his sister walked into the room.

"Good morning," Jane greeted.

Baldwin lowered the paper. "Good morning."

Jane stepped over to the buffet table and piled a plate high with food. "I thought I would eat breakfast with you this morning."

"Wonderful," he said as he brought the paper back up.

Coming to sit to his right, Jane asked, "Is there anything interesting in the morning newspaper?"

"Not particularly," he admitted. "It was announced that Lord Desmond is having a rally to garner support for his bill."

"Are you in support of the bill?" Jane inquired.

"I am not," he responded. "I am in support of workhouses in the rookeries, but I do not believe the Home Office should take over the responsibilities of overseeing them."

Jane placed her napkin onto her lap. "Then how do you suggest they be funded?"

"As they always have," Baldwin replied. "By the parishes that they are located in."

"But the parishes are unable to handle the growing number of poor people living in their borders."

"That may be true, but they can also join together to form unions to share the costs associated with the workhouses."

Jane nodded. "Those are known as Gilbert Unions. Thus, by creating large groups they are in a position to establish larger workhouses. Sadly, this was not implemented very well."

Baldwin looked at her in surprise. "You are remarkably well informed."

"I don't know why you seem so surprised," Jane remarked as she reached for her fork. "I read the newspaper nearly every morning."

"I hadn't realized you would be interested in reading the morning newspaper."

"And why not?" she asked.

Baldwin folded the paper and placed it on the table. "My apologies," he said. "I think it is commendable that you read the newspaper."

"Thank you," Jane replied as a footman placed a cup of chocolate in front of her. "I couldn't help but notice that you and Madalene appeared rather close last night at the ball."

Baldwin stiffened. "Why do you say that?"

"After dancing the waltz, you disappeared with her into the gardens for quite some time," Jane shared, a smile on her face.

"You need not worry about propriety," he started, "we were chaperoned by Miss Dowding's companion the entire time."

"I never questioned that."

"Say what you need to say and be done with it," he insisted.

Her smile grew. "You are being rather testy this morning."

"I am not."

Jane reached for her cup of chocolate as she said, "I am merely commenting that you and Miss Dowding appear to be getting closer."

"We are friends."

"Friends?" Jane asked. "I didn't think that you had too many of those."

"I don't."

"Well, I would ask that you be cautious around my dear friend, because I wouldn't want her reputation to suffer by associating with you."

Baldwin furrowed his brow. "Meaning?"

"Do you have any intention of pursuing Madalene?" Jane asked plainly.

"I do not," he replied. "Frankly, I have no thoughts of matrimony at this time."

Jane bobbed her head. "I assumed as much."

"But that doesn't mean we can't remain friends."

"Just be mindful of the gossips," Jane warned. "They can spew vicious tales and will damage reputations for their enjoyment."

"That is awful."

"It is the unfortunate truth, I'm afraid."

Before he could respond, Oliver walked into the breakfast parlor with his hair tousled and his clothes horribly wrinkled.

"Good morning," Jane said in a disapproving tone. "I see that you just got home."

Oliver winced as he brought a hand to his forehead. "I did, and I would appreciate it if you kept your voice down."

"My voice isn't raised, Oliver," Jane remarked curtly. "Perhaps you shouldn't have had so much to drink last night."

Oliver walked over to the buffet table and grabbed a piece of toast. "Where is the fun in that?"

Jane turned towards Oliver and asked defiantly, "Do you ever tire of being a despicable cad?"

Oliver swallowed the bite in his mouth. "Why are you attacking me this morning?" he asked as he leaned his shoulder against the wall.

"If you must know, it is because I rarely see you."

Oliver smirked. "You miss me, then?"

Jane shook her head and rose. "I would prefer not to spend time in your presence right now," she said before storming out of the room.

Baldwin lifted his brow. "I take it that our dear sister doesn't approve of you and your lifestyle."

Oliver sighed as he came closer to the table. "No, she does not," he replied. "She makes that abundantly clear."

"That is most unfortunate."

"The sad thing is that Jane isn't wrong," Oliver said as he sat down next to him. "Mother feels the same way."

"Has Mother said something to you?"

Oliver shook his head. "No, but I can see it in her eyes."

"We must put our duty ahead of our wants," Baldwin said.

"I know, but..." His voice trailed off as a pained look came to his face. "Have you ever wished that we weren't recruited out of Oxford to be agents?"

Baldwin lifted his brow. "No, but it would appear that you have."

"I was supposed to be a barrister," Oliver said. "I was even preparing to apply to one of the Inns of Court."

"Do you regret becoming an agent?" Baldwin asked.

Oliver frowned. "That is a ticklish question."

"Not really."

"We must put our duty ahead of our own wants," Oliver said as he rose. "I think I am just spouting nonsense because I'm tired."

Baldwin gave his brother a concerned look. "Becoming lackadaisical can get you killed," he pointed out.

"There is little chance of that," Oliver remarked dryly. "I am just babysitting schoolboys who spout radical views."

"Can you ask Corbyn to reassign you?"

"I have, but he said I was in the perfect position to spy on members of Society."

"That is a shame."

Oliver started walking backwards towards the door. "Not everyone is lucky enough to go undercover for three years and help French royalists during the war."

After his brother left, Baldwin sat for a long moment. He hadn't considered that his brother might harbor some feelings of jealousy towards him for his past assignments. They had taken such different paths after they were recruited to be agents.

A familiar voice came from the window. "I hadn't realized that

Oliver was not enjoying his cover to this extent."

Baldwin glanced over and saw Corbyn was entering the breakfast parlor by way of the open window.

"Did my butler turn you away?"

Corbyn shook his head as he adjusted his white cravat. "I didn't attempt to go to the main door."

"Were you spying on our conversation?"

"It was unintentional," Corbyn replied as he went and closed the door. "I wanted to speak to you, but I was unable to get your attention while your sister was in the room."

"Again, you could have come by way of the main door."

Corbyn stepped up to the buffet table and picked up a plate. "That would have been a waste of time," he said as he piled eggs and bacon onto his plate.

"What is it that you wanted to speak to me about?"

Walking around the table, Corbyn sat down next to him. "Morton may be right about Desmond," he shared.

"You found proof that he is stealing from the workhouses?"

"Not exactly, but the agent who reviewed the ledgers confirmed that the numbers appeared to be doctored, but has no proof," Corbyn said. "We need to find the solicitor that Morton mentioned and speak to him."

"I will see what I can do."

Corbyn took a bite of his eggs and chewed them thoughtfully. "Have you discovered anything more on the case?"

"I have not, but there is a meeting tonight at the Blue Boar."

"Excellent," Corbyn replied. "Wouldn't it be grand if you were able to meet Marie tonight and stop this growing rebellion before it escalates?"

"Yes, it would."

Corbyn pointed his fork at him and said, "I couldn't help but notice you and Miss Dowding were getting rather close during the waltz."

"Not you, too!" Baldwin huffed. "Miss Dowding and I are just friends."

"It didn't appear that way."

"Then you need spectacles," Baldwin quipped.

Corbyn leaned back in his chair. "There is nothing wrong with falling in love, especially since you are retiring as an agent after this case."

"Falling in love?" he repeated back in disbelief. "I am doing no such thing with Miss Dowding."

"Are you sure?"

Baldwin bobbed his head decisively. "I think I would know if I was falling in love with her," he asserted.

"Then I stand corrected," Corbyn said in a tone that implied he didn't believe him. "That is probably for the best, because my agents haven't been able to find any clue of Miss Hardy's whereabouts."

"None?"

Corbyn shook his head. "They have scoured London, but it would appear that Miss Hardy simply disappeared into the night."

"That isn't likely."

"I know, but our leads have been exhausted," Corbyn replied. "And I am unable to dedicate any more resources from the agency on her case."

Running a hand through his brown hair, Baldwin said, "That news is going to devastate Miss Dowding."

"It is a good thing you aren't holding a fondness for her," Corbyn remarked, amused.

Baldwin shoved his chair back and rose. "If you will excuse me, I have work that I need to see to. I trust that you can see your way out."

CHAPTER FIFTEEN

"**Y**OU SEEM AWFULLY cheerful this morning," Mrs. Foster commented as she pulled the thread through the fabric. "Is there any particular reason why?"

Madalene lowered her needlework to her lap and replied, "I find my thoughts continuously returning to the ball last night."

"Is that so?" Mrs. Foster gave her a knowing look. "Are you thinking of anyone in particular?"

"No," she replied, not daring to admit that her thoughts were repeatedly turning towards Lord Hawthorne. "The whole night was rather enjoyable."

"You sound surprised," Mrs. Foster remarked.

"Frankly, I am. I danced nearly every set, and I met the most interesting gentlemen," Madalene said.

"That is generally what happens at a ball."

Placing her needlework on a side table, Madalene admitted, "This was the first ball where I didn't feel like I was a prize to be won."

"I am glad to hear that."

Madalene reached for the teapot and poured herself a cup of tea. She took a long, lingering sip before she lowered the teacup to her lap. "I think I would like to stay in London for the rest of the Season."

Mrs. Foster's brow shot up. "Truly?"

"My mother found immense joy in London, and I'm wondering if I can find the same amount of joy, as well."

A frown came to Mrs. Foster's lips. "Is this about a handsome marquess who has somehow managed to bewitch you?"

"I know not what you are talking about," Madalene said, taking a sip of her tea.

"No?" Mrs. Foster asked. "Not only did you dance the waltz with him, but you also took a turn around the gardens."

"That is true, but nothing untoward happened."

"I never implied that it did," Mrs. Foster remarked. "I am just concerned about your welfare, and that includes your heart."

"Who said anything about my heart?"

"No one did, but it is rather obvious that you have developed feelings for Lord Hawthorne," Mrs. Foster said. "And please do not insult me by trying to deny it."

Madalene gave a half-shrug. "Perhaps I have developed some feelings for him, but that is a far cry from having my heart invested."

"Then you are lying to yourself."

Before she could respond, Graham stepped into the room and announced, "Mr. Walker is here to call upon you, Miss."

"Will you send him in?"

Graham tipped his head and departed from the room.

A few moments later, her solicitor entered with an unusually solemn look on his face.

Placing her teacup onto the tray, Madalene rose and asked, "Is everything all right, Mr. Walker?"

Mr. Walker stopped in the center of the room, his back stiff. "I hate to be the bearer of bad news, but I thought you should know before it hit the newspapers tomorrow."

"Which is?" Madalene asked hesitantly.

"I'm afraid what I'm about to share is a little indelicate," Mr. Walker said, wincing.

Madalene glanced nervously at Mrs. Foster, wondering why her solicitor was stalling. "Whatever is the matter?"

Mr. Walker took a shuddering breath before sharing, "Miss Hardy was found floating in the River Thames this morning."

Madalene gasped as she lowered herself onto the settee. "How horrible!" she exclaimed.

"The Bow Street Runner that I hired to find Miss Hardy was able to identify her at the morgue," Mr. Walker explained. "Apparently, she had been in the water for a few days."

"And this Bow Street Runner is adamant that this person found was Miss Hardy?" Mrs. Foster asked.

Mr. Walker turned his gaze towards Madalene's companion. "Yes, and her next of kin has been notified."

Mrs. Foster rose from her seat and came to sit next to Madalene. "Are you all right, dear?"

Tears burned her eyes, but she fiercely blinked them back. "I don't know what to say or do."

"That is to be expected," Mrs. Foster replied. "Edith was a dear friend of yours."

Turning her gaze towards Mr. Walker, she asked, "How was she killed?"

Mr. Walker shifted uncomfortably before saying, "It would appear that she entered the water of her own accord."

Madalene's mouth dropped open. "You think she killed herself?"

"There were no signs of foul play, and the coroner ruled it as suicide," Mr. Walker said, his eyes full of compassion.

Madalene started shaking her head profusely. "No, no, no..." she started. "That is impossible. Edith would never do that."

"I know that it may seem impossible, but we don't know if Edith was in her right mind at the time she entered the water," Mr. Walker explained.

"The coroner is wrong!" Madalene exclaimed. "Edith was abducted. Her room had been ransacked, and the perpetrator must have killed her."

Mr. Walker's eyes were full of pity. "The constable now believes that Edith ransacked her own room before she headed towards the River Thames."

"That is improbable!"

Mrs. Foster placed a hand on her sleeve. "It will be all right," she encouraged. "You are just in shock right now."

"Edith wouldn't have killed herself," Madalene asserted. "She was one of my dearest friends, and she would have told me if she was considering suicide."

"You mustn't blame yourself," Mrs. Foster said, reassuringly. "Sometimes people hide their pain from others, and they won't let anyone in."

Shifting to face her companion, Madalene replied, "She was paying off her mother's debts and trying to start a new life. Why would she do those things if she had planned to kill herself?"

Mrs. Foster offered her a sad smile. "I'm afraid I can't answer that."

"I would like to be the first to offer my condolences, Miss Dowding," Mr. Walker said. "I hope I did the right thing by telling you."

"You did," Madalene rushed to assure him, "and I thank you for coming to see me."

"You are welcome," Mr. Walker replied. "I shall see myself out, then."

Madalene rose from the settee. "Before you go, will you inform Miss Hardy's mother that I would like to pay for the funeral costs?"

Mr. Walker visibly stiffened. "That is most kind of you. However, Miss Hardy will not be allowed to be buried in a parish cemetery due to the nature of her death. She will most likely be buried at a crossroad with her head downwards."

"Then I wish to give Mrs. Hardy one hundred pounds for all the costs associated with her daughter's death. With any luck, she can start anew with the money."

"That is more than generous, Miss Dowding," Mr. Walker acknowledged. "I shall see to securing the funds and informing Mrs. Hardy of your decision."

"Thank you, Mr. Walker," Madalene said. "I do appreciate your help with this delicate situation."

Mr. Walker tipped his head. "My job is but to serve you, Miss."

After her solicitor left the room, Madalene returned to the settee, retreating into her own thoughts. She couldn't seem to process what she had been told. There was no way that Edith had killed herself. No. It was ludicrous to even think that she would.

"Madalene," Mrs. Foster spoke softly, "how are you faring?"

Madalene brought her gaze back up. "Edith wouldn't have killed herself."

Mrs. Foster sighed. "Madalene—"

"I know her!" Madalene exclaimed, cutting her off. "She wouldn't have left her mother and sister without a fight."

"We don't know what drives someone to end their life, but—"

Madalene jumped up from the settee, causing Mrs. Foster to stop speaking. "No! Nothing you say will convince me otherwise," she asserted as she rushed out of the drawing room.

She didn't stop running until she arrived at the gardens, finally giving herself permission to cry. It felt good to let the tears fall, to express her emotions so freely. There has to be a way to appeal the coroner's decision, she thought. There must be! She refused to let her friend be buried head downwards.

What if anyone discovered my mother's shame, she wondered. Would she be removed from her plot at the parish and buried at a crossroad, head down? Madalene felt the tremble of a sob as tears poured down her cheeks. No. She would never allow that to happen. She would fight to preserve her mother's legacy, and Edith's, as well.

A calm and collected voice broke through her thoughts. "Miss Dowding."

Madalene turned around and saw Lord Hawthorne watching her from a short distance away, a concerned look on his face. Without thinking of the repercussions of her actions, she closed the distance between them and threw her arms around him.

To her great relief, he encompassed her in his arms and held her without saying a word. She laid her head on his chest and listened to the calming sound of his heartbeat beneath his blue jacket. She felt protected in his arms, making her feel as if she had found a new home.

After a long moment, and with great reluctance, Madalene stepped back and dropped her arms. "I apologize for my display of emotions, Lord Hawthorne," she said, averting her gaze.

Lord Hawthorne took his finger and placed it under her chin, forcing her to look at him. "You have nothing to apologize for, Miss Dowding."

"But I do," she said. "I accosted you nearly the moment you said my name."

He smiled, a charming smile that caused her to grow weak at the knees. "You are welcome to accost me anytime you see fit."

Madalene felt her cheeks grow warm as he dropped his finger. "Well, I thank you for your kindness."

"Perhaps you will tell me what has you so upset."

With a sigh, she revealed, "Edith was found dead in the River Thames this morning."

Lord Hawthorne grew solemn. "I am sorry to hear that. How are you faring?"

"Not well," she admitted. "The coroner ruled her death as a suicide since there was no evidence of foul play, despite her room being ransacked prior to her disappearance."

His brow knitted together in a frown. "Suicide, you say?"

She nodded. "But there is no way Edith would have killed herself," she asserted. "I know her, and that is not something she was capable of doing."

Placing his hands on her shoulders, Lord Hawthorne leaned in and said, "I believe you."

"You do?"

"I do," he replied. "I will go speak to the coroner, and I will see if we can sort this mess out."

Tears formed in her eyes. "You would do that for me?"

A smile came to his lips. "I would, most assuredly."

"Why?" she found herself asking.

His smile grew. "Typically, when someone agrees to do you a favor, you just reply with a thank you."

"Thank you," she murmured.

Lord Hawthorne dropped his arms but remained close. "If you don't believe it was suicide, then how do you believe that Miss Hardy died?"

"I don't know," she admitted, "but I believe the people who abducted her must have killed her."

"People are killed in the rookeries all the time, and the coroners can't handle the workflow," Lord Hawthorne said. "Most likely, the coroner didn't give her autopsy the time it deserved."

"I am sure that was the case."

Lord Hawthorne glanced up at the sky. "Unfortunately, I have business I need to attend to this evening, but I will go speak to the coroner first thing tomorrow."

"Thank you," she responded, hoping her words conveyed her sincere gratitude. "This means more to me than you will ever know."

He brought his gaze back down to meet hers. "It is just a trivial thing, Miss Dowding."

"Not to me," Madalene replied softly. "To me, it is everything."

"You are giving me far too much credit," he said, a tender smile on his lips. "I'm afraid it shall make me full of myself."

Madalene ducked her head as she felt the familiar warmth return to her cheeks, finding it hard to find something clever to say when she was standing so close to him.

"I'm afraid I must depart," Lord Hawthorne said, taking a step back.

"Must you?" she asked boldly.

Lord Hawthorne chuckled. "I would much rather stay with you than go to the House of Lords and listen to boring men ramble on."

"You flatter me," Madalene joked, meeting his gaze.

"That was my intention." He offered his arm. "May I escort you back inside?"

"You may," she replied as she placed her hand on his.

As they walked back towards the townhouse, Madalene said, "Thank you for coming when you did, my lord."

"That is what a good friend is for," Lord Hawthorne replied, patting her arm.

Madalene smiled up at him. "I'm glad that we are friends."

"As am I."

In that moment, Madalene realized that she cared for Lord Hawthorne more than she was letting on. She was falling in love with him, and that scared her.

WITH THE MOONLIGHT brightening his path, Baldwin hurried along the cobblestone street as he headed towards the Blue Boar. He was dressed in a tattered white cotton shirt, a waistcoat that was too small for his muscular frame, and trousers held up by twine. He had yet to replace the jacket that he had given to the beggar on the street as he was racing away from the Bow Street Runner.

He arrived at the Blue Boar, ignoring the rowdy men who were lingering in front of the pub, and stepped inside. He didn't acknowledge anyone as he headed towards the back room and knocked on the door.

Baldwin was surprised when it was opened by Morton, who ushered him in.

"Good, you have finally arrived," Morton said as he latched the door closed. "We have been expecting you."

Baldwin glanced around the room and counted only six people, a far cry from the crowd that had been here just a few days ago. A woman sat at the table in the corner, her features shadowed.

"Where is everyone?" Baldwin asked.

Morton stepped into the middle of the room and raised his hands, gesturing widely. "These are the people that are going to help ignite the revolution." He pointed towards a table where two of the men were sitting. "Paul and Mark are supplying the carts and horses for the mission."

Morton walked over and placed his hand on a man's shoulder. "Tom is the solicitor that I was telling you about. He worked with Lord Desmond at the workhouse, and he has been writing articles in the newspaper about our cause." He grinned. "Anonymously, of course."

Turning back towards the woman in the corner, Morton gestured towards her. "And this is Marie."

The woman rose confidently from the chair and stepped closer to Morton. Marie was rather tall for a woman, and she had a slim frame. She was dressed in a simple pale green gown with her brown hair pulled back at the base of her neck. With her narrow face, she wasn't overly beautiful, but he could see how some men might find her attractive.

Marie eyed him critically as she asked in a thick French accent, "What purpose does this man serve?"

Morton turned to face her. "Baldwin saved me from being arrested by a Bow Street Runner. He is a deserter from the Royal Navy, and I thought he would be a good candidate to drive the wagon into the square since he has some experience with explosives."

"A deserter?" Marie asked, turning her gaze towards him. "That was rather risky, no?"

"It was, but I was tired of fighting wars for a tyrant of a king who cares nothing for me," Baldwin spat out.

Marie took a step closer to him, her eyes sparking with distrust. "Have you ever driven a wagon with a bomb strapped to the back of it before?"

"I can't say that I have," Baldwin admitted honestly.

"If you make one wrong move, then you will be blown up," Marie warned, snapping her fingers. "Are you prepared to die for the cause, Baldwin?"

"I am."

Marie nodded approvingly. "I am pleased to hear that, because this mission could very well be your last."

Baldwin straightened himself up to his full height and declared, "I am prepared to do whatever I need to for the revolution to begin."

"That is good," Marie replied.

Morton walked over and pulled out a chair from one of the tables. "Take a seat, Baldwin," he said. "We have much to discuss."

As soon as Baldwin was situated, Morton stepped back into the center of the room and declared, "It was announced that Lord Desmond is going to have a rally to support his bill tomorrow." He started pacing. "This will be our first target."

Marie gestured towards him and revealed, "Baldwin will drive the team as close as he can to the stage. When the wagon is situated, he will light the fuse and run to safety."

"How long is the fuse?" Baldwin asked.

"It is a slow match, so you shouldn't need to fear unless you are dawdling."

Frowning, Baldwin said, "The rally will be packed. Won't we have mass casualties with the bomb?"

Marie looked at him like he was a simpleton. "That is the point."

"I thought it was to assassinate Lord Desmond, not kill innocent people," Baldwin declared, his eyes darting towards the other conspirators.

"These people are not innocent," Morton interjected. "They are feeding into Lord Desmond's lies."

"But to kill them?" Baldwin questioned.

Marie shrugged, unconcerned. "It will be a quick death for most of them," she shared. "I have spent the last few years perfecting my father's machine infernale."

Tom spoke up. "What exactly is a machine infernale?"

"It is an explosive device in a barrel bound with iron hoops and filled with gunpowder, flammable materials, metal shards, and bullets," Marie replied. "Basically, it is a bomb of epic proportions."

Morton turned towards Marie and suggested, "Perhaps you should tell them about your father so they can understand your passion for this mission."

Marie tipped her head and obliged. "My father, François-Joseph Carbon, was a royalist who fought to restore the French monarchy. He hated Napoleon and vowed to see him dead. He almost succeeded with the machine infernale. It was planted along the route that Napoleon intended to take on his way to the opera, but it was detonated too late and too far away from Napoleon's carriage."

Baldwin glanced at Morton before saying, "Your father was a royalist. Aren't you in favor of the British monarchy?"

"I am in favor of the French monarchy. I have no loyalty towards the British Crown," Marie replied.

"Napoleon is exiled, and the French monarchy has been restored," Baldwin pointed out. "Why do you hold such animosity for the British?"

Marie's eyes grew hard. "After the failed assassination attempt, my father planned to flee Paris, and he turned for help from the British agents who had helped him devise the plan against Napoleon. But they had abandoned him, and he was captured. They left him to die."

Walking closer to him, Marie cocked her head and asked, "Do you know what it is like to be betrayed, Baldwin?"

"I do not," he replied.

"These British agents promised him their protection, but they turned on him," Marie said, stopping in front of him. "Instead, my father was savagely executed in front of Napoleon, the man he hated the most." She ran a finger down his cheek. "Was that fair of them?"

Keeping his face expressionless, Baldwin replied, "No, it was not."

Marie's eyes narrowed. "If my father had been successful, then the English would have branded him a hero. Instead, they abandoned him when he failed," she growled. "My father's death will not be in vain. The British will pay for what they did."

Morton spoke up from behind Marie. "After Lord Desmond is killed, we will move forward with our plans and assassinate Lord Liverpool and Lord Sidmouth," he declared. "The people will start to rally after Lord Desmond's death, and the revolution will begin."

"If everything goes according to our plan, we will continue assassinating one government leader each week until we are free of their oppressive rule," Morton explained.

Marie remained rooted in place as her eyes searched Baldwin's face. "I am not entirely sure about this one," she said. "He doesn't seem like he shares our same passion."

Morton came to stand next to her. "I can vouch for Baldwin."

"I should hope so," Marie said, turning away from him. "We both know what is at stake."

Baldwin shifted in his seat. "How will we get a cart with an explosive close enough to Liverpool and Sidmouth?" he asked.

"We aren't going to kill them that way," Marie replied, a wry smile on her lips. "Oh, no. We intend to blow up their carriages with bombs on their undercarriage."

"That is clever," Tom declared.

Marie walked back towards the center of the room. "Besides, I only have enough gunpowder to make one machine infernale," she shared. "I have made the smaller bombs for the carriages."

Morton bobbed his head in approval. "We will all need to reconvene here tomorrow." He turned his attention towards Baldwin. "You will need to be cautious as you lead the team towards Lord Desmond's rally. Avoid any dips in the roads. We would hate for the bomb to go off unintentionally."

Baldwin scoffed. "Taking me with it."

"Exactly," Morton replied.

"The bomb will be inside of a big wine cask, and I will fill it full of gunpowder before the rally," Marie informed them. "Any questions?"

Baldwin rose from his chair and said, "It would appear that I am the only one that could be arrested in this scenario."

"Not if you stick to the plan," Morton asserted. "You light the slow match and get out of there. Once the explosion happens, no one will be paying you any real heed."

"What if I can't get the wagon close enough to the stage?" Baldwin asked.

Marie shrugged. "Get as close as you can. The bomb will do the rest."

"Can't we just leave the wagon next to the stage overnight?" Tom asked.

Morton shook his head. "No, the constables would find it when they do a sweep of the square," he replied. "They also check under the stage for any explosives."

Baldwin lifted his brow. "If the intent is just to kill Lord Desmond, why don't I sneak into his townhouse and stab him through the heart?"

"No, that wouldn't work," Morton said. "We are trying to start a revolution, and we need something to ignite a flame under the people."

Marie clapped her hands together. "Are there any other questions?"

"Where are the powder kegs being stored?" Baldwin asked. "I don't want to risk the gunpowder being bad and delaying the ignition."

"I can assure you that it is being stored in a safe, dry place," Marie replied.

"That is good," Baldwin said.

Marie tipped her head. "Then let's adjourn, and we will meet tomorrow." She put her clenched fist up in the air. "To the revolution!"

"To the revolution!" everyone else said in unison.

CHAPTER SIXTEEN

"**A**RE YOU POSITIVE you would like to do this now?" Mrs. Foster asked, glancing over at her in concern.

Madalene remained rooted in her spot as she stared up at the orphanage. "Edith did not kill herself, and I need to prove it."

"How do you intend to do that?"

"I don't rightly know, but I presume we should start at the last place where she was seen alive," Madalene replied.

"I still contend this is a bad idea," Mrs. Foster said as she placed a hand on her sleeve. "Why don't we return to your townhouse, and I will pour you a nice cup of tea?"

"No, I can't just sit by and do nothing while Edith is buried in such a disgraceful manner."

Mrs. Foster dropped her hand and remarked, "I find that commendable, but it is much too soon. You haven't even had time to start grieving yet."

"I will."

"Why does it matter so much to you how Edith is buried?" Mrs. Foster asked curiously.

Madalene pressed her lips together. "It just does," she replied. "It matters greatly to me."

Mrs. Foster sighed. "Then it matters greatly to me, as well."

"Thank you," Madalene said as she approached the door to the orphanage and knocked.

It was a long moment before the door was opened, and Mrs. Kipper's eyes grew wide at the sight of them.

"Good heavens," Mrs. Kipper declared, opening the door wide. "I apologize for taking so long to answer the door, but I hadn't realized you would be visiting us today."

"No harm done," Madalene remarked as she stepped into the entry hall. "How are you faring?"

"Not well," Mrs. Kipper admitted.

Madalene gave her a sad smile. "I assumed as much," she replied. "How are the girls handling the news about Edith?"

Tears came to Mrs. Kipper's eyes as she admitted, "There have been many tears since we heard the news this morning from Mr. Walker."

"I can only imagine," Madalene said.

"But Miss Gaillard has been wonderful with the girls," Mrs. Kipper shared. "She truly has been a godsend during these terrible times."

"I am happy to hear that."

Mrs. Kipper stepped closer and lowered her voice. "We informed the girls that Miss Hardy had drowned, because we didn't want to tell the girls what truly happened."

Madalene nodded approvingly. "I think that is wise."

Swiping at the tears in her eyes, Mrs. Kipper said, "I had no idea that Miss Hardy had the capacity to hurt herself. It is such a vulgar thing to do to oneself."

"I am of the mindset that she didn't kill herself," Madalene expressed.

"But the coroner said—"

Madalene spoke over her. "The coroner could be wrong, especially since the constable originally reported her as being abducted."

Mrs. Kipper gave her a look filled with pity. "I see," she murmured. "Well, I certainly hope that you are right about that."

"We were hoping to take a look in her room and see if we can find anything that might help us prove what happened to her," Madalene shared.

Mrs. Kipper tipped her head. "Of course," she replied. "If you will follow me, Miss Hardy's room was on the second level."

They followed the housekeeper up the stairs as Mrs. Foster asked, "Has Miss Hardy's room been touched since the constable was here?"

"It has not," Mrs. Kipper replied.

"That is good," Mrs. Foster acknowledged.

Speaking over her shoulder, Mrs. Kipper said, "I'm not sure what you will find considering the constable already did a thorough search of her room, but I wish you luck."

As they came to a stop in front of a door, Mrs. Kipper pulled a key out from the pocket of her apron and unlocked it. She pushed the door open and stood to the side to grant them entry.

"Look at this mess!" Mrs. Foster exclaimed as they stepped into Edith's room.

Madalene's eyes scanned the room. Clothes had been thrown haphazardly on the floor, the dressing table chair was tipped onto its side, and the drawers on the wardrobe were left open.

"I still contend that something terrible happened here," Madalene murmured as she started picking up the gowns and draping them over her arm.

"How do you know that Miss Hardy did not live this way?" Mrs. Foster asked.

Madalene placed the gowns on the bed and said, "I lived with her at boarding school, and her area was always neat and orderly."

"People change," Mrs. Foster contended.

"Not that much."

Mrs. Kipper spoke up from the doorway. "I must agree with Miss Dowding. Miss Hardy's room was always tidy."

Walking over to the chair, Madalene picked it up and placed it next to the dressing table. Then, she placed her reticule on the table. "I just refuse to believe that Edith left here of her own accord. It is just ludicrous to think that she purposefully left her room in such shambles."

While Mrs. Foster and Mrs. Kipper cleaned up Edith's room, Madalene searched the dressing table, looking for anything out of the ordinary. But she found nothing.

Her eyes scanned the room, hoping she could find a place that Edith may have been hiding something. But, again, she couldn't find anything.

What about under the mattress, she thought. That would be a perfect place to hide something that you wouldn't want anyone to see.

Walking swiftly, she approached Edith's bed and lifted up the mattress. Only to find nothing. Madalene let out a sigh as she dropped the mattress back down onto the frame. There was nothing in this room that would vindicate Edith.

Mrs. Foster walked up to her and placed a hand on her shoulder. "Perhaps I should go down and prepare some tea for us."

Madalene gave her a weak smile. "Thank you," she murmured. "I would like that."

"Then I shall see to it," Mrs. Foster said before she departed from the room.

Walking over to the window, Madalene looked out onto the courtyard. A small brick outbuilding was along the far wall and a wagon with a covered load was positioned next to it.

"When did the orphanage acquire a wagon?" Madalene asked.

Mrs. Kipper came to stand next to her. "It belongs to Miss Gaillard. It arrived the day after Miss Hardy disappeared," she informed her. "Mr. Walker gave her permission to store the wagon in the courtyard."

"I see," Madalene replied. "Do you know what is in the back of the wagon?"

"Furniture and whatnot," Mrs. Kipper replied. "Her cousin passed away recently, and she inherited some pieces."

"Miss Gaillard hadn't mentioned that to me."

"I am sure it just slipped her mind."

As the housekeeper was speaking, Miss Gaillard stepped out from the outbuilding and closed the door behind her.

"Why was Miss Gaillard in the outbuilding?" Madalene asked as she watched the French teacher walk across the courtyard.

"Miss Gaillard expressed an interest in transforming the outbuilding into a living space for herself, and Mr. Walker granted her permission," Mrs. Kipper explained. "Poor Miss Gaillard spends hours nearly every day in that outbuilding. I have even seen her working in there at night."

"Is the outbuilding habitable?"

Mrs. Kipper looked at her with a curious expression. "Mr. Walker toured it with Miss Gaillard and deemed that it was. Why do you ask?"

"No reason," Madalene replied. "I'm afraid I haven't given the outbuilding much thought."

"Neither have I, but I think it is admirable what Miss Gaillard is attempting to do."

"I would agree."

Mrs. Kipper took a step back. "Now, if you will excuse me," she said, "I need to see to the girls before they resume their lessons."

"Of course," Madalene replied, her eyes remaining on the outbuilding and wagon.

Something didn't feel right about Miss Gaillard using the outbuilding and storing a wagon in the courtyard. After all, she had no doubt that Edith would never have granted her permission to do either, especially since the courtyard was the only place the girls could safely play outside.

She needed to see what Miss Gaillard was up to.

With her decision made, Madalene hurried out of Edith's room and down the stairs. She didn't slow down until she exited the rear door and started crossing the courtyard. She approached the wagon, which was covered with a thick sheet securely tied down over the load. There was no way to peek under the sheet without loosening the rope.

Drat.

Turning her attention towards the outbuilding, she approached the door. She didn't even hesitate as she opened it and stepped inside. It was a one room structure with a table in the middle. Crates lined the walls, making it nearly impossible to walk around the table.

On the ground in front of the table were four barrels that were secured by rope. She stepped closer to the table and saw piles of bullets, metal shards and a white substance that appeared to be flour.

The door opened, and Miss Gaillard stepped into the building. She closed the door, a sneer on her thin lips.

"I see you found what I have been working on for the past few days," Miss Gaillard said in a tone that was anything but pleasant.

Madalene met her gaze. "What exactly are you working on?"

"You are clever, girl," Miss Gaillard said. "What do you think I am doing?"

Madalene's eyes scanned the barrels as she replied, "These barrels must have gunpowder in them, since they are tied by rope and not metal in order to avoid sparks."

"That would be correct."

"And the bullets and metal shards lead me to believe you are building a bomb," Madalene rationalized.

"But not the flour?" Miss Gaillard asked.

Madalene gave her a baffled look. "I am not entirely sure what the flour is for."

"Flour is extremely flammable, given the right circumstances," Miss Gaillard explained. "Also, orange peels are flammable, as well. But it is rather difficult to acquire enough oranges right now to do the job justice."

"I had not realized."

"I am not surprised, but my father knew," Miss Gaillard said. "He always knew exactly what was needed to make the perfect bomb."

"Are you trying to blow up the orphanage?"

Miss Gaillard laughed. "Heavens, no," she replied. "I find it admirable what you are trying to accomplish with these girls."

"Thank you," Madalene said hesitantly.

In a swift motion, Miss Gaillard lifted her skirt and removed a pistol that was strapped to her leg. "But that doesn't mean I am going to let you go. At least, not yet," she remarked, pointing the pistol at her. "If you are a good girl, then I might let you live."

Miss Gaillard walked over to a crate and produced some rope. "I must admit that I was pleased when I first saw you snooping around my wagon," she said as she stepped closer to her. "I knew that it was only a matter of time before you stepped inside of the outbuilding."

"Why was that?"

"Because we are a lot alike," Miss Gaillard stated. "We both are curious creatures."

Miss Gaillard put the pistol on the table. "I am going to tie your hands now," she instructed. "If you try to reach for the pistol, I will kill you." The way she spoke those words, Madalene knew she was in earnest.

"I understand," Madalene replied, knowing she needed to bide her time until she could find a way to escape.

Miss Gaillard stepped closer and roughly tied her hands tightly together. Then, she reached down and ripped a large section of Madalene's gown off.

"I can't have you yelling for help, now can I?" Miss Gaillard asked before she shoved the fabric into Madalene's mouth.

"Oh, there is one more thing," Miss Gaillard said nonchalantly as she picked up the pistol. "Unfortunately, this part is going to hurt."

Madalene watched as Miss Gaillard pulled her arm back, and she attempted to brace herself the best way she could. As the pistol slammed against the side of her head, everything went black.

BALDWIN LEANED BACK in his seat and took a sip of his drink before saying, "Marie is mad."

"Why do you say that?" Corbyn asked as he sat across from him.

"She despises the British for what they did to her father," Baldwin explained, "but I believe her hatred to be misdirected."

Oliver nodded. "I would agree, but it isn't as if she could go after Napoleon. He is exiled on the island of Elba."

"Her plan could kill hundreds, if not thousands, of innocent people," Baldwin said. "Lord Desmond's rallies always attract a large crowd, and constables are on hand to ensure no violence breaks out."

"Do you think the mass killing will be the start of the revolution that they are planning?" Oliver asked.

"It very well could be," Baldwin replied, "especially since the people have been stirred up for less before."

Corbyn leaned forward in his seat. "After you drive the wagon away from the Blue Boar, our agents will raid the pub, and we will capture Marie, Morton, and the other conspirators."

"Where will you take the wagon?" Oliver asked.

"I am not sure," Baldwin replied. "It isn't safe to go very far with a bomb strapped to the back of it."

"I would drive it to the docks and toss it into the river," Corbyn advised. "The water will neutralize the gunpowder, rendering the bomb useless."

"That is a good idea," Baldwin acknowledged.

Corbyn smirked. "You sound surprised, but that is why I am the one in charge," he remarked. "I will have agents standing by on the docks to assist you in removing the bomb very gently from the wagon."

"I would appreciate that," Baldwin said before taking a sip of his drink. "I can't help but comment on how evident it is that Morton and Marie intend for me to be the scapegoat. Frankly, I don't think they care whether I survive the explosion or not."

Rising, Oliver responded, "You make an interesting point." He walked over to the drink cart and poured himself another drink. "To them, you are expendable."

Corbyn raised his glass. "I see that they sized you up correctly," he joked.

Baldwin chuckled.

"If we knew where Marie was storing the bomb, then we could seize it tonight," Oliver said, bringing the glass up to his lips. "Do you have any idea where she is hiding out?"

"The only hint that she gave was that the gunpowder was in a secure place," Baldwin replied.

"That could be anywhere," Oliver mumbled.

Baldwin nodded. "My thoughts precisely."

A knock came at the door.

"Enter," Baldwin ordered.

The door opened, and his butler stepped into the room. "I am sorry to disturb you, milord. But a Mrs. Foster would like a moment of your time."

"Mrs. Foster, you say?" he asked, wondering why Miss Dowding's companion was here to call on him.

"Yes, and she says that it is most urgent," Pratt asserted.

Leaning forward, he placed his drink on the table in front of him and rose. "Send her in."

Pratt tipped his head and departed from the room, leaving the door open.

"Why do you suppose Miss Dowding's companion is calling on you?" Oliver asked with a puzzled look on his face.

"I was just asking myself that very same question," Baldwin muttered.

Fortunately, he didn't have to wait long. Mrs. Foster rushed into the study, her eyes frantically seeking him out.

"Whatever is the matter?" Baldwin asked as he hurried over to her.

Mrs. Foster placed a hand up to her forehead. "I'm sorry for barging in on you at this late hour, but I didn't know where else to go."

Baldwin placed a hand on her sleeve and led her towards an upholstered chair. "Why don't you start by telling me what is wrong?"

After she was situated, Mrs. Foster looked up at him and asked, "May I have something to drink?"

"Yes, I can get you some tea," Baldwin suggested. "That should help calm your nerves."

Mrs. Foster shook her head. "I need something much stronger than that," she replied. "Do you have any brandy?"

Baldwin blinked in surprise. "Yes, I do have brandy." He walked over to the drink cart and poured a glass, then walked back and handed it to her.

"Thank you, my lord," Mrs. Foster said as she accepted the glass with a shaky hand.

Pulling a chair closer to her, Baldwin sat down. "Can you tell me what is wrong?"

"It's about Miss Dowding," Mrs. Foster said hesitantly, "she's gone missing."

Baldwin could feel the air rushing out of his lungs at her stunning announcement. But in the next moment, he grew solemn and alert, knowing he had to keep all of his wits about him. He knew he needed to find out as much as he could about Miss Dowding's disappearance, and quickly.

"I want you to start from the beginning," Baldwin ordered, his eyes never straying from hers.

Mrs. Foster took a sip of her drink. "We went to the orphanage to look for any clues about Miss Hardy's disappearance, but we didn't find anything. Not that I thought we would," she rambled. "I told Miss Dowding that but—"

"I need you to focus, Mrs. Foster," Baldwin said, speaking over her.

Mrs. Foster gave him a repentant smile. "My apologies," she replied. "I tend to ramble on when I get nervous."

"There is no reason to be nervous here," Baldwin assured her.

Mrs. Foster glanced over his shoulder, and he followed her gaze. Corbyn and Oliver were both standing there with stern looks on their faces.

Turning his attention back towards Mrs. Foster, Baldwin remarked, "Don't concern yourself with them. They will be able to aid in the search for Miss Dowding."

Mrs. Foster nodded. "As I was saying, we didn't find anything in Miss Hardy's room, so I thought Madalene would benefit from some tea. But, when I returned from preparing the tea, Madalene was gone."

"Do you have any idea where she went?"

Mrs. Foster shook her head. "We searched the entire orphanage before we called for the constable," she said. "Then, we searched it again and again."

"Are there any other buildings that she could have visited?"

"There is an outbuilding, but Miss Gaillard was kind enough to search it for us," Mrs. Foster said.

Corbyn spoke up. "Who is Miss Gaillard?"

"The French teacher at the orphanage," Mrs. Foster explained. "She was temporarily appointed as headmistress after Miss Hardy went missing."

"I see," Corbyn replied. "So, she must be a trustworthy individual."

Mrs. Foster bobbed her head. "Oh, yes. The girls love her."

"Can you think of any reason why Miss Dowding might have left the safety of the orphanage?" Baldwin asked.

"Not one," Mrs. Foster answered. "She is smart enough to know that it is not safe to wander in that part of Town."

"Was she carrying her pistol?"

Mrs. Foster gave him a blank look. "I didn't even know that she owned a pistol."

"Did no one witness Miss Dowding leave the building, whether by the front or the back?" Oliver asked.

"We questioned all the girls, but no one saw her leave the building," Mrs. Foster replied. "The constable even spoke to our driver and footman, but they didn't see anything, either."

Baldwin ran a hand through his hair, attempting to squash his growing irritation. "How can someone just disappear without leaving a trace?"

"Have you considered that Miss Dowding didn't want to be seen leaving the building?" Corbyn asked.

Baldwin turned to face Corbyn. "Meaning?"

"Perhaps she had an errand she needed to run," Corbyn proposed.

"No, that is impossible," Mrs. Foster said firmly. "Besides, we don't frequent any businesses in that part of Town."

Corbyn gave him a knowing look. "What if she found a clue to Miss Hardy's disappearance and left to investigate it?" he asked. "After all, it wouldn't be the first time Miss Dowding has visited disreputable establishments."

"You have a point," Baldwin admitted reluctantly. "But what could she have found that would have caused her to leave the orphanage, unescorted and without any word?"

"I don't know," Corbyn replied with a shake of his head.

Mrs. Foster interjected, "The constable searched Miss Hardy's room, but didn't find anything that would give a reason as to why Madalene disappeared."

"What of the people that work at the orphanage?" Oliver asked.

"There are three teachers, a housekeeper, and a cook," Mrs. Foster shared. "They did recently hire a man to do odd jobs around the orphanage, but he wasn't assigned to work today."

"Was Miss Dowding in a disagreement with anyone?" Corbyn questioned.

"No, everybody loves Miss Dowding," Mrs. Foster asserted.

Baldwin abruptly rose from his chair and walked over to the darkened window. They were missing something. He could feel it. And time was of the essence.

Rising, Mrs. Foster said, "I am sorry for burdening you with this, my lord, but Miss Dowding seemed to believe that you have a knack for finding missing persons."

Baldwin turned back to face her. "You did the right thing coming to me. I will begin making inquiries immediately, and we will bring Miss Dowding back home."

Mrs. Foster bobbed her head, but he could see the fear in her eyes. She didn't seem to believe his words.

"May I escort you home?" Baldwin asked.

"I thank you for the offer, but I would prefer it if your time was spent trying to find Miss Dowding," Mrs. Foster said.

Baldwin met her gaze and promised, "I won't rest until we have found her."

"Thank you, my lord," Mrs. Foster said, turning to leave.

After she left the room, Corbyn and Oliver turned their gaze towards him.

"We need to start making inquiries from the other agents to see if anyone has heard from or seen Miss Dowding," Baldwin ordered.

Corbyn tipped his head. "I will see to that."

"Good," Baldwin said, striding towards the door. "I will be searching for her, as well."

Oliver's voice stopped him from exiting. "Where, exactly, are you going to start searching?"

"I will start at the orphanage," Baldwin shared, "and then I will search every blasted building in the rookeries if I have to."

Oliver frowned. "You are letting your emotions cloud your judgment," he said. "Wandering around the rookeries is a good way for you to end up dead."

"Then what would you have me do?" Baldwin exclaimed. "Sit here and do nothing?"

"No," Oliver replied. "We need a plan."

"A plan?" Baldwin repeated back incredulously.

Oliver nodded. "Yes, we need to carefully think this through."

"How about this for a plan?" Baldwin mocked. "We find Miss Dowding and bring her back home."

Corbyn approached him. "I agree with Oliver," he said. "You are entirely too invested in this, and you need to take a step back."

"I will not!" Baldwin exclaimed, pointing at the door. "Miss Dowding is somewhere out there, alone and afraid, and I will not abandon her."

"We have agents in the field who can search for her, but we need you to prepare for tomorrow's mission," Corbyn asserted. "There are hundreds, if not thousands, of innocent lives at stake if you screw it up. You must think about them, as well."

Baldwin reared back. "Are you truly asking me to stay home and do nothing?"

"No," Corbyn replied, crossing his arms over his chest, "I am ordering you to stay home and prepare for tomorrow."

For a long moment, Baldwin stared at Corbyn, his mind reeling with all the horrible tragedies that could have befallen Miss Dowding. *No.* He wasn't about to stand by and do nothing. In a collected voice, he said, "Then I quit."

Dropping his arms to his sides, Corbyn questioned, "You don't truly mean that, do you?"

"I do," Baldwin declared. "If you are making me choose between Miss Dowding and being an agent, I have made my choice."

"What about tomorrow?" Oliver asked.

Baldwin shifted his gaze towards his brother. "I know my duty," he replied. "I will be at the Blue Boar per the plan, and I will stop the bomb from ever reaching its destination. You have my word."

Without waiting for their response, Baldwin turned and headed towards the entry hall. He hadn't even reached the main door when his brother caught up to him, matching his stride.

"Don't even try to stop me," Baldwin growled.

Oliver glanced over at him. "I won't," he said. "I'm going with you."

"You are?"

"Don't sound so surprised."

"Aren't you afraid Corbyn might dismiss you for coming along with me?"

Oliver grinned. "It is a risk I am willing to take to ensure that my brother doesn't get himself killed."

"I won't get myself killed," Baldwin grumbled.

"Perhaps, but I don't really want to be the next Marquess of Hawthorne," Oliver joked. "So, I am going along just to make sure of that."

As they reached the main door, Baldwin placed his hand on the handle and said, "I do appreciate you accompanying me, Oliver."

"You would do the same thing for me," Oliver replied.

"I most assuredly would," Baldwin stated as he opened the door wide. "Have no doubt about that."

CHAPTER SEVENTEEN

MADALENE GROANED. SHE felt as though she had been run over by a carriage. The entire left side of her head throbbed, and her whole body seemed to ache with every breath. As she moved to touch her forehead, she was reminded that her hands were bound together.

"Good," a familiar voice from above her said. "You are finally awake. I was worried that I might have killed you with that blow."

With great reluctance, Madalene attempted to pry her eyes open and was met by the smiling face of Miss Gaillard.

"The effects will wear off soon enough," Miss Gaillard remarked as she turned back to tinkering at the table. "I removed your gag so we could talk before I depart."

Madalene sat up and rested her back against a crate. "Where are you going?" she asked, her voice sounding hoarse to her own ears.

"I am going to blow up Fieldstone Square and, hopefully, everyone in it."

"Why would you want to do that?"

"Why, indeed?" Miss Gaillard asked, glancing over at her. "Because I hate the British and everything you stand for."

Wincing in pain, Madalene remarked dryly, "At least you have a reason."

Miss Gaillard laughed. "You are funny, no?"

"I'm not attempting to be."

"I could have killed you," Miss Gaillard said, turning to face her. "It would have been rather easy, but I didn't. And do you know why?"

Madalene shook her head, and immediately regretted it.

"Because I respect you, Mademoiselle Dowding," Miss Gaillard said. "You have created an orphanage filled with love, and you impressed me with your dedication to the girls."

"Thank you."

A pained look came to Miss Gaillard's eyes. "After my father died, I was sent to an orphanage, and I became just a number. Frankly, the headmistress didn't care if I lived or died. We were always half-starved and cold." Miss Gaillard shuddered. "We were always so cold during the winter months."

"I'm sorry you were forced to endure those terrible conditions," Madalene said, compassion in her tone.

"Don't be," Miss Gaillard replied. "That is why I ran away and lived on the streets of Paris with other like-minded individuals."

Not entirely sure what to say, Madalene decided to remain quiet.

"I knew if I killed you, I would regret it later," Miss Gaillard shared. "But I have no regrets about killing the headmistress."

Madalene's eyes grew wide. "You killed Edith."

"Was that her first name?" Miss Gaillard asked with a shrug. "I would have thought her to be a Jane or Catherine."

"Why did you have to kill her?"

Miss Gaillard crouched down in front of Madalene. "Because she started asking too many questions, so I needed her to disappear," she answered.

"Why not just abduct her but keep her alive?"

"Then I would have been forced to take care of her, and that was too much trouble," Miss Gaillard remarked without a hint of remorse. "Instead, we just threw her unconscious body off the bridge."

"We?"

Miss Gaillard rose. "Your solicitor, Mr. Walker, helped me. He is a good man. It is a shame that he will be hung for treason."

"Treason?" she asked. "Why?"

"After we depart from the Blue Boar, I have no doubt that agents will raid the pub, and they will arrest all of the conspirators."

"But not you?"

With a shake of her head, Miss Gaillard replied, "I intend to ride with your suitor to Fieldstone Square myself. We are to attend Lord Desmond's rally, and I don't dare miss it."

"You are mistaken. I don't have a suitor."

"No?" Miss Gaillard asked. "You are not being courted by Lord Hawthorne?"

"I am not."

Miss Gaillard tilted her head. "That is a shame, no? Not only is he handsome, but he is quite rich, as well."

"He is handsome," Madalene admitted, "but we aren't courting."

"Do you object to him being a spy?"

Madalene looked up at Miss Gaillard in confusion. "Pardon?"

Miss Gaillard gasped in delight and brought her hand up to cover her mouth. "You didn't know he was an agent of the Crown, did you?"

"I did not." Madalene felt like a fool that she hadn't pieced that together sooner.

Lowering her hand, Miss Gaillard said, "When my partner first informed me of Baldwin, I had my own suspicions. I decided to follow him one night, and I saw him leaving the rookeries in ragged clothes and renting a hackney. You can only imagine my surprise when he pulled up in front of Hawthorne House and entered by way of the main door."

A self-satisfied smile came to Miss Gaillard's lips. "Lord Hawthorne wasn't even aware that I continued to follow him over the course of a few days, including when he repeatedly met with you. If our circumstances were different, I would even be hoping that you two would marry."

"Wonderful," Madalene muttered.

"I take it that you are displeased, and I will inform him of that when I speak to him."

"That won't be necessary," Madalene asserted. "I shall speak to him when I have the chance."

Miss Gaillard's lips dropped to a frown. "I'm afraid that is impossible," she shared. "I intend to kill him in a few hours."

Madalene felt her heart drop at Miss Gaillard's remark. "Why would you kill him?"

"I know he has no intention of driving the wagon to the rally, so I am going to have to blackmail him to force his hand," Miss Gaillard announced proudly. "That is where you come in."

"Why me?"

Miss Gaillard gave her a concerned look. "I fear that my blow to your head has rattled your brain. I believe I have properly explained it, but I will explain it in more simple terms for you." She paused. "Lord Hawthorne will drive the wagon to the rally because your life will depend on it."

"Please don't do this," Madalene pleaded as she attempted to loosen her bonds.

"It is either your life, or he will detonate a bomb that will kill hundreds of people," Miss Gaillard said. "Which one do you think he will pick?"

Madalene shook her head. "He won't pick me."

"I wouldn't be so sure," Miss Gaillard remarked. "I have seen the way he looks at you. He looks like a man who is besotted."

"Regardless, my life is not worth killing hundreds of innocent people."

Miss Gaillard leaned down and patted her cheek. "I am wagering that Lord Hawthorne will think differently."

"Why are you doing this?"

"My father was betrayed by British agents," Miss Gaillard said. "Do you know who one of those agents was?"

She shook her head, more gently this time.

"Lord Desmond," Miss Gaillard replied. "When the bomb goes off in the crowd, I will be a short distance away with a rifle to ensure that he doesn't leave the podium alive."

"You don't have to do this," Madalene asserted. "You can just walk away from this, and no one else has to die."

Miss Gaillard gave her a sad smile. "A part of me died the day my father was executed, and every day a little more of me dies inside."

"Let me help you," Madalene attempted. "I can give you money, lots of it, and you can just return to France."

"This isn't about the money," Miss Gaillard said as she took a step back. "This is about revenge."

"Miss Gaillard, please—"

"My name is Marie," she said, speaking over her, "and I am tired of living a lie."

Marie picked up a bullet from the table and placed it on the ground next to Madalene. "If you try to escape before the sun sets," she threatened emotionlessly, "I won't hesitate to kill you the next time we meet."

Madalene's eyes grew wide as she bobbed her head. It was evident that Marie meant every word.

"I'm glad that we can see eye to eye, Mademoiselle Dowding," Marie remarked with a sinister smile. "Although, I am sorry that I have to kill Lord Hawthorne, but I have no doubt that you will have another suitor before long."

Not bothering to wait for her response, Marie left, closing the door behind her. Madalene didn't dare move from her spot until she heard the sound of the wagon being pulled away by a team of horses.

When it grew quiet once more, Madalene struggled to stand, then glanced out the curtained window. There was no one in the courtyard, and nothing that could help her. She turned back towards the table and saw a large shard of metal.

Madalene picked it up with her fingers and started rubbing it back and forth over the rope. It finally started fraying after what felt like hours but was probably only moments. She continued using the metal shard until the rope was weak enough that she was able to break through it.

As the rope dropped to the floor, she took a moment to run her hands over her reddened wrists and inspect the cuts on her fingers from the metal shard. She wondered what she could possibly do to warn Lord Hawthorne of Marie's evil designs.

"Think," Madalene said, thinking out loud. "What would Lord Hawthorne do?"

Madalene frowned, knowing exactly what he would say to her at this precise moment. He would have chided her for leaving the muff pistol in her reticule, which she had left on Edith's dressing table. She hadn't thought that through when she went to search the wagon and outbuilding. Then again, who would have thought that Miss Gaillard was mad and intended to use the wagon to blow up hundreds of innocent people?

Either way, she needed to retrieve the muff pistol and somehow find a way to stop Marie from killing anyone else.

Madalene opened the door and ran across the courtyard. She raced up the steps and nearly collided with Mrs. Kipper at the top of the stairs.

"Where have you been, Miss Dowding?!" Mrs. Kipper exclaimed in astonishment. "Whatever happened to you?"

"Follow me," Madalene ordered as she ran towards Edith's room. "I need you to send word to the constable that someone is planning on blowing up a bomb at Fieldstone Square during Lord Desmond's rally today."

"I beg your pardon?" Mrs. Kipper asked with labored breath as she stopped at the doorway.

Madalene picked up her reticule and reached inside for the muff pistol. She pulled it out and held it in her hand. The housekeeper's eyes grew wide.

"Miss Gaillard is not who we thought she was," Madalene explained. "She is mad and wants to kill hundreds of people."

Mrs. Kipper frowned. "That is impossible. Miss Gaillard is such a nice woman."

"We were all deceived by her, but she admitted to me that she killed Edith," Madalene replied, returning the pistol to her reticule. "We need to stop her before it is too late."

Mrs. Kipper's face paled. "Why would she kill Edith?"

"That isn't important right now," Madalene asserted as she slipped the reticule around her right wrist, wincing at the pain from her earlier bonds. "I need you to focus, Mrs. Kipper. Can you go inform the constable of what Miss Gaillard intends to do?"

With a nod, Mrs. Kipper replied, "I will go myself."

"Good," Madalene replied as she hurried out of the room.

Mrs. Kipper called after her. "Where are you going?"

"I am going to find a way to stop Marie from killing Lord Hawthorne!" Madalene shouted over her shoulder.

"Who is Marie?" Mrs. Kipper yelled back.

Madalene didn't have time to stop and explain. Instead, she ran out the main door and approached a hackney that was parked down the street from the orphanage.

"I need a ride!" she shouted up at the driver.

Keeping his gaze straight ahead, he replied dismissively, "I don't give rides to ladies."

"But you must!"

He met her gaze and frowned. "Are you aware that you have dried blood in your hair and on your face?"

Ignoring his question, she said, "I will pay you a pound if you take me to the Blue Boar right now."

He eyed her curiously. "You don't want to go to the Blue Boar, Miss. It is deep within the rookeries, and it ain't safe for a young miss like you."

"You won't take me?"

He shook his head. "Not even if you paid me two pounds."

"Five pounds."

"Pardon?" the driver asked in disbelief.

Stepping closer to the hackney, she said, "I will pay you five pounds if you take me to the Blue Boar."

"Do you have that kind of money on you?"

Madalene shook her head. "I do not," she admitted. "I only have two pounds in my reticule." She pointed at the building behind her. "But this is my orphanage, and I live on Grosvenor Street. If you come by tomorrow, I will gladly give you the rest of the money."

She could see the uncertainty crossing the man's face, and she knew she needed to continue to plead her case. "I assure you that it is a matter of life and death," she asserted.

The man gestured towards the door. "Get in before I change my mind," he barked.

Madalene rushed to open the door to the coach and was met with a pungent odor that managed to assault all of her senses. How she wished she had a handkerchief with rosewater on it at this precise moment.

"Is there a problem, Miss?" the driver asked impatiently.

"Not at all," she replied as she stepped inside, attempting to ignore how the bottom of her boots were sticking to the floor.

After she closed the door, she sat down on the bench that was worn so thin that it offered little cushion. She truly hoped that she arrived at the Blue Boar before Marie did. If not, she didn't even want to think about the possibilities.

———————◆———————

SITTING ON THE straw mattress in his rented room, Baldwin yawned as the back of his head rested against the wall.

"You look terrible," Oliver muttered.

"I feel terrible," Baldwin replied. "We spent all night searching for Miss Dowding but found no trace of her."

Oliver took a bite of his bread. "You need to eat something," he advised.

"I'm not hungry," Baldwin said, glancing down at the piece of bread in his hand. The thought of food didn't appeal to him right now, not when Miss Dowding was still missing.

"We will find her," Oliver assured him.

Baldwin turned his attention towards his brother. "We both know there is a good chance that we will never see her again. People disappear in the rookeries all the time, and no one gives it any heed."

"But you are Falcon," Oliver pointed out. "I daresay there is nothing that you can't do."

A knock came at the door, and they both reached for their pistols.

"Enter," Baldwin ordered.

Corbyn stepped into the room and closed the door behind him. "I assumed you would both be here," he said. "I came by to inform you that agents are standing by to raid the Blue Boar after you drive the wagon away."

"Thank you." Baldwin rose and tucked his pistol into the waistband of his trousers, covering it with his waistcoat.

Corbyn gave him a concerned look. "I take it that you didn't find Miss Dowding?"

"No," he replied, "and we searched all night."

"The other agents have all reported back that no one saw a woman fitting her description anywhere near the rookeries," Corbyn shared.

Baldwin sighed. "I assumed as much." He held up the bread towards Corbyn. "Hungry?"

Corbyn accepted the bread. "I can always eat."

"I suppose it is time that I head over to the Blue Boar and meet with Morton and Marie," Baldwin said as he removed his jacket and tossed it onto the ground. "I can't show up looking too presentable."

Corbyn watched him with a frown on his lips. "I daresay that won't be an issue. You look terrible."

Oliver spoke up. "I said the same thing."

"Don't worry," Baldwin responded. "I am a trained agent. I know my role in all of this."

"About that," Corbyn said, "I have decided not to accept your resignation yet."

Baldwin let out a disbelieving huff. "Why does it matter?" he asked. "I am set to retire after this mission anyway."

"That may be true, but I don't want to do any more paperwork than I have to," Corbyn remarked. "Frankly, I don't want to have to explain to anyone why I had a dismissed agent working on a case, especially if it turns into a disaster."

"It won't."

"Let's hope not," Corbyn asserted.

As Baldwin moved to open the door, he asked, "Will you both be with the agents that raid the Blue Boar?"

"Oliver will be, but I have someplace I need to be," Corbyn said.

"Which is?"

Corbyn's eyes grew dark. "It is best if you don't know."

"Understood." Baldwin knew better than to ask his friend more questions when his responses were cryptic.

Baldwin opened the door and departed from the room. He needed to focus on the mission, but his thoughts kept returning to Miss

Dowding. What would he do if he never saw her again? He couldn't imagine a future that didn't involve her.

His steps faltered on the street at that realization. He wanted a future with Miss Dowding. He needed her in his life. But would she even welcome his advances? He knew she wasn't completely immune to his charms, but that was a far cry from her agreeing to a courtship. Regardless, he needed to find her first, and he wouldn't stop searching until he did.

The Blue Boar loomed up ahead, and Baldwin knew he needed to put Miss Dowding out of his mind for the time being. He had a mission he needed to accomplish.

Baldwin stepped inside and headed towards the back room. He knocked on the door and it was opened by a man he was unfamiliar with. The room was crowded with men as they sat around the tables and some were even resting their shoulders against the walls.

"Baldwin!" Morton shouted from the front of the room. "The man that we have all been waiting for."

A few of the men turned towards him and lifted their tankards towards him. "Baldwin!" they repeated.

Baldwin approached Morton. "What are all these people doing here?" he asked.

"They are here to witness history," Morton replied. "After the machine infernale is detonated, these men are going to flood the streets and rally the people to revolt!"

"To the revolution!" a man shouted at the table, lifting his tankard in the air.

"To the revolution!" everyone said in unison.

Baldwin glanced around the room. "Where is Marie?"

"She will be here shortly," Morton replied, eyeing him with interest. "Are you nervous?"

With a shake of his head, Baldwin said, "There is nothing to be nervous about. I light the slow match and run as fast as I can out of

Fieldstone Square."

"You are a good man," Morton remarked. "Don't let anyone tell you otherwise."

The door opened, and Marie stepped into the room. She was dressed in a simple blue gown and her hair was pulled tight into a chignon.

"Baldwin!" she shouted. "Are you ready to start a revolution?"

"I am," he replied as he approached her.

Marie nodded approvingly. "Let me show you the machine infernale, then."

He followed her out of the pub and saw a wagon parked in front. In the back was a large wine cask that was held together by rope. A twine fuse was positioned in the back of the cask.

Marie stepped closer to the wagon and pointed at the fuse. "You light the slow match and you quickly leave Fieldstone Square without attracting too much attention."

"That fuse isn't very long," Baldwin commented.

"It doesn't need to be," Marie remarked. "It is slow burning and will only present a small glowing tip after you light it."

Baldwin lowered his voice and asked, "What do you estimate the blast radius to be?"

Marie met his gaze. "I would just run, and don't stop running until you are as far away from the blast as you can be."

"I understand."

Placing a hand on the wine cask, Marie ordered, "Get the wagon as close as you can to the stage and let the machine infernale do the rest."

Baldwin's eyes scanned the bomb. "I will do my best."

"If you don't succeed, I will kill you," Marie said in a stern voice.

His eyes snapped back to hers. "I understand my job."

A smile came to Marie's lips. "Good, but I am coming with you to ensure that we have no mishaps along the way."

Fearing he'd misheard her, he asked, "Pardon?"

Marie lifted her brow. "Is that a problem?"

"No, you are more than welcome to come along."

Walking around the wagon, Marie stepped up to the driver's bench. "Shall we?" she asked. "I would hate to miss Lord Desmond's rally."

Baldwin's eyes scanned around the buildings before he sat next to her on the bench. As he urged the team forward, he felt something jab him in the ribs.

He glanced over in surprise and saw Marie holding a pistol in her hand.

"Don't look so surprised," Marie said. "I knew you had every intention of betraying us, just as I intend to betray your countrymen."

"How do you know?"

Marie smirked. "Morton is a fool, and he trusts entirely too easily. But I had my suspicions about you from nearly the moment he told me about you," she explained. "He just saw you as the perfect scapegoat, blinding him from the truth."

"Which is?"

"That you are Lord Hawthorne," she said. "I followed you one night out of the rookeries to Hawthorne House. I doubt you ever suspected a woman was following you."

"I did not," he replied, keeping his gaze on the street.

"Women are often overlooked here, are they not?" she asked. "The British don't seem to think women make very good spies, but France has been using women for years in subterfuge."

Marie tilted her head. "Although, you may have noticed me following you, if you hadn't been so distracted by Mademoiselle Dowding."

He clenched his jaw so tightly that a muscle below his ear began to pulsate. "Did you abduct her?" he growled.

"I did," she replied unabashed, "but I have no intention of killing her, assuming you move forward with our plan."

"Where is she?"

"In the outbuilding behind the orphanage," she answered.

Baldwin glanced over at her. "You are lying," he declared. "That building was searched by a teacher at the school."

Marie smiled victoriously. "That would be me."

"You worked at the orphanage?"

"I was the French teacher," she shared. "Mademoiselle Dowding's solicitor helped arrange the job for me so we had a place where I could build a bomb without causing suspicion."

"Am I to assume you were the one who abducted and killed Miss Hardy?"

With a shake of her head, Marie replied, "I don't know why you sound so surprised. Miss Hardy started asking too many questions, and she became a liability. You, of all people, should understand that."

"You didn't need to kill her."

"But I did," Marie said. "I don't like having too many loose ends."

Adjusting his grip on the reins, Baldwin asked, "Why did you betray Morton?"

"I have no doubt that your agents raided the Blue Boar the moment we drove away," Marie said. "I could have warned him, but I found him rather irksome."

Baldwin slowed the wagon as a street urchin ran into the street, passing right in front of the horses.

"I was sent by a group of radicals in France that wanted to ignite a revolution in Britain," Marie continued. "But I decided I would much rather seek revenge on Lord Desmond. After all, he was one of the agents that betrayed my father."

"I had no idea that Lord Desmond was even an agent."

"Soon, it won't matter," Marie said. "After the machine infernale blows up Fieldstone Square, Lord Desmond will be dead."

"If your entire plan revolves around killing Lord Desmond, why do you intend to kill all those innocent people?"

"No one is truly innocent," Marie spat out. "Your people are fools for living under the oppression of the mad King George and his worthless son, Prinny."

"Your logic is faulty."

"Perhaps, but at the end of the day, I will still be alive, and you won't."

They had just passed the buildings that lined Fieldstone Square when Baldwin pulled back on the reins, knowing this action could very well be his last. Up ahead, he saw a large crowd had assembled, and they were all standing around a stage that had been erected for the rally. He could scarcely make out Lord Desmond's words as he directed his comments towards the crowd.

"I won't drive this cart into the crowd," he declared, dropping the reins.

"Then Miss Dowding will die."

"So be it," Baldwin replied as he kept his face expressionless. He knew that Miss Dowding was rather clever, and he hoped she had already managed to get herself to safety.

Marie shoved the pistol further into his ribs. "And you will die."

"I have no doubt that you planned to kill me either way," Baldwin said. "You might as well do it now and save us a load of trouble." He paused. "Although, firing a pistol so close to a bomb might not be the smartest idea."

"You are right," Marie said, pulling back the pistol slightly.

That was all the encouragement he needed, and he swiftly brought his hand up and shoved the pistol away from him and the wagon while simultaneously elbowing Marie in the jaw.

The pistol discharged, and he could feel and hear the bullet whiz within inches of his chest. Then, he heard the deafening explosion of the shot.

He saw Marie jump off the side of the wagon, and he did the same as he vaguely heard people screaming in the distance. He ran around the wagon and saw her hastily attempt to light the fuse with steel and flint.

"It is over!" Baldwin removed his pistol from the waistband of his trousers and pointed it at her.

"If you discharge that pistol this direction, then it will cause the bomb to ignite and we will both die, taking everyone else with us," Marie informed him, keeping her hands near the fuse.

Baldwin nodded as he kept his gun pointed at her heart. "I am well aware of that fact."

"And you would still do it?"

"I would."

Marie scoffed. "Then you are the mad one."

"So be it."

Marie's eyes grew frantic as she looked over his shoulder. "They are coming!" she shouted. "You need to let me leave, *now!*"

"Why would I do something so stupid?"

"I refuse to go willingly," Marie cried out. "If I am going to die, I might as well take you with me."

As she moved to strike the flint, a shot rang out over the square, and Marie fell to the ground, dead. A pool of blood began to emerge from under her head, staining the worn cobblestone.

Baldwin turned his attention towards the red brick building where he heard the shot fired and saw Corbyn standing in the third level window with a Baker rifle in his hand. In the next moment, Corbyn disappeared from his view.

The sound of booted steps approaching him caused him to slowly turn around, and he counted five constables.

"Put the pistol on the ground," one of the men ordered, each one of them pointing their own pistols at Baldwin.

In a calm and collected manner, Baldwin complied without protest. He knew that these men were only doing their job, and he didn't want to give them any reason to shoot him.

Before they could give another order, a coach pulled up beside them and the door was thrown open. Miss Dowding stepped out, but she became suddenly rooted to the spot when she saw Marie on the ground.

Her pale face looked up at him, and he saw the questions in her eyes. Even though her hair was disheveled, her dress ripped, and she had dried blood along the left side of her face, he had never seen her look more beautiful.

He gave her a reassuring smile, and he thought his heart might burst with joy when she returned it.

At some point, Oliver had come to stand next to him and was speaking to the constables on his behalf. "I could use your help here," his brother muttered under his breath.

Turning his attention back towards the constables, Baldwin said, "I have a letter that will clear this up."

A dark-haired constable scoffed. "Not bloody likely," he declared. "Not unless it is from the Prince Regent himself."

"If that is the case, this matter should be resolved nicely," Baldwin replied, nodding his head towards the pocket of his waistcoat. Oliver reached in and pulled out a folded piece of paper, then extended it towards the men.

One of the men snatched it and his eyes grew wide as he read the paper. He looked up at Baldwin in surprise. "This *is* from the Prince Regent," he declared. "It says that you are under his protection, and that we take orders from you."

"That is correct," Baldwin said, accepting the letter back. "I am going to take this wagon out of Fieldstone Square, and I would appreciate it if you could remove the body."

"Who is she?" the dark-haired constable asked.

"Her name is Marie," Baldwin replied, "and that is all you need to know about her."

"Did you kill her?"

Baldwin shook his head. "I did not. A sharpshooter took the shot from that building," he revealed, pointing towards the brick building.

The dark-haired constable let out a low, approving whistle. "That was an impressive shot. That building is over a hundred yards away."

Another constable placed his hand on the wine cask. "What is in the barrel?" he asked curiously.

"A bomb that could blow up this entire square," Baldwin replied honestly, and was gratified to see the constable remove his hand and step back.

Turning back towards Miss Dowding, he closed the distance between them in a few strides. "I need to do a few things before I can call on you," he said. "Do you have a ride home?"

Oliver spoke up from behind him. "I can see her home in your new hackney."

"My hackney?" Baldwin asked, turning to face him.

Oliver smiled ruefully. "When Miss Dowding pulled up at the Blue Boar, she was frantic to see you and informed us of Marie's plan. So, I bought this hackney from the driver and drove us here."

"You bought a hackney?"

"You misunderstood me," Oliver said. "*You* bought the hackney. The previous owner will be coming by Hawthorne House tomorrow to collect his money."

Baldwin lifted his brow. "What am I going to do with a hackney?"

"Not my concern," Oliver teased as he went to step up onto the driver's box. "Perhaps you can sell it back to him at a reduced price."

Chuckling, Baldwin turned back to Miss Dowding. "My brother is an idiot," he muttered.

She smiled, her eyes lighting up. "I am so happy to see you alive," she said.

"I feel the same way about seeing you." He took a small step closer to her.

Miss Dowding tilted her head to look up at him. "I feared that we wouldn't arrive in time, especially since Marie was determined to kill you and everyone else in Fieldstone Square."

"I had the situation in hand," he assured her.

A line creased her brow as she asked, "Was that letter truly from the Prince Regent?"

"It was."

She went up onto her tiptoes and whispered next to his ear, "Do all agents get one of those?"

He stared back at her, not knowing what to say. He could lie, but he found he didn't want to. He was tired of keeping secrets, and he wanted to let Miss Dowding in.

"Marie told me," she whispered. "I hope this means you won't have to kill me now."

His lips twitched in amusement. "No, but it means we will need to have a serious talk later."

"I shall be looking forward to it."

Baldwin offered his arm and assisted her into the hackney. "I don't know when I shall see you next, but I'll be counting the moments until I do."

"I understand."

He closed the door and watched the hackney drive away until it turned a corner. Then, he turned back towards the wagon, knowing what needed to be done.

It was time to get back to work.

CHAPTER EIGHTEEN

BALDWIN ADJUSTED HIS white cravat as the coach jostled back and forth. "Let's get this blasted meeting over with," he muttered.

Corbyn chuckled. "I take it that you are not a fan of Lord Desmond."

"No, I am not," Baldwin replied. "Desmond used to take swipes at my father when he was still alive, and I find him to be rather insufferable."

"Then I would imagine you should be looking forward to this meeting."

Baldwin shook his head. "I do not delight in the misfortune of others."

"That is an interesting remark from a spy," Corbyn observed.

Glancing out the darkened window, Baldwin remarked, "I work as an agent to keep England safe from domestic and foreign threats."

"After this meeting, you will officially be retired as an agent of the Crown," Corbyn said. "How does that make you feel?"

The image of Miss Dowding came into his mind, and he smiled. "I believe life as a civilian will suit me very nicely."

"You are thinking of Miss Dowding, aren't you?"

"I am," he replied, unabashed.

Corbyn bobbed his head. "She is a strong woman. I heard that she hired a hackney to take her to the Blue Boar to try and stop Marie."

Baldwin chuckled. "I must admit that she was the last person I expected to see in Fieldstone Square."

"I can't imagine you had any complaints," Corbyn remarked knowingly.

"I did not, but it did make explaining my presence a little more troublesome to the constables."

Reaching into his waistcoat pocket, he removed the letter from the Prince Regent and extended it towards Corbyn. "I won't be needing this letter anymore."

"Keep it," Corbyn said. "You never know when you might need it again."

Baldwin returned the letter to his pocket. "Should the need ever arise, you can count on me to defend England's interests."

Corbyn smirked. "I think you might be too busy entertaining a new wife."

"That is assuming I can convince Miss Dowding to marry me."

"You will."

"How can you be so sure?"

Corbyn's eyes grew reflective, as if recalling a painful memory. "Eyes don't lie, and Miss Dowding's eyes light up every time she sees you."

"That pleases me immensely to hear."

"Frankly, it is almost sickening," Corbyn joked.

Baldwin chuckled before growing serious. "I want to thank you for taking that shot in Fieldstone Square."

"I only did what needed to be done."

"If you hadn't shot Marie, I most assuredly would have."

Corbyn nodded. "I know, but I was worried that if you discharged your pistol so close to the bomb, it would ignite."

"As was I, but it was a risk that I was prepared to take."

"Well, I wasn't prepared to lose one of my best agents," Corbyn remarked.

"That was rather a nice thing of you to say," Baldwin said with a smug smile, "especially since you're losing me to retirement anyway."

Corbyn huffed. "Don't get used to it."

"That was quite the impressive shot," Baldwin remarked. "If you had missed—"

Corbyn spoke over him. "I don't miss," he said firmly. "Years of training with the Ninety-fifth Rifle Regiment ensured that. Besides, it was only a hundred-yard shot. I can shoot nearly twice that length with my Baker rifle."

"How did you know to position yourself in that building?"

With a frown, Corbyn admitted, "It was a gamble. I knew you would try to avoid the crowds at all costs, but I hadn't expected to see Marie next to you on the bench."

Realization dawned on him, and Baldwin said, "You were there to shoot me."

"Only if things turned out poorly and I had no other choice," Corbyn replied. "If it was between you and saving hundreds of innocent people, I would have taken the shot."

"You always were one to have a backup plan."

Corbyn eyed him curiously. "You aren't angry?"

"No," Baldwin responded. "I would have done the same thing, given the circumstances."

The coach came to a stop in front of a white, three-level townhouse with an iron fence surrounding the front.

They exited the coach and approached the main door. After they knocked, they each retrieved their calling cards.

The door was opened, and a tall, middle-aged butler greeted them. "Good evening," he said. "May I help you?"

Baldwin extended his calling card. "We would like to speak to Lord Desmond."

"I will see if he is available for callers," the butler responded.

"I am afraid we must insist," Corbyn asserted as he handed his calling card to the butler.

The butler tipped his head in acknowledgement before he opened the door wide and ushered them in. "Please wait in the entry hall while I go speak to Lord Desmond."

After the butler walked off, Baldwin glanced around the entry hall, admiring the collection of art on display over the pale green papered walls.

The sound of the butler's heels on the tile drew back his attention.

"Lord Desmond will see you," the butler revealed, coming to a stop in front of them. "If you will follow me to his study."

They followed the butler down a narrow hall towards the rear of the townhouse. The butler stopped at an open door and gestured that they should enter.

Baldwin stepped into the room first and heard the crackling of the fire in the hearth. Wood paneling dominated the walls, making the room very masculine.

Lord Desmond rose from his chair with a drink in his hand. "To what do I owe this great pleasure, that Lord Hawthorne has descended from on high to see me?" he asked in a mocking chide.

"I see we will forego the usual pleasantries, then," Baldwin commented dryly as he came to stand across from Lord Desmond. "That should save us a considerable amount of time."

Desmond's eyes roamed over Corbyn. "Who did you bring with you? I don't believe we've met...Lord Evan," he probed, pausing as he examined the cards his butler had given him.

"Who I am is not important," Corbyn replied as he moved to stand by the mantel over the fireplace.

Desmond grunted. "This should be interesting," he muttered under his breath.

"We are sorry about your rally earlier," Baldwin said. "It was most unfortunate that shots were fired in Fieldstone Square, causing everyone to flee."

"That was most unfortunate," Desmond agreed, "but I was informed that the perpetrator was shot trying to detonate a bomb."

"That is correct, but Marie referred to it as 'machine infernale'," Corbyn shared.

Desmond's face paled slightly. "That is impossible," he muttered. "I haven't heard that term in years."

"We discovered that Carbon had a daughter who was just as capable of making bombs as her father was, and she was harboring quite the hatred for you, even after all these years," Baldwin said.

"Why me?"

Corbyn picked up a vase off the mantel and replied, "You were one of the agents assigned to ensure Napoleon was assassinated, but when Carbon failed, you abandoned him and his fellow conspirators."

"I don't know what you are speaking of," Desmond declared.

Corbyn placed the vase down. "It matters not," he replied. "You did your job, and I have no doubt that you followed your orders. We just wanted to inform you that Carbon's daughter had every intention of assassinating you today at the rally."

"But we foiled her plans," Baldwin interjected, "along with a group of radicals who were planning a revolution."

Desmond looked at him with newfound respect. "You are an agent," he said. "Of course, that is why you were gone for so many years."

"Not anymore," Baldwin replied. "This was my last case."

Desmond offered him a sad smile. "The desire to be an agent will never go away. The danger, excitement..." His voice trailed off. "I miss it every day."

Corbyn's voice drew back his attention. "Unfortunately, we do come bearing some bad news."

"More of it?" Desmond asked.

Corbyn shook his head. "Informing you about Marie was more of a professional courtesy, but we wanted to give you a warning before this news became public."

Glancing between them, Desmond inquired, "Which is?"

"One of the radicals arrested today was your solicitor, Mr. Tom Walker," Corbyn shared.

Desmond waved his hand dismissively. "I work with many solicitors, so his arrest will hardly impact me."

"Mr. Walker has decided he doesn't want to die for the cause, and he has offered something up in exchange for his life," Baldwin explained.

"Which is?"

"Proof that you stole money from the workhouses that you are contracted to run," Baldwin replied plainly.

Desmond chuckled, albeit nervously. "That is a horrendous accusation."

"It is, and Mr. Walker says that he has been compiling proof over the last few years," Baldwin shared. "Apparently, he really loathes you."

"That is impossible," Desmond declared. "He has no proof. He is clearly lying."

"I am relieved to hear that, because if he does have any proof, it will discredit you," Corbyn said. "And it will ruin your chance of ever running for Prime Minister."

"Furthermore, you will be forced to resign as the contractor for those workhouses, and I can't imagine how the public will react to an earl stealing from the poor," Baldwin remarked.

Desmond's face paled further. "I am being set up," he insisted. "I have done nothing wrong."

"Then you have nothing to fear," Baldwin asserted.

"You must believe me, Hawthorne," Desmond appealed, panic in his eyes. "Mr. Walker is just trying to save himself."

"Frankly, I don't," Baldwin replied. "I believe you were culpable in stealing that money from the workhouses."

"Regardless, we need more workhouses in the rookeries," Desmond pressed. "The Poor Laws are outdated, and we need a new way to fund building them."

"I agree, but you won't be contracted to run them," Baldwin replied.

Desmond frowned. "You aren't going to help me push this bill through Parliament, are you?"

"No," Baldwin responded with a shake of his head, "but I will recommend that we update the Poor Laws to incorporate new laws on workhouse conditions."

"That isn't enough," Desmond said, his voice rising.

Baldwin took a step closer to him and replied, "If you hadn't profited off the poor, then your passionate argument may have worked on the other members of the House of Lords. But I am not fooled by you, no matter how loudly you speak."

As Baldwin turned to leave, Desmond's defeated voice met his ears. "It was such a trifling amount of money," he said. "What if I returned it to the workhouses?"

"That would be a start," Baldwin remarked, "but it won't solve all of your problems. Nor should it."

Not bothering to wait for Desmond's response, Baldwin walked out of the room and Corbyn followed closely behind. They didn't speak until they stepped back into the coach and it started rolling down the street.

"Do you suppose we did the right thing by informing him of the investigation?" Corbyn asked.

"I do," Baldwin replied, "but it won't matter now if they don't press charges. Just the allegations will ruin his reputation."

"He will never be Prime Minister now."

Baldwin shook his head. "No, he most assuredly won't."

"Now on to things that are much more pleasant," Corbyn said. "It is time for you to travel to Miss Dowding's townhouse and woo the lovely young lady."

"It is," he replied. "I hope it isn't too late for her to receive callers."

Corbyn pounded on the top of the coach, and the coach started slowing down. "This is where I get out."

"Why?"

Corbyn smirked as he opened the door. "I need to get back to work. We have a cell full of rebels that need to be interrogated before they are deported or hung for their treasonous acts, including their leader, Morton," he said as he stepped out.

"Would you care for some assistance?"

Corbyn chuckled. "Need I remind you that you are retired?"

"You work too hard."

"Someone needs to," Corbyn replied before closing the door.

Baldwin watched as Corbyn headed down the pavement, disappearing into the first alleyway he came to.

As the coach continued down the street, Baldwin decided it was time to rehearse the speech he intended to say to Miss Dowding.

DRESSED IN A white gown, Madalene stared out the darkened window as she waited for Lord Hawthorne to call on her.

"I wish you would step away from the window," Mrs. Foster said from the settee behind her. "You wouldn't want Lord Hawthorne to see you in the window *if* he comes to call."

"He will come," Madalene remarked firmly.

"How can you be so sure?"

Madalene turned away from the window and met her companion's gaze. "He told me he would."

Mrs. Foster lifted her brow. "When was this?"

"When we spoke last."

"Which was?"

Walking over to an upholstered armchair, Madalene sat down. "It matters not," she replied dismissively.

Mrs. Foster frowned. "When you arrived home earlier, you looked terribly disheveled, and you told me quite the story about Miss Gaillard."

"It wasn't a story," Madalene defended.

"I know, and I believe you," Mrs. Foster said. "But you failed to mention anything about Lord Hawthorne or Lord Oliver being present."

"They weren't there when Miss Gaillard abducted me or when I freed myself."

"Then how was it possible that Lord Oliver brought you home?" Mrs. Foster asked. "And in a hackney, no less."

Madalene pressed her lips together, unsure of how to respond. She didn't dare confess that Lord Hawthorne or his brother were agents of the Crown. That was not her secret to share, and she would never betray them.

Mrs. Foster sighed. "I am not a simpleton, my dear," she said. "It is evident that you are keeping more secrets from me."

Madalene lowered her gaze to her lap. "I'm afraid it is not my place to say anything else."

"Just as I thought," Mrs. Foster replied. "But I should warn you that secrets can consume you, assuming you let them."

"I understand."

Mrs. Foster reached for the cup of tea on the table in front of her. "I do hope that Miss Gaillard got what she deserved for abducting you and killing Miss Hardy."

"I can assure you that she did."

Mrs. Foster bobbed her head in approval. "That is good," she said, bringing the cup up to her lips.

"I am sorry—" Madalene attempted.

"You have nothing to apologize for," Mrs. Foster said, speaking over her. "You have a right to your secrets, and I respect that."

"Thank you."

Mrs. Foster lowered the teacup to her lap. "It sounds like you had quite the adventure," she remarked.

"I did," Madalene responded. "I most assuredly did."

"You never were one who enjoyed being idle for too long," Mrs. Foster said fondly. "Perhaps Lord Hawthorne is a good fit for you after all."

Madalene looked at her in surprise. "You approve of him?"

Mrs. Foster laughed. "Let's not be too hasty," she replied. "I merely think he isn't as terrible as I once led myself to believe."

"How did you reach that conclusion?"

"When you went missing, I went over to Lord Hawthorne's townhouse, and I spoke to him," Mrs. Foster revealed. "He was very attentive, and I could tell he was quite worried about you. It made me realize that I may have misjudged him."

Madalene smiled. "I am happy to hear you say that."

"Are you sure you wouldn't be interested in a boring lord who sits around the library reading all day?" Mrs. Foster joked.

"I would not."

"I assumed as much," Mrs. Foster replied dramatically. "Perhaps it is time for me to do something else with my life."

"No, no, no..." Madalene declared, moving to sit on the edge of her seat. "You are my companion. You can't leave me alone."

Mrs. Foster's face softened. "I would never leave you alone, but I can't help but wonder if you will be married soon."

"Lord Hawthorne hasn't declared his intentions."

"I believe he will, and you won't be in need of a companion anymore."

Madalene shook her head. "I will always need you in my life."

Placing her cup on the table, Mrs. Foster said, "I was thinking about applying for the position of headmistress of the orphanage."

"Pardon?"

"Those girls are going to need someone to tend to them, especially after losing Miss Hardy and Miss Gaillard so closely together," Mrs. Foster remarked. "I would like to help advance your mother's legacy."

"That is a splendid idea, but I am not ready to say goodbye to you," Madalene said dejectedly.

Mrs. Foster smiled reassuringly at her. "That is the brilliant part. I won't be so far away from Hawthorne House, and you often visit the orphanage anyway."

"The girls would love having you as a headmistress," Madalene commented.

"But you will need to hire someone to handle the ledgers," Mrs. Foster asserted. "After all, I would like to spend as much of my time with the girls as possible."

Madalene nodded. "I could do that."

"Cheer up, Madalene," Mrs. Foster said. "You look as if you are being led to the executioner."

"What am I going to do without you?" she asked, her eyes filling up with tears. "You have been with me since before my mother died."

"And that won't ever change," Mrs. Foster stated. "I couldn't love you any more than if you were my own daughter."

Graham stepped into the room and met her gaze. "Lord Hawthorne is here to call on you, Miss."

Madalene blinked back the tears that were threatening to fall and rose from her seat. "Please send him in."

Mrs. Foster gave her a knowing look. "I will give you and Lord Hawthorne a moment alone," she said, "but I shall be in the next room."

As Lord Hawthorne walked in, Madalene felt her breath hitch at the mere sight of him. He was impeccably dressed in a blue jacket, ivory waistcoat, and buff trousers. His hair was neatly brushed forward and his sideburns had been recently trimmed. She had to admit to herself that he was, by far, the most handsome man she had ever met.

He stopped and bowed. "I hope I am not calling too late."

Madalene opened her mouth to reply but found she couldn't formulate any words. Thankfully, Mrs. Foster took pity on her and spoke up. "Not at all, my lord. We only just finished supper."

Lord Hawthorne directed his gaze towards her. "May I speak to you privately, Miss Dowding?"

She nodded slowly.

His lips twitched at her lack of response.

Rising, Mrs. Foster said, "I shall give you two a moment alone."

After Mrs. Foster stepped out of the room, Lord Hawthorne asked, "How are you faring?"

"I am well." Madalene was pleased that she was finally able to find her voice. "And you?"

Lord Hawthorne took a step closer to her. "I am well."

Madalene smiled nervously. "I am glad that we are both well."

Chuckling, he replied, "I am not the one who was abducted by a madwoman and still managed to secure a hackney to travel to one of the most disreputable public houses in all of the rookeries."

"I have had harder days," she joked.

"I can only imagine." Lord Hawthorne grew serious. "I must assume that you have some questions for me."

"I do."

Lord Hawthorne took another step closer to her, making them only a few feet apart. "What would you like to know?"

"You will be honest with me?"

With a thoughtful nod, he replied, "From here on out, I will never lie to you again." Madalene could tell he was in earnest.

"It pleases me immensely to hear you say that," she said. "I am going to start with an easy question first."

"Whatever you would prefer."

With a solemn look, she asked, "What is your favorite dessert?"

Lord Hawthorne's eyes twinkled with amusement. "Sugar biscuits."

"That is a wise choice, my lord," she joked. "But I'm afraid the questions will become increasingly harder now."

"Yes, I imagined that would be the case."

Madalene glanced over at the door and lowered her voice. "How long have you been an agent of the Crown?"

"I was recruited out of Oxford."

"Is that why you disappeared for three years?"

Lord Hawthorne nodded. "I was working with a group of French royalists on the island of Jersey as we tried to stop Napoleon."

"Why didn't you come home when Napoleon was exiled?"

"Because we were still tracking down people who were loyal to him," he explained. "I only came home when I heard that a French spy was coming to England to meet with a group of radicals."

"The French spy being Marie?"

"Yes, it was."

"Did you have to kill her?"

"I wasn't the one who killed her," he revealed. "Another agent took the shot."

"Was it Oliver?" she boldly asked.

"It was not."

"But he is an agent, as well?"

Lord Hawthorne bobbed his head. "He is."

"Does Jane know?"

He winced slightly. "No, she does not," he replied, "but I assure you that it is much safer if she doesn't know the truth."

"Why is that?"

"The less people that know about us, the better."

Madalene pursed her lips together as she found the strength to ask her next question. "Was anything that you told me the truth?"

"Most of it."

She shook her head. "I can't imagine that to be true."

"A good lie always has some elements of truth to it," he shared. "I just left out the parts that would incriminate me as an agent."

"I feel as if I don't even know the real you," Madalene said as she turned away.

Madalene stopped when Lord Hawthorne placed a hand on her sleeve and replied, "You know the real me. I have been here the whole time."

"But you have another life I know nothing about."

"That is true," he said, "but you should know that I am no longer an agent."

Her lips parted in surprise. "You aren't?"

"This was my last case," he informed her as his hand dropped to his side. "My days will now be filled attending Parliament and managing my properties and investments."

"That doesn't sound very exciting."

Huffing, Lord Hawthorne replied, "No, it does not."

"Whatever will you do to alleviate your boredom?"

He gazed intently into her eyes. "About that," he started in a solemn voice, "we do have a problem."

"Which is?"

"How can I be certain that you won't tell anyone about my being an agent?" he asked with an uplifted brow.

"You shall have to take me at my word."

Pressing his lips together, he replied, "I'm afraid that is not good enough."

"It's not?"

"No, it is not." He took a step closer to her, forcing her to tilt her head to look up at him. "I propose a union between us."

"So I won't reveal your secret?" she asked hesitantly.

"Among other things."

Dropping her gaze to the lapels of his jacket, she felt disappointed by his offer. She didn't want a marriage of convenience to Lord Hawthorne. The thought of marrying him when he didn't return her affections caused her heart to ache.

"I'm afraid I must decline your offer," she murmured as she reluctantly stepped back.

The surprise was evident on his face as he asked, "Why?"

"I am not interested in a marriage of convenience."

He stared at her blankly. "Is that what you think I am offering?"

"Isn't it?"

Running a hand through his hair, Lord Hawthorne declared, "Heavens, no!"

"Then I'm afraid I don't understand."

Lord Hawthorne met her gaze, and she refrained from smiling at his tousled hair. "I am not good at giving speeches, Madalene. But I want you to bear with me."

He took a deep breath before he began. "You are the most intriguing young woman I have ever met. You are beautiful, compassionate, kind, clever, and incredibly headstrong." He chuckled. "At times, you may almost be too stubborn, but I am willing to overlook that."

"Are you trying to compliment me or insult me?"

Lord Hawthorne reached for her hand. "Compliment you," he replied. "I don't hesitate when someone is pointing a pistol at me, but I'm growing increasingly anxious at the prospect of offering myself to the woman that I love."

She blinked. "Love?" she repeated. "You love me?"

"Yes, how could I not?" he asked. "I don't know exactly when I started to fall in love with you, but I suspect it was when I first saw you in that coffeehouse."

"Truly?"

A slow smile came to his lips. "You have no idea the effect you have on me," he shared. "When I am with you, I am a better man. But you must know that I will never be truly worthy of you."

"I disagree," she replied. "I think you are perfect for me."

"Do you mean that?" he asked, his eyes searching hers.

She blinked back the tears that came to her eyes. "I do," she asserted, "and I love you, as well."

Lord Hawthorne reared back slightly. "You do?" he asked. "I mean, I hoped you did… or at least held me in some affection—"

In a bold, swift move, she went up on her tiptoes and pressed her lips against his, effectively silencing him.

As she leaned back slightly, she asked, "Has anyone ever told you that you talk too much?"

He chuckled. "No, I can't say that anyone ever has."

Smiling, she said, "I think I found my favorite way to silence you."

His eyes dropped to her lips. "Is that so?"

"Yes," she replied, taking a deep, shuddering breath in anticipation of what Lord Hawthorne was about to do.

In the next moment, he pressed his warm, soft lips to hers. His arms came around her, drawing her closer to him. She parted her lips and kissed him back with an ardor that she had never felt before. And with every moment, she found herself growing more in love with this wonderful man.

Lord Hawthorne broke the kiss and rested his forehead against hers. "You never did answer my question."

"About what?" she breathed.

"Will you marry me?"

Madalene pretended to consider his words. "I suppose a union between us would be a good idea," she finally replied.

"Yes, it most assuredly would," he said, "especially since I never wish to be parted from you ever again."

"Then I agree, assuming you will let me kiss you whenever I

want."

A charming smile came to his lips. "I can agree to those terms."

"Wonderful."

The word was barely out of her mouth before Lord Hawthorne pressed his lips against hers. Not that she was complaining. She rather enjoyed kissing her fiancé.

Her companion's voice caused them to jump apart. "I hope this means that there will be a wedding," Mrs. Foster said in a firm voice.

"Yes," Madalene replied as she brought her hand up to her tingling lips. "Lord Hawthorne asked me to marry him."

"Baldwin," he corrected gently.

Madalene smiled over at him in response.

Mrs. Foster rushed forward and embraced her. "I am so happy for you," she said as she stepped back. "For both of you."

Baldwin met Madalene's gaze, his eyes conveying his love. "Now that I have secured your hand in marriage, I will depart and call upon you tomorrow to discuss the particulars."

"I shall be looking forward to it."

"Very good."

Madalene watched as Baldwin walked to the door and spun back around. "I love you, Madalene, and you have made me the happiest of men."

Surprised by his outburst, it took her a moment to respond. "I love you, too."

Baldwin smiled, his eyes full of a love such as she had never known. "Until tomorrow, then."

EPILOGUE

Six months later

"WHERE ARE YOU taking me?" Madalene asked as she sat next to him in the dimly lit coach.

Baldwin grinned at his wife's exuberance. "You can stop pestering me with questions," he said. "I am not going to tell you."

"We have been traveling with the drapes closed for hours."

He chuckled. "It has been closer to twenty minutes."

Madalene gasped as she turned to face him. "Are you abducting me again?"

"I am not."

"Are you taking me to the orphanage?"

He shook his head. "Why would I need to keep that a secret?"

"Good point," she said, fidgeting with the reticule in her lap. "Although, I thought we were done with secrets."

"This isn't a secret."

"It isn't?"

Smiling, he replied, "No, it is a gift."

"But I don't need any more gifts from you," she objected. "I daresay that you have spoiled me with all the jewelry you have given me. I mean it when I say that I am more than content with just being your wife."

"It pleases me immensely to hear you say that."

Bringing her face closer to his, she murmured, "You should know that I love you more with each passing day."

Unable to resist, he bent his head and kissed her on the lips. He leaned back and said, "I could stay in the coach and kiss you all day."

"Then why don't you?" she asked coyly.

"Don't tempt me."

Her nose scrunched and she brought her hand up. "We are definitely in the rookeries," she announced.

"Why do you say that?"

"Because it smells like the inside of a chamber pot."

"That it does."

Madalene offered him a curious look. "Do you miss working as an agent?"

"Part of me does," he admitted. "I miss the danger and excitement of being a spy, but I do not regret my decision to retire."

"No?"

He shook his head. "Lord Desmond may have been discredited when his solicitor testified against him, but he isn't the only peer that is corrupt."

"That is most unfortunate," Madalene murmured.

Before he could reply, the coach came to a stop.

"I want you to close your eyes," he said.

She gave him a puzzled look. "Why?"

"Just trust me, please."

"Fine," Madalene said before she closed her eyes tightly. "I can't see anything."

"Allow me to escort you," he said, placing his hand on her arm.

After Baldwin gently led her out of the coach, he stopped her in front of a brown brick building.

Baldwin turned to face her because he wanted to see her reaction to her gift. "Now, open your eyes," he ordered.

Madalene opened her eyes, and he was gratified to hear her gasp in delight. "When did you have time to accomplish this?"

"I generally find the time when something is important to me." He turned to face the building. "Does it please you?" he asked, as they both gazed at the sign over the main door that read, *"Elizabeth Dowding Workhouse and Infirmary"*.

"Immensely," she replied, "especially since you used my mother's name."

Baldwin reached for her hand. "I know you are worried about your mother's legacy, but between the workhouse and the orphanage, your mother's name will live on for good for generations to come," he explained. "I have hired a contractor to oversee the managing of the workhouse, but I thought it would be prudent if he reported back to you."

Tears came to his wife's eyes, but he knew they were happy tears. "I don't know what I did to deserve you," she murmured.

"I suppose you are right," he joked. "You are quite lucky to have me."

She laughed, as he hoped she would.

"But, as it turns out, I have a gift for you, as well," Madalene said as she turned to face him.

Placing his hand on her right cheek, he replied, "Every day with you is a gift."

"Do you truly mean that?"

"I choose you, and I will keep choosing you for as long as I live," he promised, hoping his eyes conveyed his sincerity.

A tear slipped out of her eye and rolled down her cheek. As he went to wipe it away, she surprised him by saying, "I am with child."

Fearing he misheard her, he asked, "I beg your pardon?"

She smiled tenderly as she repeated, "I am with child."

Leaning back, he asked, "Are you sure?" He glanced down at her stomach. "I mean… have you spoken to the doctor—"

His words were stilled when she pressed her lips against his, earning disapproving looks from people that walked past them on the pavement.

"You talk too much, Baldwin," she said, leaning back.

"I am just flabbergasted," he declared, running a hand through his hair.

"Does it please you?"

He chuckled at the absurdity of that question. "Nothing could please me more than to have you be the mother of my children."

"I am relieved to hear you say that," she replied. "I was planning on telling you over supper tonight, but I found I couldn't wait."

"I have no doubt that my family will be elated when we share the good news."

She gave him a sheepish grin. "I'm afraid I may have already confided in Jane."

"That does not surprise me," Baldwin remarked. "You two have only appeared to have gotten closer since we wed."

"That we have."

Baldwin glanced at the building. "I had intended that we should take a tour of the workhouse and infirmary before it officially opened up to the public," he said. "But perhaps we should take you home to rest."

"I am perfectly capable of touring the workhouse," Madalene said stubbornly as she approached the door. "You do not need to coddle me now that I am with child."

Taking a step around his wife, he opened the door wide and replied, "That is exactly what I intend to do. I can't risk anything happening to you or the baby."

"You need not fear," she said with a smile. "We will be together for the rest of forever."

Baldwin offered his arm to her. "You promise?"

"I do," Madalene replied, leaning against him. "I don't intend to ever let you go."

The End

About the Author

Laura Beers is an award-winning author. She attended Brigham Young University, earning a Bachelor of Science degree in Construction Management. She can't sing, doesn't dance and loves naps.

Besides being a full-time homemaker to her three kids, she loves waterskiing, hiking, and drinking Dr. Pepper. She was born and raised in Southern California, but she now resides in South Carolina.

Made in United States
Troutdale, OR
06/25/2023

10785581R00166